INTRODUCTION

Mississippi Mud by DiAnn Mills
Roberta Kate Dixon, commonly known as Berta, is the owner of Bert's Dirts—a bulldozing business. Berta has a reputation to maintain in Calista, Mississippi—and bills to pay. She's putting away her money to attend a school in Biloxi to fulfill her dream of becoming an opera singer and leaving Mississippi far behind. But God has other plans, and romance is on the way.

Not on the Menu by Martha Rogers
Widowed Dottie Jean Weaver is sailing along in contentment as owner of the Catfish House in Calista when an old flame from high school reappears and dredges up all the hurts from the past. Her pride causes her to keep her distance even though her heart dictates otherwise. Before love can blossom, she must bury her past and accept the offer of love in the present to brighten her future.

Gone Fishing by Janice Thompson
Whenever Sassy Hatchett's temper flares, she heads to the pier for a time of prayer. Rumor has it the cantankerous fifty-nine-year-old catches enough fish to keep Calista's diner stocked. Wendell Meeks, local postman, is a gentle, soft-spoken soul. He's still single at sixty but thinks it's time to change that. When he sets his sights on Sassy, everyone in town is amused. And confused. Will this somewhat fishy relationship prove that opposites really do attract?

Falling for You by Kathleen Y'Barbo
The two most unlikely people in Calista, Mississippi, to fall in love are about to make New Year's resolutions. When an accidental fall from a ladder outside the Rhonda-Vous House of Beauty lands beautician Sue Ellen Caldwell in hot water with Deputy Bud Briggs, she decides to _____ attend a New Year's Eve party with _____ Little do they know their midnigh_____ ows of another kind.

Sugar and Grits

Southern Hospitality
Enriches Four Mississippi Romances

DiAnn Mills

Martha Rogers

Janice Thompson

Kathleen Y'Barbo

BARBOUR
PUBLISHING

Our mission is to publish and distribute inspirational products offering exceptional value and biblical encouragement to the masses.

Member of the
Evangelical Christian
Publishers Association

Printed in the United States of America.

Mississippi Mud

by DiAnn Mills

Dedication

To Julie Garmon, a Southern girl with true grit

For God did not give us a spirit of timidity,
but a spirit of power, of love and of self-discipline.
2 TIMOTHY 1:7

Chapter 1

Berta Kate Dixon didn't have a care in the world that bright June morning—until she ran her bulldozer into a hill of rattlesnakes.

"Oh no!" A million rattlers, or so it seemed, wiggled on the blade. Berta grabbed the left joystick and moved the huge scoop up and down. Still she had snakes lifting their angry heads and squirming all over the rich, black dirt. Grasping the right joystick, she raised the blade. Peering out the cab at her tracks, she saw several more rattlers creep up her dozer tracks and threaten to take retribution.

They were coming after her for disturbing their peace.

Berta couldn't jump because the snakes covered the ground like a mound of ants, so she had no choice except to jam the machine into reverse and tear back from whence she'd come.

"Oh, Lord, I haven't always been real good, but I sure need Your help now."

The dozer hit a rut, sending her bouncing a good foot off the seat. One of the rattlers jumped up from the track on her left side. Definitely an unhappy fella. She kicked him off with her boot.

Berta swallowed hard. *Adam and Eve have nothing on me. They just had one nasty serpent; she had more than she could handle. Oh, Lord, this is not how I planned to meet You.*

She didn't see a clearing large enough to turn around, which sent her farther in reverse through more brush and screaming at her crew at the top of her lungs.

"Get out of my way! Ran into a hill of rattlers!"

Since it was still early morning, the sun hadn't yet heated up the day, yet sweat trickled down the side of her face and rolled off her jaw onto her neck. The tickle caused her to gasp as though the first snake had met her body and was ready to sink its fangs into her flesh.

Glancing to the right and left, she saw a few pesky rattlers still clinging to her tracks. By all rights, they should have been squashed and gone to meet their Maker. She had a hard time coming to terms with God's creating those pesky boogers. Someday she'd ask Him about it, but hopefully not today.

The county road behind her loomed in the distance. Her three-man crew had fled—most likely to their trucks. Who'd want to be in the way of a bulldozer heading backward while slinging rattlesnakes in every direction?

Once Berta hit the paved road, she swung around and pulled the machine off into a clearing, barely missing a shiny silver sport utility vehicle parked on the side of the road.

Sure hope that's not some fancy inspector looking over my job. Worse yet, it had better not belong to Matthew Jordan VanMichael III. The large fee she had requested from the Biloxi businessman lost its appeal once she hit the hill of rattlers. If she hadn't spent his deposit on supplies and banked the rest, she would return it.

Her credibility as the sole bulldozer operator in the county just hit bottom. After making sure no more snakes clung to the sides of her machine, she shakily climbed down.

"Watch out. I see a rattler wedged in the right track," Bubba Lee Crawford pointed out.

Berta flashed a look but saw that the snake no longer posed a problem. "Thanks. See any more?"

"Nope. You all right?" Bubba's leatherlike face was etched with deep worry lines. Some days his overprotectiveness bothered her, but at the moment, she could hug his burly neck.

"I'm fine, just shook up a bit and mad as a wasp booted out of his nest at those rattlers. Now I've got to get them all out of there." She wiped her face on her shirtsleeve. "Got any ideas other than a healthy dose of snake bait?"

"Hey," a voice called out behind her.

She swung her gaze in the direction of a man's voice—right beside the expensive sport utility vehicle. Because of the sweat stinging her eyes, she couldn't make out much about his appearance, except to see he wore a dark three-piece suit. He gave the door of his SUV a gentle push.

Oh, brother. Who is this guy? A gnawing fear told her it was Matthew Jordan VanMichael III.

"I'm looking for the owner of Bert's Dirts," he said. "Don't imagine he's around with all of this commotion."

"The owner's here." Bubba Lee snorted and stepped between Berta and the stranger. He crossed his arms over his massive chest and straddled the path. "What do you want?"

Berta had to stifle a laugh. Bubba Lee used to wrestle at the county fairs and had long since taken on the role of her body-guard. Underneath his baseball hat—two sizes too small—was a head as bald as a rock from the Gulf. Most folks had smarts enough not to rile him, unless they were hankerin' for a tongue-lashing. Truth be known, Bubba Lee wouldn't harm a soul. He'd given up fightin' and drinkin' several years back after a preacher got ahold of him during a countywide revival.

Blinking back the stinging sweat from her eyes, Berta made her way around Bubba Lee to the fancy-dressed man and pulled off her work glove to offer him a shake. "I'm Berta Dixon, owner of Bert's Dirts. What can I do for you?"

His eyes grew wide, and for the first time she noted his good looks. That is, looks that might be appealing to a girl who didn't have a lick of sense and went for a city man.

He grasped her hand firmly. The manicure she'd gotten yesterday from Sue Ellen Caldwell, the owner of the Rhonda-Vous House of Beauty, had come in handy.

"I'm Matt VanMichael III. I understand you're clearing land to begin my house today, and I drove out to take a look." His words were as smooth as glass. Good-looking or not, Berta didn't trust any man whose voice sounded like thick honey. Made her wonder if he'd taken some communication course in college that guaranteed to have folks melting like butter.

"Yes, sir. I did start this morning, but I ran into a little problem back there in the woods."

He raised a brow. "The noise I just heard?"

"Rattlesnakes, Mr. VanMichael. A whole hill of them right in the middle of the plot where you intend to build your house."

He let out an exasperated sigh. "How do you plan to get rid of them?"

By this time the other guys from her crew had inched closer. They'd be talking about this for a long time. She dragged her tongue over dry lips. "Usually we set traps. They look a whole lot like mousetraps. Of course, we use frogs for bait, and we have to put an order in at Sassy's Bait and Tackle in town to get a plentiful supply. Shouldn't take too long. Frogs multiply pretty fast this time of year. Ought to have them rattlers taken care of in no time at all." She was babbling like a plumb fool and stretching the truth longer than the Mississippi River.

Mr. VanMichael scowled, which did nothing for his refined features. "Miss Dixon, don't take me for an idiot. Just because I don't live in the country doesn't mean I haven't any common sense."

Ouch, I need to watch my tongue. Hadn't the Lord just delivered her from an abominable death? And here she was condescending to a man simply because he dressed better than the whole town of Calista.

"I'm sorry, Mr. VanMichael. Don't know what got into me, except I just got the wits scared out of me back there." She nodded in the direction of the cleared trail. "Guess it put me in a spiteful mood, and I took it out on you."

"Apology accepted. That was some pretty quick thinking, though." A faint smile tugged at his mouth, a full mouth like that of one of those male models she once saw on a magazine cover. Thick dark hair, too, the kind that picked up hints of red in the sunshine.

She returned his smile. "Would you like some water? We

could discuss your site and your. . .uh, tenants."

"I already have a bottle in the truck, but thank you."

Fancy citified water? Oh, Lord, what is wrong with me today? Must be spending too much time with Sassy Hatchett. Dad warned me I was going to end up spitting nails at every person who crossed me wrong if I didn't stop spending so much time with her.

"Well, I can't do much more today until I get rid of those snakes. I'm sorry, but I need to make a few calls."

"How long will it hold up progress?" Mr. VanMichael slipped a hand into his pants pocket.

"Hard to tell. I want to say a few days, but I'll let you know. I know you're anxious—"

"Miss Dixon, your crew's safety is what's most important. I surely don't want any of you bit by a rattlesnake."

"Thank you." *I don't imagine you want a lawsuit, either.*

The man did have more courtesy than she'd displayed. Berta whirled around to the oak and elm trees amid the thickly brushed area where he planned to pour a long driveway and build a six-thousand-square-foot home. "This is a beautiful piece of land, one of the prettier parcels in the area."

He nodded, and she noticed his deep-set dark eyes. Rather mysterious looking. "I agree. At first I considered some acreage along the Gulf, but this property suits my needs. I want privacy, and these trees will do just the trick. Do you suppose there are more snake beds other than the one you just disturbed?"

"I surely hope not. I nearly had an out-of-body experience with that one."

He chuckled and seemed to relax. "I need about ten acres cleared other than the two for the house, and another ten simply cleaned up. The rest will stay natural."

"Are you planning to have horses?"

"Not sure yet. Depends on too many things to list." He walked toward the cleared area leading back to his proposed building site.

"I wouldn't advise taking a walk," Berta said. "You'll need to be a mite more cautious out here than in the city." She turned to bend and study her dozer in all the likely spots that a rattler could hide.

"I'm not," he said. "City folks do understand danger."

I had that coming. "Are you heading back to Biloxi?"

"After lunch," he called over his shoulder. "I could use some company, if you're interested."

She shrugged. "I might have an answer about the snakes by then."

He turned abruptly and headed back her way, grinning wildly. "One of your shaky friends is lurking by that elm. Looks like a poacher to me."

"He won't give up easily."

"Neither do I," he said. "And I intend to build a house right back there."

"I'll send an eviction notice."

Mr. VanMichael exploded in laughter. "Say, doesn't Calista have a catfish restaurant?"

The morning sun glittering off his three-piece navy blue suit gave a silvery cast.

"Yes, owned by the sweetest lady you'd ever want to meet, Dottie Jean Weaver, and her pecan pie is fantastic. Can't miss it on the main street of town."

"Meet me there at noon?" He revealed a dimple in his chin. It may have won his mama, but Berta was all business.

"Sure." She walked with him to his SUV and saw he drove one of those hybrids. She thought about asking him about his gas mileage, but he might misinterpret her question as changing the subject. "We've got a quiet, peaceful little community here, Mr. VanMichael—"

"Matt."

"All right, Matt. Anyway, you'll find the country people here real friendly. Though some are a little suspicious of strangers."

"Particularly strangers from the city?"

"Possibly." She laughed. "Give them time to get to know you."

Matt pulled his keys from his pants pocket. "I'll try real hard."

Berta stepped back for him to open his door. "Won't be long before the sun's gonna be beating down hard. I might not be real presentable for lunch."

"Oh, Miss Berta Dixon of Bert's Dirts, I think you'll do nicely."

As she watched him drive away, curiosity wound its way through her mind. *Do nicely for what, Mr. Matt Jordan Van-Michael III?* If he planned to make fun of her, he could find someone else to dig his foundation—rattlers and all.

Chapter 2

Matt used the keyboard on his cell phone to calendar his appointment with the architect. "Yes, I'll be there in the morning around ten. I'd like to go over some of the modifications to my home. Thanks. See you then."

He disconnected the call and pressed a selection on his speed dial options to return another call. "Hey, Landon, this is Matt. I've run into a little hitch that might delay getting the house completed on time."

"What kind of hitch?"

"The company I hired to clear the land for the foundation of my house unearthed a huge hill of rattlesnakes right where I wanted to build."

"That's not good, and we're working on a tight schedule."

"You're not telling me anything I don't already know. I'm meeting with the dozer owner at noon."

"Put the heat on if you have to. It's critical, Matt. You can't afford delays."

"I don't want anyone in town getting suspicious." Matt fired up the SUV engine and punched the air-conditioning button. Soon coolness rushed over him. And he needed it.

"Some well-meaning citizen could halt the whole project."

"Landon, I purchased the one hundred acres to do with as I saw fit. As long as what I'm doing is not illegal, I'm safe. I understand the problem with time. It's keeping me awake at night."

Landon chuckled. "We'll see how the good folks of Calista respond to your plans."

"I'll keep you posted." Matt snapped the phone shut and held it in his hand for several seconds. He'd done some fancy number crunching to build this home and estate, and he wasn't about to let any delays hold him back. If only time didn't play such an important factor in all of this. Business. Couldn't live without it, but the stress was giving him gray hairs and high blood pressure.

Bert's Dirts. What a name for a bulldozing business. And to think that cute little lady with the sun-streaked hair was the owner. She couldn't be over twenty-five. He laughed despite the bad news about the delay, especially at the size of her bodyguard, or whatever he was. His name was probably Bubba. The rest of her crew looked like they'd pounce on Matt at the wink of an eye.

That's what he got for purchasing land out in the boondocks. But his project required distance and privacy from the city life.

Rubbing his temples, he laid his phone on the console and glanced around for a coffeehouse. According to his secretary, Calista hadn't made it to the Starbucks level, but they'd built a

Wal-Mart on the outskirts of town—away from his property.

The catfish restaurant across the street looked inviting. It sat back from the main thoroughfare with steps leading up to a wide porch. Hanging ferns and rockers across the front reminded him of his grandmother's home before Hurricane Katrina.

It's only ten o'clock. Maybe the Catfish House will let me work on my laptop until noon. He could sit near the windows where he could see up and down the main street. The town had a sleepy, peaceful feel to it. A perfect place to hide what he planned for his new home.

Matt gathered up his computer and phone, then set his sights on a pot of good strong coffee. He shed his jacket and loosened his tie. Maybe Miss Berta Dixon-Dirts wouldn't feel intimidated at lunch.

He made his way to Calista's Catfish House. The sign on the door said CLOSED UNTIL ELEVEN FOR LUNCH. Ignoring the ten o'clock hour, he knocked and peered inside. Two women bustled about, one younger and one older. He banged on the door again. And again. Finally he heard the click of a key, and a rather short older woman with a heavy layer of silver hair faced him.

"We're not open until eleven," she said.

"I know, but I was wondering if I could just sit at a table and have some coffee until noon. I'm meeting someone here."

The woman appeared to contemplate his request. "I guess it's all right. Come on in, and I'll get you a cup of coffee."

"A whole pot, if you wouldn't mind?" He smelled coffee brewing and something else that made his mouth water. He stepped inside the air-conditioned restaurant. To his surprise, it was tastefully decorated with a bit of fishing memorabilia. "I drove over from Biloxi this morning. Is that pecan pie I smell?"

She smiled. "Baked fresh daily. There's two things the Catfish House is noted for—fried catfish and pecan pie."

"I'll have to try them both later." He headed toward a table by a huge window.

"We don't have wireless," she said. "Just dial-up from the office."

"That's all right. I have connectivity on my phone."

"One of those newfangled kinds that does everything but peel potatoes?"

He laughed. "That's it."

"Plays music, too?"

He nodded.

"And it will work anywhere?"

"Not just anywhere. Some places I can't get service, but Calista is near the interstate."

"Glad you like it. Me? I have enough trouble setting my alarm clock. Can't even use a computer." She raised her finger and pointed to the young woman rolling silverware into red and dark blue cloth napkins. "My daughter wants us to be computerized. Says I run this restaurant like I got lost in the fifties." She shrugged. "Nothing wrong with that, I say. Now, you just have a seat, and I'll bring your coffee. I'm Dottie Jean, the owner. Holler if you need something else."

She disappeared, and he chuckled. Living in this town promised to be a whole new experience.

Berta sat in her truck and listened for the third time to the message machine at Snag-A-Snake. "We're out of the office until June twelfth. Got a hankering to go fishing. If you have trouble with snakes, use a hoe until we return."

"Very funny." She could clear other parts of the acreage until then, but she'd gotten the distinct impression that Matt VanMichael III wasn't used to waiting for folks to get back from fishing trips.

She dropped her phone into the ashtray—the only clean spot in her seven-year-old pickup—and slammed the door shut. A little harder than necessary.

"No luck?" Bubba Lee asked once she made it back to her crew.

She frowned. "Snag-A-Snake won't be in the office until the twelfth."

"So whadda we do?" As foreman, he had a right to know.

"I've got to meet with VanMichael at noon." She lifted her baseball cap and cooled her forehead. "I hate to contact anyone in Biloxi. They'll want an arm and a leg to come over here and get rid of these snakes."

"We've killed half a dozen since you've been on the phone."

"And we don't need anyone bitten by those demons. For now, let's work on clearing the area on both sides of the rattler mansion." She started toward her dozer. "It's a good two hours before lunch. Let's see what we can get done."

Two and a half hours later, Berta took a quick glimpse at her watch and saw it was already noon. Rats. She switched off the dozer and raced to her truck. VanMichael needed to be impressed, and here she was late. She grabbed a roll of paper towels from behind her seat and wiped the grit from the back of her neck. Two more towels later, she rubbed the dirt and grime from her face and throat. Used to be, she attempted to wear makeup while working. What a mistake. Now she was a take-it-or-leave-it gal.

Her nose attested to the heat of the June morning, but too late. She had a meeting with a man who'd decided to build a house so big that most folks would call it sinful. Maybe he was married with a dozen kids. But she hadn't seen a ring on his left hand, and she'd looked. Shame on her, but a man who had a wife usually was a little easier to deal with.

The truck bounced along the county road until she got to the highway. At least she could now think a little more clearly without juggling her brains. Clearing out the rest of his property made sense, but not if he had a contractor sitting by waiting on his turn.

Berta swung the truck into the parking lot. As much as she loved catfish, she'd not taste the food today. Oh, but didn't she look like a redneck? She had the tanned neck to prove it. Grabbing a shirt to cover most of her black tank top, she tossed her John Deere lid onto the seat and took a quick glimpse into the mirror. Cringing at the ponytail, damp along the ends and the rest a curly flat mess as a result of the cap, she clamped it back on her head and hoped for the best.

With her clipboard in hand and her cell phone in the front pocket of her jeans, she decided to face the music with Mr. Matthew VanMichael III. Once on the porch of the Catfish

House, she spotted him inside the restaurant bent over his computer. If he'd lift his nose from the screen, he'd see he selected the perfect spot to watch folks coming and going on Main Street. She laughed. He had a Bluetooth stuck in his ear while his fingers flew over the keyboard.

It all added up to stress, and she was about to give him another generous helping.

Once inside, she dashed to the ladies' room to wash her hands and splash some water onto her face. On the way, she spotted Dottie Jean.

"Help me, Dottie Jean. I'm late for an appointment with that fella over there by the window. The one wired up with all the modern technology. He's the one who's building that huge house."

"Right, Berta. He's gone through two pots of coffee waiting on you. Been here since ten."

"Great. Simply great. It's been one of those mornings I'd like to forget. Do you have a nailbrush? I wear gloves and still my hands look like I dig worms for a living."

Dottie Jean laughed. "Go on in and start washin'. I'll be right there. And I'll go tell your young man that you're on your way."

"He's not my young man; he's—"

Too late, Dottie Jean was clipping along toward the glass wall where Matt pecked away—reminded her of a chicken.

With soap up to her elbows, Berta wished she had some cologne for an "eau de cologne bath." A clean pair of jeans and shirt would help. The check for this deal would get her out of debt and on toward her dreams.

Dottie Jean stuck her hand inside the bathroom. "Here, sweet girl. What about that dirty baseball cap?"

"I have a bad case of the sweat-head."

"I see. I'll look for a cleaner one in the back room."

"You're a doll. I'd hug you, but I'm soapy."

"I want you heading off to get your master's degree, and I know this deal will do it."

Berta blew her a kiss and went to work on her filthy nails. All the while she prayed God would blind Matt's eyes and nose. And get Snag-A-Snake back to work. She rinsed her hands and dried them with paper towels as she dashed out the door.

"Sorry to keep you waiting." She eased into the chair.

"No problem. I had plenty of work to do." He removed the Bluetooth and disabled it from his phone. With a smile that would rival sunshine streaming through a church on Easter morning, he closed his laptop and slipped it into its case. "How many rattlesnakes are left?"

"About six less than when you were there this morning."

He frowned. "Is there a problem?"

"A delay is more like it. My source for ridding those pesky creatures is out of the office until next Monday."

"That puts me a week behind schedule."

"I understand. My men are working on clearing the other areas."

"That doesn't help what needs to be done to pour the foundation."

Berta had met his type a few times. While they glimmered with good looks, charm, and impeccable manners, they expected, rather demanded, peak performance like that of a finely tuned engine. Matt needed to understand he was in a tractor town.

"I'm sorry. What would you like for me to do?"

"Put on some pressure. Get the job done."

"The folks are on vacation until the twelfth."

"Hire another company."

"There isn't one." Berta started to say more, but Dottie Jean had arrived with the menus.

"What would you like to drink?" Dottie Jean asked.

"Water for me, please." Berta smiled up at the woman who had been her surrogate mother since her own mother died several years ago.

"I'll take the same," Matt said. "A twist of lime, please."

"We just have lemon." Dottie Jean planted her hands on her hips.

"That will do fine."

"Do you know what you want to order?" Dottie Jean asked.

"I'll have catfish and hush puppies—the luncheon special with coleslaw." Berta handed her the menu.

Matt gave Dottie Jean his menu. "The same here. Make sure I have a generous slice of that pecan pie with ice cream for dessert."

Dottie Jean hurried toward the kitchen, greeting several customers as she went.

Maybe the pie would sweeten his disposition. "Sometimes I have pie and ice cream instead of lunch," Berta said.

He grinned. "Are you thinking I'm a bit sour?"

Before she could answer, Sassy Hatchett made her way toward them. If Berta could have ducked under the table, she'd have done so and held her breath until the Second Coming.

"Hey, Berta. Dottie Jean said you were sitting over here with a good-lookin' city fella, so I came to see for myself."

How do you explain Sassy Hatchett to a businessman from Biloxi who's investing money into one hundred acres and a six-thousand-square-foot house? For that matter, Berta wondered how to explain Sassy to anyone. With a red bandanna tied around her forehead and jeans resting a good six inches above her ample waistline, Sassy teetered on her heels.

"Speak up, girl. Cat got your tongue?"

"Hi, Sassy. I'm having a business lunch with a customer. This is Mr. VanMichael." She turned to Matt, who appeared to wipe a grin from his face. "This is Sassy Hatchett."

Sassy reached out and grabbed Matt's hand and pumped it like a water pump. "I own the local bait and tackle shop." She frowned. "Not much of a handshake there, son. Don't you exercise?"

"Yes, ma'am. I do."

"Work on it a little more. Lift some weights. Do some real work besides pushing a pencil behind a desk and kissing on the secretaries."

Berta searched desperately for Dottie Jean to save her from utter humiliation.

"I'll do that very thing."

"What do you do for a living, anyway?"

Matt fidgeted. "I work for the IRS."

Chapter 3

Did you say the IRS, as in the Internal Revenue Service? You must have lost your mind! Couldn't you get a better job than that? Where's your mama? How do you sleep at night?"

Matt stared up at the woman with the fiery red hair and a temperament to match. "I've worked for the IRS since college. It's a respectable job." He found no need to head for the defense line. People like her who judged him because of his job irritated him.

"Comin' down on folks to squeeze out their life's savings?"

"That's not what I do at all."

Sassy stiffened. " 'Scuse me while I go fetch my rifle."

Dottie Jean slid up beside Sassy and wrapped her arm around the woman's waist while another young woman set the food before Berta and Matt.

"Let it rest, Sassy," Dottie Jean said. "Come on over and talk to me a little while I have a lull."

"You don't have a lull. You're busier than a bumblebee in May."

Dottie Jean raised a brow.

"All right, but one of us has got to talk to Berta about the company she keeps. I know she needs money, and there ain't no prospects around here for marriage. . ."

Matt didn't hear the rest because the two women ambled toward the kitchen. He avoided Berta's gaze.

"I'm sorry about Sassy." Her face held the sheen of a polished apple.

"Is she always like that?"

"No. Today's a good day."

He hoped Sassy wasn't a good representation of the town's reception. Too late now. "Can we talk about the snake problem?"

When her lips turned up and she covered her mouth, the humorous side of the rattlesnakes and Miss Sassy hit his funny bone. He laughed until he realized half the restaurant watched him and Berta. Finally, he was able to contain himself.

"We'd better eat before this gets cold," he said. "Haven't laughed like that in a long time." He stabbed a hush puppy and popped it into his mouth. It melted on his tongue. Mmm, he could get used to this.

"Sweet Sassy will have you either laughing or crying. Truth is, she has a heart of gold."

He doubted if Sassy had a soft spot anywhere, but he wasn't going to pick an argument with Berta. Making her mad might mean looking for another dozer company.

"Seriously, is there anything you can do to speed up the extermination of those snakes?"

She shook her head. "Snag-A-Snake is the only company around here who'll take care of the problem. I do promise you that as soon as they return, I'll work seven days a week and nights to catch up."

"I believe you would. I might have to help." He studied the young woman seated across from him. Usually he kept the company of socialites who wouldn't dare set foot in public without perfect hair, rosy cheeks, and shiny lips. Yet Berta Dixon, owner of Bert's Dirts, had a fresh beauty that he appreciated—right down to the splattering of mud on her jeans. His mind wandered on to the topic of a boyfriend, like that self-proclaimed bodyguard at the building site.

Matt glanced at his plate and realized he'd eaten everything.

"Seconds are free," she said.

"You're tempting me, but then I wouldn't have room for the pie."

She smiled, and the blue of her eyes, like the depths of the ocean, seemed to penetrate his soul. "I think I'll have a piece, too."

"With coffee?" he asked.

"Absolutely. Coffee with lots of cream and sugar."

"Why drink it if you're going to disguise the taste?"

"I started drinking coffee at eleven years old. My dad had his cup every morning, and I wanted to be just like him. Only I couldn't handle the strong taste." She smiled a delicious sugar-and-cream smile.

"Are we doing better now?" he asked. "I mean, we got started on the wrong foot."

"I think so."

"Are you certain there's no one else to take care of the snakes?"

She nodded. "Not unless you want to hire a couple of good ol' boys with rifles on a Saturday night."

"Don't tempt me. I've already regretted a million times not hiring a contractor to take care of the whole thing instead of subcontracting the work myself. That's what I get for being a hands-on type of guy."

⸙

Before the Snag-A-Snake folks returned from their fishing trip, word had spread through every corner in Calista that an IRS man intended to live in their town and Berta Dixon was clearing his land. Overnight folks frowned at her instead of smiled—thanks to Sassy. Didn't they understand that Matt VanMichael III would find another company to clean up his property if she backed down from the job?

One item bothered her immensely—how did a man working for the IRS earn enough money to build a huge house? The whole idea left a bitter taste in her mouth, like the tax collectors in the Bible who grew rich at the expense of others. Was Calista a place to hide from those he'd exposed for nonpayment of taxes?

To make matters worse, Matt had a likable personality. She would've much preferred him to be old and ugly and reek of bad breath.

Berta pulled her truck behind Dottie Jean's double-wide trailer, which sat behind the Catfish House, and turned off the engine. Tonight was their weekly Bible study with Dottie Jean, Sassy, and her best friend, Sue Ellen. The four had reserved every Tuesday night since Berta and Sue Ellen were in high school. They were an odd foursome—different as earth and sky—but they were devoted to each other.

Dottie Jean opened the door before Berta had a chance to knock. Sassy and Sue Ellen were already there.

"Always-Late-Kate is here," Sassy said.

Every time Sassy made that remark, Berta regretted revealing her middle name, Kathryn: Roberta Kate Dixon. The same as her deceased mother.

"You'd be disappointed if I arrived on time. Besides, then you'd have to come up with another nickname." Berta plopped her keys onto the kitchen table beside a pie layered a foot high with toasty meringue. She inhaled deeply. *Lemon meringue*.

"Oh, I've been working on a special ditty just for you," Sassy said.

"Do I really want to hear it?"

"It's kinda like a poem. Here goes. . . Berta thinks she's done her best by working for a man from the IRS. When she's collected her well-earned fee, he'll build a house out of taxes from you and me."

"That's terrible, Sassy." Berta bit back a few caustic words.

"But true."

"You're not being fair," Berta said. "Somebody has to make sure we all pay the government what we owe."

"My granddaddy would have filled the fella's expensive pants with buckshot. Good-for-nothing revenuers."

"You don't even know him."

"And you do? Sitting goggle-eyed across from a man at lunch doesn't qualify you as an expert on his character."

"Hey, you two," Dottie Jean said. "Sassy, you're overstepping the boundaries of love and friendship here."

The woman startled, as though Dottie Jean's words shocked her. "Of course I love Berta. I'm just looking out for her, that's all. I don't want her hurt or losing the respect of the citizens of Calista over a no-good IRS man."

Berta prayed for patience—no, not patience, for then Sassy would get worse. Grace and mercy sounded better. "He's a customer who is paying me quite well to clear out his property. Can't we talk about something else, like our Bible study lesson?"

"I agree," Sue Ellen said. "Are we still in James?

"Uh-huh." Dottie Jean picked up her Bible. "We're on James 3, taming the tongue."

"Did you do this on purpose?" Sassy stuck her fingers inside the straps of her overalls and tipped her chair up on its back legs.

"It's simply the lesson for this week. Maybe you're feeling guilty for what you said to poor Berta."

Sassy slumped in her chair. "I only wanted to help. If I've hurt your feelings, Berta, then I'm sorry."

Berta wrapped her arms around Sassy's shoulders. "That's all right. I know you mean well. I have no idea what branch of the IRS Matt works for, but he must work from home or plans to quit in order to live so far from Biloxi."

"You might be right. It's not as if you're going to marry him—just collect his money so you can get your master's in music." Sassy sniffed.

Berta glanced up at Sue Ellen, who pressed her lips together to keep from laughing aloud. Poor Sassy. She really meant well. If only her brain would engage along with her tongue.

Matt rose at 4:00 a.m. to drive to Calista. This was the day Berta could start work on his home site. Yesterday, the snakes were to have been terminated, exterminated, and asphyxiated. The last thing he needed was a fat rattler slithering up his steps. He envisioned the huge home with a massive wraparound porch and lots of rockers, similar to the Catfish House, but he'd pass on the red roof.

He tuned the radio to a Christian talk show and listened to a pastor expound on the virtues of doing business in a godly manner. Matt chuckled, but not because he thought the words were humorous—he believed in every one of them. He had learned from the negative legacy left by his father, Matthew VanMichael II, who had suffered from alcohol abuse and had been unfaithful to his wife. Matt's grandfather had run a chain of shady liquor stores in Biloxi and had drunk more than he sold until it killed him. Neither man was the epitome of a role model, but God had spoken to Matt at a church camp when he was sixteen years old, and he'd never strayed since then.

That's why this project in Calista meant so much to him. Granddad had left him a sizable inheritance, and Matt felt he had no choice but to use it for the Lord. Even so, time ticked by and he couldn't afford any more delays. Matt trusted God; he believed in answered prayer. Yet the lives of precious people teetered on the balance.

His hybrid SUV, true to its claim to good gas mileage, took the turn down a country road and bumped along to the hundred acres that he'd affectionately termed Kozy Korners.

He powered down his windows and heard the music of nature and then. . . Yes! The song of a bulldozer clawing through brush was the best tune of the morning.

Once he parked, he stood and observed the team, busy at work. Not one man stood idle. Berta sat atop one of two dozers, advancing into the brush and undergrowth like a hungry animal. Matt laughed. What a great and glorious day. All those years sitting in the office had never prepared him for the elation of watching the beginning works of his dream.

Matt shed his coat and tie, tossing them into his vehicle. The project would take nine months, like birth. That meant next spring he could move in and begin a new career from home.

He watched the progress for the next hour, much like a little boy in awe of the huge machinery and the muscular men. However, his gaze often strayed to the young woman who doggedly attacked the undergrowth. After what Miss Sassy had said about his weak handshake, he'd spent more time at the gym this week. He even hired a personal trainer. Even if the woman disliked him for his job with the IRS, at least she could say he got himself buffed.

Berta had been so embarrassed.

He'd thought about the owner of Bert's Dirts all week, but he kept his sentiments to himself. Landon would never understand, thinking the visionary Matthew VanMichael III had fallen for a backwoods country girl.

Berta was anything but backwoods. Any woman who could take on a man-sized business and count herself as one of the men had his admiration and respect. Was she a Christian? He hoped so. Better yet, he hoped he had the opportunity to find out.

As the noon hour approached, Matt waited around to see if he could take Berta to lunch. Right on time, the dozers stopped and the group headed toward their trucks. Only Berta stayed behind, as though surveying what needed to be done.

"Can I help you?"

Matt focused on the big guy who would give a wrestler a run for his money—the same fellow from the last visit. "I'd like to speak with Berta."

"I'm her foreman. Whatcha need?"

This guy doesn't budge an inch. Matt stuck out his hand. "I'm Matt VanMichael, the owner of this property. I wanted to congratulate her on the progress done this morning."

The man reluctantly returned the shake, a real gripper. "I'm Bubba Lee Crawford. My two brothers and me have worked for Berta since she started the dozer business four years ago. The tall one is Mark. We call him Mule. The bald one, like me, is Luke, and we call him Bull. We kinda take care of details for her."

Am I a detail? Or am I a threat? "I see. She's lucky to have you."

"Berta and I have been close since we were kids. Know what I mean?"

"Of course."

"What else do you need?"

"I'd like to talk to her about the job here."

"If you'll give me your card, I'll give it to her."

"Doesn't she take a break for lunch?"

"Not today. She's eating on the dozer."

Sure enough, Berta crawled back onto her machine and started it up. He saw a sandwich in one hand and a joystick in the other. Matt reached into his shirt pocket and pulled out a card.

"Tell her I was here and to give me a call."

"Be glad to." Bubba Lee grinned. "You have a nice day, ya hear? We'll get this job done for you in no time at all." He walked toward a mud-coated pickup and then whirled around. "Don't expect a call on Tuesday night, 'cause that's when she has Bible study, or Wednesday night, 'cause that's choir night and Midweek Lift. We're working sunup to sundown except for church on Sunday morning. But I'm sure she'll get back with you real soon."

Chapter 4

Berta didn't know that Matt had been to the site until Bubba Lee handed her his business card.

"When was he here?" she asked.

"I spoke with him at noon, but Mule said he was here about an hour before that."

"I wonder what he wanted."

"He said to congratulate you on the progress made this morning."

She smiled. "Good. Thanks for taking care of him for me. I'll return his call in a little while."

Bubba Lee took on his familiar stance—crossed his arms over his chest and stood with his feet wide apart. Sort of reminded her of a sumo wrestler.

"What is it? You have that afraid-to-ask look on your face."

"Aw, Berta. Can't you make things easy for me just once?"

She laughed. "No. I like to see you squirm."

"Can I take you to choir practice this week?"

She tilted her head. "I love you—"

"Like a brother, I know. But I'm one stubborn guy."

"Maybe *you* should be called Mule." She touched his arm. "I may be late in leaving the church after practice. I'm singing this week, and I need to rehearse in the sanctuary."

"I'll wait."

"Why do this to yourself? How long's it been? Since junior high?"

He lifted his cap and brushed his hand across his bald head. "Some habits are hard to break."

"What's being broken is your heart." Berta sensed a lump jump into her throat. If only she could find a nice girl for Bubba, one who would love him for all of his goodness. Ever since he walked her home from school many years ago and she found her mama had died from a stomach aneurism, he'd been looking after her. She wished she loved him the way he wanted. She really did.

"So I'll pick you up around seven twenty."

"All right." Berta downed the rest of a bottle of water and climbed back on the dozer. Already she regretted giving her consent. "Back to work."

The situation with Bubba Lee was getting worse instead of better. Sue Ellen insisted the man was obsessed and she needed to be careful. Berta shook her head. Bubba was devoted and believed he loved her after what they shared years ago. A few times she attempted to explain that love was more than a one-sided affair. It involved unselfish giving for both the man and the woman. Bubba said he didn't care; he'd wait until she learned to love him. She wasn't sure what to do, and allowing him to take her to choir practice had been a bad idea. Except she hated to hurt his feelings. He had this look. . .not sappy. . . just sad and lonely.

Tonight, after work, she'd stop by to see Dottie Jean. The dear lady housed more wisdom in her gray head than a dozen professors. Until then she'd pray God would guide her through the painful process of trying to help Bubba see he needed to find someone who would love him as he deserved.

Remembering Matt's call, she laid his card on her leg and punched in the numbers. He answered on the second ring.

"Hi, Matt, this is Berta. Bubba Lee said you stopped by the site before noon."

"I did. And I was impressed with how much you'd gotten done in one day."

"Actually, we started late yesterday afternoon after the Snag-A-Snake people left."

"No more tenants?"

"If they try to sneak back in, there's a chemical around the perimeter of the building site that will cause them to disintegrate."

"That's a comforting thought."

"Matt, I have a question."

"Fire away. I sure hope this isn't about another delay."

"Not at all. Was Bubba Lee rude today?"

"Can't say that he was. Is there a problem?"

"Sometimes he gets a little carried away in making sure the boss's stress doesn't hit the explode level. My idea of professionalism doesn't always agree with his."

Matt laughed. "Is he succeeding in keeping you stress-free?"

Berta laughed lightly. "Sometimes. He's a sweet man, and

I've known him since I was a kid."

"He mentioned that."

Flares popped into every corner of her mind. "In the future if you need to talk to me, use my cell. It's always in my pocket."

"Will do. I'm planning to drive up on Sunday after church."

"Do you want to attend mine? After all, you'll be living in the Calista area and will want a church of your own."

"What time are the services?"

"Ten thirty. We have just one. And the church is on Main Street—Calista Community Church—opposite end of the Catfish House. We have a good preacher."

"I can do that."

"Great. I'll see you then. I'll need to get to the site afterwards."

"I'd rather you not work on Sunday. I'm a firm believer that God will honor the other six days when we give one day back to him."

"All right. But if you change your mind, let me know."

"I won't on that decision."

The call disconnected. Suddenly she remembered what was happening on Sunday. *Rats. I'm singing. He'll think I'm showing off.*

When evening shadows threatened the safety of her crew, Berta sent the men home and phoned Dad to tell him not to expect her until late. She drove to Dottie Jean's with her head swimming in the whirlpool of what to do with Bubba Lee. An age-old problem with no easy solution.

Dottie Jean always left the restaurant at eight o'clock, which gave her time to rest up a few minutes before Berta arrived.

"Sweet girl, Bubba Lee will not let up on pursuing you until you tell him the truth and stick by it."

"But it's only choir practice." Berta knew Dottie Jean was right, but she hated to admit it. She lifted a glass of lemonade to her lips.

"Doesn't matter if he helped you empty the trash. To him, it's a date."

"I can't seem to get him to understand that I'm just not interested."

"You shouldn't have made him foreman."

"He does a great job."

Dottie Jean shook her head. "Of course he does. He's working for the woman he loves. Now, eat your dinner."

Berta took a bite of the seafood salad. Her stomach had growled for the past several hours, but the ache in her heart made the food tasteless. "Tell me what to do, and this time I'll follow through."

"Why now? Has that man from Biloxi taken your eye?"

Berta smiled. "I don't know a thing about him, but as long as Bubba Lee chases him away from the site, I won't ever get to know him."

"Bubba Lee's obsession with you is not healthy."

Berta's eyes widened. "Now you sound like Sue Ellen and Sassy. He's harmless—"

"He's a man in love with a woman who isn't interested. It's like tossing a stray dog a bone."

"Dottie Jean!"

"Let me finish. Bubba Lee will never find the right woman for him as long as you give indications that you might someday fall in love with him."

"You're right."

"Of course I am." Dottie Jean laughed.

"I'll talk to him on the way to choir tomorrow night. I'll make sure he hears the truth."

"He may need to find another job."

"Which means I might lose a good man along with his brothers."

"God will provide, Berta. Honor Him, and He'll take care of you."

Berta finished her supper and toyed with the right words to say to Bubba Lee. For certain, God would have to lead her. "I'm going to see him tonight while I have the nerve. He and his brothers were having dinner with their folks. I can catch him there."

"Probably a good idea. I'll be praying for you."

Berta shivered. "Do you have any idea how I despise hurting him? Bubba Lee's one of the kindest men I've ever met."

Dottie Jean tilted her head. "Then give him the respect he deserves."

All the way to the Crawford farm, Berta prayed. By the time she drove down the long lane to the lighted house, her courage had dissipated. *Okay, Lord. I'm relying totally on You.*

Bubba Lee must have seen her drive up, because he met her on the front steps with two coon dogs.

"Is anything wrong?" he asked. "Is your daddy all right?"

For once, she'd like for him not to be so sensitive to her needs. "Everything's fine. I came to see you."

"Me?"

The crickets seemed to echo his question.

"Who's there, Bubba?" Mrs. Crawford asked.

"Berta, Mama. She's here to see me."

"Invite her in. I've got chocolate cake left from supper."

This was getting harder by the minute. "No thanks, Mrs. Crawford. I just ate. You doing okay?"

"Pretty good. The garden's coming in, and that keeps me busy."

"Yes, ma'am. You always have a beautiful garden."

"Sure you don't want something? You could come in and give me a hug."

The idea of visiting with Mrs. Crawford pleased her a whole lot more than telling Bubba Lee she'd never love him more than a brother. "I'd be glad to."

Forty-seven minutes later, Berta and Bubba Lee sat side by side on the front porch swing.

"I know this isn't good," he said. "I can tell by the way you aren't joking."

The crickets continued to serenade—a sad, mournful song. He slipped his arm around her shoulder.

"Don't. Please."

He hastily drew back. "So this is about us."

"There *is* no us, Bubba Lee. I'm not the girl for you."

"You've been the only one for me since you were thirteen years old."

"Not if I don't love you like a woman is supposed to love a man." Her heart thudded like that of a scared rabbit. She turned on the swing to face him. "Bubba, you have a heart of pure gold. I could ask you for anything, and you'd do it for me.

You're gentle and soft-spoken. You've gotten me out of more scrapes than my own daddy."

"I don't want to be your daddy."

She slowly exhaled. "I understand what you want. You deserve a girl who loves you so much that it makes your head spin. She should think about you the moment she wakes in the morning and just before going to sleep—second only to God."

"You could be that person if you'd try."

Berta felt the tears slip from her eyes. "I've tried, Bubba. For over twelve years I've prayed that my love went only to you."

"It's that VanMichael fella, isn't it?"

"Would it make any difference if it were him or one of your brothers? The truth is, I've hurt you repeatedly for too many years. I want us to be friends. Nothing more."

"What you're asking is hard." He glanced away into the darkness.

"I want more for your life than disappointment over my decisions," she whispered. "But you've got to leave me behind."

"I can't stop loving you all at once." He turned back to her. "Working with you every day. . ." He shook his head without finishing. "Who will take care of you?"

"God will help me."

He rubbed his face.

Please don't cry. I already feel horrible.

"If you don't want to work for me anymore, I understand. Can't blame you for quitting."

"I need to think on it. Might be easier if I left Calista for a while. Easier on both of us."

"You know I'm saving to go back to school."

"I doubt if I can wait till then."

They sat for several minutes in silence. She had nothing else to say. Bubba Lee needed to work through this, and the longer she stayed, the more he'd play on her compassion. He didn't mean to appeal to their years of friendship. This had always been his way, convincing her she couldn't get along without him. The ploy wasn't healthy for either one of them.

Berta stood. She refused to touch him. "I'm leaving now. If you decide not to show up for work tomorrow, I understand."

"Do you, Berta? I can't look at you and not see the little girl who found her mama dead on the kitchen floor. I held you that day, remember? I decided right then that I'd always take care of you."

"No more. It ends right here." Berta made her way to the edge of the porch, down the steps, across the gravel crunching under her work boots, and to her truck. Tears streamed down her face for a man who deserved so much more.

God, help him. He's a fine man. Just a little mixed up about me.

Chapter 5

Matt examined the brick samples on his living room floor. How could selecting a color of red brick be so confusing? He should have hired an interior decorator, and this was only the beginning. How would he ever put together paint samples, cabinetry, flooring, hardware? The choices ahead gave him a horrendous headache. Tomorrow he'd hire a decorator, one who could help him with the whole project.

His phone rang, interrupting his near choice of brick. Frustration inched through him as the William Tell Overture alerted him again to the caller. When he recognized the number, he snatched it up.

"Yeah, Landon. What's going on?"

"Got some bad news."

"That seems to be your specialty. I'm ready."

"Mr. Phillips wandered off today, and it took the home five hours to locate him."

"Is he all right?" Matt pictured the elderly man, frail

and weak, succumbing to the intense Mississippi heat. And medicine. . .he took daily insulin injections.

"Two of the staff members found him. He was badly dehydrated but is doing better now."

"Did a doctor check him out?"

"Yes. Sent him home."

Matt sighed. "I find it hard to believe that Mr. Phillips has no family."

"None of them do, and time is running out."

"I believe the house will be done before I'm faced with a real dilemma."

"That's the rest of my bad news. The date's been moved up. We now have six months."

Matt tightened his fist. "What changed?"

"The house has been condemned."

"No surprise there." Matt picked up a sample. "Here I am wasting brain cells on brick samples while good people are being forced into the street."

"They won't be on the street."

"Right. The government will find a home for them, but they'll all be separated. After Katrina, I promised all of them they'd never be separated. You know how much I love those people."

"You shouldn't have made a promise you couldn't keep. They've probably forgotten what you said. Mrs. Devereaux doesn't even know who you are."

"Too late. I made a commitment, and I intend to find a solution."

"Hey, I'm sorry. Representing you is not what I signed up

for at law school, but it's never boring. This whole situation is frustrating, and I'm taking it out on you. Give it to God. Aren't you the one always telling me that?"

Matt snatched a pillow from his sofa and lay back on the wood floor, tucking the pillow beneath his head. "Guess I should practice what I preach. I really expected the building project to go much more smoothly."

Landon chuckled. "You committed to a God-sized project, and you weren't expecting problems the size of China?"

"Right. What was I thinking?"

"You've followed all the guidelines and mandates from the state. You have two nurses ready to take residence at your new home. In the meantime, is there a place in Calista where your friends can live?"

"I don't think so."

"You'd best be talking to someone who can help."

Berta? The local pastor? "Is the current nursing home maintaining standards until it closes?"

"According to the owner, she will fulfill her obligations until the doors close. The residents talk about her visits and how kind she is to them."

"Good. One less concern. I'm heading to Calista on Sunday to see if I can come up with a solution. I'll call you on Monday and let you know what I learn."

Although Matt had plenty of work to keep him busy the rest of the week, the hours dragged by. He trained in the evening for his position as a software consultant in Calista, a job he could perform at his new home. Actually, he enjoyed his current job of keeping the software programs updated for the ongoing needs of the IRS. Too many people just naturally thought the organization was the enemy instead of realizing they were all on the same team. He'd had women cancel dates with him once they learned where he worked, and one of the pastors at his church avoided him as though he carried a dread disease. Sometimes Matt referred to the misconception as one of the hazards of the job, and other times he called it comic relief.

Sunday morning he awakened early enough to get himself on the road by five. The idea of a hotel in Calista appealed to him, but the sleepy town didn't have one. Resting beside him in the console was a steamy cup of coffee. The fresh nutty aroma hinted at morning despite the darkness surrounding him. Slowly the sky lightened to a dark blue with a hint of sunrise within the hour. His stomach growled, and he stuck his hand inside a white paper bag containing a sausage and cheese kolache and a bear claw. His fingers wrapped around the pastry. Why were the tasty things in life not good for you?

Then he remembered Berta.

She'd be wearing something other than jeans this morning. *Excuse me, Lord, if that's not proper.* Seeing her was worth the early morning drive. Driving north, he missed the splendor of an eastern sunrise, but the pastel colors of pink and coral were painted across the sky.

With a stop for gas and another cup of coffee, Matt drove into Calista a few minutes before ten. Perfect. The church members used both sides of the street to park, and a small sign indicated a parking lot in back. He chose to slide in close to the curb farther down the street in order to leave plenty of room for older folks and families with small children. From the many cars, he wondered if the church offered Sunday school at an earlier hour. His present church called it small group. Same thing.

Folks smiled as he walked in. Obviously Sassy hadn't passed around his picture with her news about his infamous position with the IRS. He laughed as he climbed the steps to the entrance.

After accepting a bulletin from a bubbling teenager, he made his way to an empty pew in the middle of the right-hand side of the sanctuary. Voices hummed around him. A laugh here and there. He loved being with God's people, even if he didn't know a soul. Matt hadn't asked Berta where they should meet. For now he would simply read the bulletin and keep his eyes and ears alert for her.

"I do declare. The last person I expected to see this morning." Matt recognized Sassy's voice without lifting his head.

"Good morning, Miss Sassy."

She wore a purple dress. It went well with her carrot-red hair and fire-engine-colored lipstick. She held a straw purse to her chest as though it contained pure gold.

"Feelin' guilty?" she asked.

"Should I?"

"Well, you're in the right place to shed your sins. I hope after you get moved here, you'll find a respectable job. I could always use a little help at the bait shop. Probably digging worms. I pay a nickel more than minimum wage."

"Thank you. I'll remember your offer, but I'm all set." He clamped his teeth down on his tongue to keep from laughing.

Sassy leaned in closer and grasped his pew and the one in

front of him. "When the altar call comes and you realize your choice of profession isn't God-honoring, I'll be glad to pray with you."

"I appreciate that."

She nodded and proceeded down the aisle, stopping and greeting folks as she went. He swallowed to keep his mirth in check and opened the bulletin. A hymnal rested in front of him. He hadn't cracked one of those in a long time. His church used an overhead to display whatever songs had been chosen for the day. Then he spotted something rather peculiar. Berta Dixon was the special music. She was to sing "Great Is Thy Faithfulness." How nice. He paused a moment to think about how her voice must sound. He imagined a Faith Hill type, since she, too, was born in Mississippi. But he'd settle for whatever lifted the rooftops in small-town Calista.

A moment later, Berta scooted in beside him. She smelled faintly of the ocean and wore a little makeup. She shook his senses. The pale green in her dress complemented her tanned face. She was far too appealing for a man who was determined to concentrate on worshiping God.

"So glad you came," she said. "I'm sorry about this morning. I forgot I was supposed to sing."

"No problem. I'm looking forward to it."

She wiggled her nose. "Hope you're not disappointed."

"I'm sure I won't be. Did you tell your crew that work was called off today?"

"Sure did. They were real glad to rest up before another busy week. Mule and Bull have families."

"Are you busy after church?"

"Just fixing lunch for my dad. Want to join us?"

"I won't be intruding?"

"Absolutely not. I planned to ask you anyway."

He smiled into those ocean-depth eyes. "Thanks. I'd like to discuss something with you later."

"We'll make time for it. I've got to move up front now until after I sing. Then I'll join you."

Matt thought since he was accustomed to attending a large church that Calista's service might not be as meaningful. He'd forgotten God didn't require a specific style or mega crowds. He dwelled where folks wanted to worship. The presence of God rested on Matt like the dew on a morning flower.

The time came for Berta to sing. Matt held his breath and prayed she'd sing well. The piano began her intro. Oddly enough, he felt anxious for her. But the moment she opened her mouth, he was mesmerized by her deep voice that rang clear and strong. His blood ran hot and cold at the same time. He'd heard many trained voices that lacked her perfect pitch and passion. In short, he was transported to the throne room of God. When she eased down beside him, just before the sermon, all he could mumble was, "A beautiful song," when he wanted to stand and clap until the sun went down.

The pastor took a passage of scripture and applied it to Matt's life as though the reverend had been informed about all the problems plaguing him. Trust was the focal point, right out of the Old Testament where King Saul chased David and his small band of men. His worship experience this morning showed him that living in Calista would meet all of his needs.

Afterward, he met many of the people, including a tall

woman, whom Berta introduced as Sue Ellen, and Berta's dad, a frail man who used a walker. Mr. Dixon reminded him of those he wanted to help, reinforcing the need to find housing for Grandma's friends. Thankfully, Sassy made no broad announcement of his working for the IRS.

Matt followed Berta's pickup about a mile out of town, down a dirt-and-gravel road, to a bungalow type of home. Well kept and sparkling with a new coat of paint and a sprinkling of blooming flowers, the home welcomed him with tasteful charm. A dog bounded up to them—or rather a mixture of about ten varieties of the species.

"He won't bother you," Mr. Dixon said. "Brushhog, leave the man alone."

Brushhog? "I never met a dog I didn't like." Matt let the animal sniff his hands, and in a moment the two were fast friends.

As soon as Berta opened the front door, he inhaled the tantalizing aroma of roast beef and vegetables.

"Mmm. Something smells wonderful," he said.

"Good. Lunch isn't burnt. That's a good sign." The older man hobbled through to the kitchen after Berta, and Matt followed. "With Berta, food is always a mystery." Her dad laughed.

"Dad, don't give away all my faults before he's here five minutes."

"I think hearing her sing would cover a dozen bad meals," Matt said. "When she sang, I thought heaven had sent one of its own."

Berta blushed. A trait he hadn't expected from the owner

of Bert's Dirts. This woman was full of surprises. He shivered. *Am I falling in love?*

"Just have a seat and I'll have lunch on the table in a few minutes."

"No way. I'm helping." He hoped his eagerness didn't show, but sitting around while others waited on him wasn't his style. "My grandma brought me up better than that."

A strange look passed over her face. "Did your grandmother raise you?"

He nodded. "My folks were killed in a car accident when I was six months old. I was with Grandma at the time, and she just kept me."

"How is she now?"

A twinge of bittersweet, a mixture of longing and a sense of peace, inched through his heart. "She went home to Jesus right after Hurricane Katrina. With the power out in her little community, no one knew she'd fallen. By the time I could get to her, it was too late."

"I'm so sorry." Berta covered her mouth.

"She's in a better place."

"I understand."

And from the look on her face, he believed she really did. "Can I set the table?"

"I never turn down help." She pointed to a cupboard. "The dishes are there, and the silverware is in the drawer below. We eat in the kitchen."

"Sounds good to me. That's where the food is. Mind if I take off my tie and jacket?" Before she had an opportunity to respond, he loosened his tie.

"Throw them over my shoulder, and I'll take care of it," her dad said.

"Are you sure?"

"Ah, you'd be surprised what an old man can do with this walker—run races, shove people out of the way in lines, get the best parking spaces."

Matt laughed. He would love calling Calista home. He obliged Mr. Dixon, then grabbed three plates from the cabinet. He peered out the window. "You have close neighbors."

"That's the Crawford place. Bubba, Mule, and Bull's folks."

So she and Bubba had grown up together. Understanding trickled through him along with a hint of jealousy. He pushed it away in hopes he didn't have a reason to fill his heart with envy.

"Can I ask you some questions?" he asked.

"About your property?"

"No, an entirely different matter."

"Fire away, but I'm warning you, I don't hand out recipes."

Chuckling, he reached for the glasses. "I have a problem. The home I'm building is not just for me. Five others will be living there, too."

She tossed him a puzzled look.

"You see, my grandmother lived in a community of older folks. All of them were hit hard by the hurricane. Their homes were destroyed. A local nursing home took them in, but it hasn't turned out to be a good situation. Before the hurricane, the home was an upscale property, but the folks who owned it decided not to make the necessary repairs. In short, the nursing home is closing. Those people were my aunts and uncles while

I was growing up, and they were all friends with each other, too. When Grandma died and they were grieving for her and their lost homes, I promised them they'd never be separated again. So that's when I got the idea of taking some of my inheritance money and building a home large enough for all of us. I chose Calista because the real estate is affordable and the area is beautiful."

"How wonderful." Berta sighed. "I bet your grandma is smiling down at you from heaven. I'm very touched by what you're doing, but I don't understand your problem."

"The nursing home has been condemned, and the new home won't be finished in time. In short, I'll break my promise to them unless I can find someplace where they all can stay for a few months—preferably here in Calista. I can pay a nurse and a cook and provide a handicap van and whatever else they need, but where? I've driven the streets of Calista, but I didn't see anything for sale or rent that would accommodate five elderly people."

Berta tapped her chin with her finger. "That's a tall order. Let me think about it and ask around." She stared into the living room where her dad had set up residence on the sofa, Bible in hand. "I'm concerned about how long Dad can continue to stay by himself during the day while I'm working," she whispered. "If he'd fall and suffer until I found him. . .well, that would be a nightmare."

"I'm debating whether to add another thousand square feet to the house. Maybe he could join my adopted family."

"Thanks." She swiped at her cheeks. "It's real hard watching him grow old and not be able to do all the things he once enjoyed."

"Berta, I may not be the man I once was, but I still have my hearing." Her dad laughed. "Thanks, sweetheart. Don't be worrying about me. You take care of yourself."

The look on her face nearly melted Matt's heart. He wanted to take her into his arms. Maybe that day would come.

Chapter 6

Tell me one more time why you're confused about finally meeting a man you're actually interested in." Sue Ellen lifted her scissors and paused from her task of thinning Berta's ultra-thick hair. "I may be blond, but this doesn't compute."

"Don't talk too loud. If word gets out about this, I'm toast."

Sue Ellen bent down. "You mean with Sassy or Bubba Lee?"

"Both. Sassy dislikes him because of his job with the IRS, and Bubba Lee thinks I've ended our so-called relationship due to Matt." Berta shook her head. "And now that I have nearly enough money to get my master's in music, I meet this wonderful man. I really, really would like to get to know him better. Now do you see why I'm confused?"

"Absolutely. All you've ever talked about is moving away from Calista and using music as a ministry."

Berta nodded, but she couldn't voice her deepest desires. "Then there's the home he's building."

"I'm still in the dark, girlfriend. You mean the house is so huge, and you don't want to toss your chances to live there?" Sue Ellen tugged on both sides of Berta's hair and peered into the mirror to make sure it was cut even.

"No, not that. He's building it to house five elderly people who were victims of Hurricane Katrina. You see, his grandmother, who raised him, died after she fell during the storm and couldn't get help. He'd been raised in the area and considered all her neighbors as aunts and uncles. He simply couldn't abandon them when their homes were destroyed. They've been living in a nursing home, but now it's closing. He promised them they'd never be separated."

Sue Ellen continued staring into the mirror. Her eyes moistened. "That is the most beautiful story I've ever heard."

Berta studied her best friend. She wore her hair in a ponytail because she was always too busy fixing everyone else's hair to do anything with her own. Sue Ellen had no idea about her natural beauty, an endearing trait for an endearing friend.

"His story caused me to think about Dad. He's getting slower and slower. The day is coming when I'll have to find someone to help me with him."

Sue Ellen smiled sadly. "I'm really blessed that my parents are in good health."

"Well, he's all I have left. Matt mentioned Dad coming to live with him. Isn't that sweet?"

"Makes me want to fall in love with him. So what's stopping you?"

"My point. He's almost too good to be true. There has to be something horribly wrong with him. I just haven't discovered it yet."

"Maybe he plans to do an audit of Bert's Dirts."

"With the way I keep records? I'll be outta business and doing hard time."

"Duh, girlfriend, have you considered that God has put Matt VanMichael III in your path for a reason?"

"If Sassy and Bubba Lee don't kill him first."

Sue Ellen giggled. "You poor girl. But what about your music career?"

Berta shook her head. "With Daddy's health, my business, and my fledgling love life, I'm not sure what I should do."

"I know who does."

Berta smiled. "I've pleaded my case. Now I'm waiting for God to answer."

"I may not have any solutions to your problems, but I have an idea how to help Matt with his housing problem."

Matt spent his lunch hour looking for a nursing home that would take five senior citizens for three months, one of whom had dementia. He'd reached a dead end. Either the residences didn't have room or their policy insisted upon a yearly contract. He understood the business end of it all, but the frustration in dealing with it had made him tense and irritable. These were people, not just names and social security numbers. His only other idea was to lease a single dwelling for a few months and hire a nurse to come in on a daily basis. Even that solution would be difficult to find. Homeowners wanted their property leased a year in advance.

To make matters worse, he needed cable for Internet connectivity for his new job, and the cable company that took care of Calista had just pushed back two months the availability to his property. Satellite or dial-up service wouldn't work. He sat back in his office chair and wondered if all his problems were supposed to instill patience. If so, he had a long way to go. One of his grandmother's sayings danced across his mind. "Life is a game of trust. A lack of it means you've demoted God to a mortal." He smiled. She was right, as usual.

He missed his grandmother more than he cared to admit. If he dwelled on his memories of her for very long, he'd tear up like a kid. She'd fulfilled three roles: grandmother, mom, and dad. And she'd done so when the rest of her friends were starting to take life easy. While other women her age took trips and made quilts for needy families, Grandma showed him how to hit a baseball, attended parent-teacher conferences, and washed his mouth out with soap for spouting bathroom words. He laughed. Grandma had taught him how to love and work hard. Someday he hoped to pass on those same values to children of his own— but not the washing out of their mouths with soap. He'd hated that. Of course, all it took was one time, and he never repeated the word again.

Grandma would have liked Berta—beauty, brains, and tenacity. Except Grandma couldn't sing. Oh, she'd taught him hymns, but Berta's voice rivaled the voices of the angels. Next Sunday he planned to attend Calista's church again and spend some time scouting around for a possible solution for his friends. Maybe Berta would tag along. He'd call her tonight about that very thing.

From the corner of her eye, Berta saw Bubba Lee pull up in his truck. He hadn't quit. At least not yet. Mule and Bull arrived right behind him. They were only fifteen minutes early instead of the customary thirty. Maybe they had a talk this morning about future plans. The idea of hiring three men who didn't know her routine didn't sit well at all. But she'd deal with it. Coaxing them to stay would be selfish. Berta waved at the three men and made her way toward them to discuss the day's work.

To Berta, clearing land this morning was going far too slow. The dozer seemed to creep forward by inches instead of feet. At least tall leafy oaks shaded the area, and a light breeze cooled her face. Matt specifically requested that as many trees as possible were to remain standing, which made their job a little harder. She'd love to see his house plans. Maybe he'd show her this Sunday when he came for church.

She nearly laughed aloud at Sue Ellen's suggestion for housing the elderly people until their new home was completed. Tonight she'd make the initial call to see how far-fetched the idea really was. Funny how God worked out the strangest of circumstances.

Berta glanced to her right, where Mule worked an area with a wheel loader. As usual, he wore headphones. That man lived and breathed country-western music. Whether it be Hank Jr., Garth, Willie, or George Strait, Mule knew the words, but not the pitch. From what she heard of his activities on Saturday nights, he should be listening to a little gospel music.

She held her breath. What was he doing? Didn't he see Bubba Lee to the right of him pulling out brush by hand? Bubba wasn't paying attention, either.

"Bubba, get out of there!" She shouted so loudly that her

throat hurt. "Mule, watch where you're going!"

Berta lived and breathed safety on the job, but neither man acted as though they'd ever heard a word. She whipped around to get Bull's attention, but his back was to her.

"Bubba, you're going to get hit!" She switched off the dozer and jumped down. Pure anger flared through her veins. She ought to fire both of them for their stupidity.

Mule's dozer crept closer toward Bubba. Dangerously close. Fear nearly paralyzed her. In the next instant, she raced toward them, shouting, praying. Within twenty feet of the dozer, Mule hit reverse, swinging the front-end loader to a wide right—knocking Bubba Lee down hard.

The screams rose and fell in her throat. Mule immediately saw what had happened and stopped his wheel loader. He was on the ground and at Bubba's side in an instant. She held her breath at the sight of Bubba's body. Blood streamed from his temple and cheek on the left side of his face, and his arm was mangled and twisted into a hideous mass of torn flesh. His closed eyes frightened her.

"Bubba, can you hear me?" she asked.

Nothing, not even a moan, but his eyelids fluttered.

"Hold on. I'm calling an ambulance now." She whipped out her cell phone and hit speed dial. Thank goodness she'd had the foresight to preset the county's ambulance service in case of an emergency.

Bubba slowly opened his eyes and looked up at her with a pain-glazed expression. "I'm all right. Just my arm."

"Bubba, I'm real sorry." Mule knelt at his brother's side, his face as pale as Bubba's. Mule swiped at the blood on his brother's face with his shirtsleeve.

"What happened?" Bull asked from behind them. "Is Bubba hurt?" He stopped cold. "Oh no."

"You'd best get back—" Bubba slipped into unconsciousness.

Berta slid her cell phone back into her jeans pocket. "The ambulance is on its way. Mule, go get the first-aid kit out of my truck. I want to check the bleeding."

Bubba looked like an animal caught in a trap. More dead than alive. Blood everywhere. Was it her fault? Had she hurt him to the point he didn't heed her warnings?

Dear God, please don't let him die.

<hr/>

Eight o'clock. Berta should be home by now. Matt picked up his phone and punched in her cell number. She might be tired. Whose fault was that? Guilt bombarded him for his insistence upon getting his land cleared. A woman shouldn't have to work that hard.

He settled back on his sofa and waited for her sweet voice. She answered on the third ring. Her voice quivered.

"Berta, this is Matt. What's wrong? Have I called at a bad time?"

"Something is terribly wrong." She paused. "Bubba Lee was in an accident at the site this afternoon."

"How bad?"

She sniffed. "His brother hit him with the wheel loader."

"I'm sorry. What have the doctors said?"

"He just came out of surgery. Internal injuries."

"Do you want me to come there?"

Silence.

"Berta, I'm asking."

"Would you do that?" Her voice sounded weak, distant.

"Yes, I can leave here in a matter of minutes."

"I don't know what to say."

"Who's there with you now besides Bubba's family?"

"My dear friends—Sue Ellen, Dottie Jean, Sassy."

The latter woman was a bit of a sore subject with Matt, but if Sassy Hatchett was a source of comfort to Berta, he could swallow his pride. "What about your dad?"

"He's alone. Sassy drove out there before coming to the hospital and made sure he was okay."

His opinion of Sassy raised a few notches more. "Good. Where are you?"

"Closer than you might think. I'm in Hattiesburg. City General Hospital."

"All right. I'll be there in about two hours."

He disconnected the call and wrapped his fingers around his keys.

Chapter 7

Bubba Lee's family visited him in critical care while Berta leafed through nameless magazines in the uncomfortable chairs of the sterile waiting room. Dottie Jean, Sassy, and Sue Ellen kept her company. They'd all prayed for Bubba and sought comfort in the chapel. Now Berta found it difficult to concentrate on conversation. She couldn't stop feeling that Bubba's accident was her fault.

"If you don't stop blaming yourself, I'm going to up and whip you." Sassy slapped her magazine shut and tossed it on the table. "This wasn't any more your doing than me causing the moon to shine."

Sassy meant well.

"I really hurt him," Berta said.

"Then blame me," Dottie Jean said. "After all, I'm the one who insisted you tell him the truth about your relationship."

"No one pushed Bubba Lee in front of Mule's wheel loader." Sue Ellen stood and paced across the small room. "It was an accident, plain and simple. We've been to the chapel. We're praying, and we're here for the family. That's all we can do. If we're all going to be here, let's do something constructive."

Berta stared up from the magazine. "Like what? I can barely think."

"Remember when you told me about Matt's problem?"

"Praise God," Sassy said. "Is he quitting the IRS?"

"No, Sassy." Berta sensed her temper about to skyrocket. "The house he's building is not just for him. He's planning to take care of five senior citizens who were friends of his deceased grandmother and left homeless after Hurricane Katrina."

Sassy's eyes widened. "You mean there's a shred of decency in that boy?"

"Put a lid on it, Sassy," Sue Ellen said. "He's a man, not a boy, and you've up and judged him without taking the time to know what he's all about."

"Just who do you think you are, Miss Priss?" Sassy asked. "Have a little respect for your elders."

"Hey, stop it right now, you two." Dottie Jean's voice rose over Sassy's, a feat in itself.

"I'm sorry." Sue Ellen shook her head. "I'm being judgmental, not helpful."

"I don't have an excuse," Sassy said. "Except I hate to see Berta upset about something that's not her fault." She pulled herself up from the sofa, made her way to Berta's side, and wrapped her arms around her shoulders. "I have a mouth as big as the Gulf, but you know I love you."

Berta nodded and kissed the older woman's cheek.

"Now tell me about your friend's problem."

Just as she opened her mouth to describe the sad situation

with Matt's friends, the subject of their conversation appeared in the entrance of the waiting room.

Sassy cleared her throat. "Speaking of the devil."

"Hi, Miss Sassy, Miss Dottie Jean, Sue Ellen." Matt smiled at Berta. "How are you doing?"

"All right." *Much better with my friends close by.* "Bubba's in critical care."

Sassy grasped the edge of the chair beside Berta and wiggled until she stood. "Sit here. What's your name again?"

"Matt."

"Okay, Matt. All I could think of was revenuer, but none of us makes moonshine."

He patted her shoulder. Obviously he'd dealt with the Sassy type before. "Thank you, ma'am."

Once Sassy ambled over and settled herself beside a smiling Dottie Jean, Matt swung his attention to Berta. The tender look in his eyes and that I'm-here-to-ease-your-heart look caused her to gape, until she caught herself.

"You look tired," he said. "Can I get you anything? Have you eaten?"

"I can't think of doing anything until I find out how Bubba Lee's doing."

"I can only imagine how his brother feels."

Not any worse than I do. "He took the accident real hard. The Crawfords are a close family. And don't worry about your land. I'll get the job finished this week."

He frowned. "Clearing my property wasn't a consideration."

"I know, but we do have a business arrangement." Why was she a short stick away from being rude to a man who'd just driven two hours to keep her company? She started to apologize, but Mule stepped into the waiting area.

"Berta, he's awake and asking for you." He tossed Matt a look that would stop a category five hurricane.

She stood on shaky legs. *Thank You, Lord.* "I'm ready." She smiled at Matt and hoped he saw she hadn't lost all of her manners. "I'll take you up on getting something to eat when I get back."

Mule cleared his throat, and she followed him down the hall with its glaring lights and slamming of metal. How did anyone ever rest in these places?

"Is he in a lot of pain?" she asked.

"Some. But you know Bubba Lee. Won't admit to anything. He's hooked up to a morphine drip, and I saw him use it."

"How long will he be here?"

"Doctor hasn't made that call yet."

She took a deep breath. "Are you doing better?"

Mule shrugged. "How's a man supposed to feel when he's nearly killed his brother?"

"It was an accident."

"No matter." He paused. "I thought I killed him."

An image of Bubba Lee's bloody body scrolled through her mind. "God was looking out for him."

"I've been thinkin' about that. Reckon it's time I grew up and got myself into church."

"That's a good decision. How are your folks doing?"

"Mom's real upset, but Dad's holding up."

They stopped outside a closed door. Mule studied her face. "He still don't look too good."

"Mule, I have to ask you something. Did Bubba Lee tell you what happened the other night when I stopped by at your folks' place?"

He nodded.

"Do you suppose I hurt him so bad that he wasn't paying attention today?"

Mule shook his head. "You already said it was an accident to make me feel better. Now I'm telling you the same thing. But you two will work out your problems."

He opened the door, and she walked inside. The sight of the huge man hooked up to an IV pole and a heart monitor and wearing a body full of bruises and stitches was a little more than her emotions could take. She covered her mouth and sobbed.

Bubba attempted a faint smile. "I expected a better reception than this. Are you trying to tell me that I can't enter Calista's beauty contest?"

"Not this year." She swallowed a sob. "You have to be a female."

"Shucks. Just when I was about to ask you for singin' lessons."

Berta gave Mr. and Mrs. Crawford a hug and acknowledged Bull.

"He gave us quite a scare," Mr. Crawford said, his face tanned by the Mississippi sun and aged by its relentless heat. He turned to his wife. "Come on, Mama, let's get us some coffee and let these young people talk."

"I'll go with you," Mule said. "I need to call the wife and the kids."

"I should do the same," Bull said.

The idea of being alone with Bubba Lee sat like mashed potatoes in the pit of her stomach.

"I'm glad you're going to be all right," she finally said.

"Me, too. It'll take awhile. Best you find someone to replace me. Temporarily or permanently."

"What would you like?" She reached for his hand, and he squeezed it lightly.

"I like my job."

"I'll be selling the business once I leave for New York in a few months."

"That's where you'll be going to school?"

"Uh-huh."

"Hope I'll be getting around good by then."

"Of course you will." She despised the small talk, especially with the tension between them. "Remember the snake pile I ran into?"

He forced a laugh. "How could I forget?"

"I kind of feel those rattlers are wiggling between us."

Bubba Lee closed his eyes. "That's why I wanted to talk to you. You know, get it all straightened out."

"I'm sorry."

"For what? Bein' honest?"

"For hurting you."

He glanced away and bit into his lip.

"Take a shot of the morphine, Bubba Lee."

"Not yet. Doc says it might make me sleep. I want to say I'm sorry for stalking after you like a lovesick dog for all these years. You tried to tell me how you felt a hundred times, but I refused to listen."

A tear trickled down her cheek.

"You go on to New York and be a star or whatever it is you want to do. Just remember your biggest fans will always be back home in Calista, Mississippi." He shook his head. "I'm not sure all of this is coming out right. What I mean is I understand you have your own life. I won't be getting in your way anymore."

"You're the best friend I've ever had."

"Don't tell Sue Ellen that. She might come after me with a pair of scissors and a bottle of nail polish."

She laughed. "Sue Ellen's here, and so is Sassy and Dottie Jean."

"The Fearsome Foursome." He closed his eyes and winced. "I'm leaving you alone now. Get some rest."

"I will. And you head on home. A fella can't get well with a bunch of people hanging around."

She squeezed his hand lightly. So many thoughts rushed through her head, but not one made it to her lips. "I'll check on you tomorrow."

<hr />

"I hear you're planning to put old people in that house you're building," Sassy said.

Old? Matt didn't think Sassy was far behind Grandma's age. "Yes, ma'am. I think they'll enjoy how pretty it is there."

"I hear you have a problem. Something to do with the house?"

Dottie Jean touched Sassy's arm. "Maybe Matt doesn't want to talk about it right now."

Sue Ellen lifted her gaze from filing her nails. "Oh, I think he should."

The ladies reminded Matt of a few of his grandma's friends—or maybe it was simply the way of women.

"My problem is that the home I'm building won't be done before their nursing home closes. I'd like to find a house around here that's big enough for all of them until my house is completed."

"Is that all?" Sassy slapped her leg. "I've got just the place for you."

"Where?" he asked.

"Why, me and Joe's place. We had this huge house when the kids were growing up, and after he died I couldn't part with it. I've been meaning to fix it up a little to sell for a long time. I could get the painting and minor repairs done so those folks could live there until your house is done and then sell it."

Had he heard correctly? Had Sassy Hatchett, the feisty woman who appeared to despise him, offered to help him with Grandma's friends?

"Not sure what to say," he said. "I'd about given up on finding a solution. I'm real grateful."

"You don't understand that Berta is real special to all of us. If she takes a shine to someone, then we have to look out for her best interests."

"You see," Dottie Jean said, "the four of us look like a mismatched set—and we are—but God put us all together when Berta's mom died several years ago. We meet every Tuesday evening for Bible study and just talk about life. I took over as her mom, and the rest of us filled in the other missing spots."

"But Berta is there for us, too," Sue Ellen said. "It's not one-sided like she's an emotional mess or something. That's what makes our relationship special. We have unique personalities." She glanced at Sassy. "And we have a way of complementing each other."

Matt thought back to when he was growing up and how Grandma's neighbors had taken care of him. He understood more than what they might think. "I'm going to enjoy living in Calista. Biloxi is a fine city, but I miss the small-town friendliness."

"I sure wish you had another job," Sassy said.

He smiled. Dare he delight in letting her believe that he planned to continue working as an IRS agent once he moved? "Aw, Miss Sassy, as long as you pay your taxes, you don't have a thing to fear from the IRS."

She scowled. "It's the principle of the thing. You tell me why they're having you live out here unless it's to spy on folks. And since when did the IRS pay a person enough to build your fancy house?"

"Now, Sassy, just when you're getting to know Matt, you get cantankerous," Dottie Jean said.

Matt waved his hand. "I think I've had enough fun at Miss Sassy's expense. Although my current job is needed and respected, once I'm in Calista, I'll be working from home for a computer company."

"Praise God." Sassy fanned herself. "So you plan to live respectable here? Too bad Berta is leaving."

"Leaving? Where is she going?" His gaze swept over each woman.

"Berta has a dream." Dottie Jean stood from the sofa and

walked to the edge of the waiting room. She peered up and down the hallway as if she didn't want Berta to hear what she had to say. "Berta could sing before she could talk plain. Her mother made sure she had voice lessons. Sacrificed a lot for her little girl to learn from the best, no matter how far she had to drive or how much it cost. When Berta's mother died, her dad continued with the lessons. Berta won every singing contest around. It comes natural for her, like breathing is for the rest of us. She went away to college on a music scholarship, but her daddy wanted her to get her master's and be someone famous. Berta has always done exactly what her parents wanted. Of course, Bubba Lee encouraged everything she ever did."

"That's 'cause he loves her," Sassy said. "That man has loved her since they were kids."

"She is extremely talented." Matt didn't know what else to say. Selfishness washed over him like mud.

"She started Bert's Dirts to get the money needed to go on back to school," Dottie Jean continued. "Most likely she'd do that at the end of the summer."

"I'm sure she'll be a success," he said. How could he fall for a woman in such a short time and then learn she was leaving? What about Bubba Lee? Were the two of them destined to be together? He felt like a fool.

Chapter 8

Berta left Bubba Lee alone to sleep and heal. His pain must be unbearable for the big man to take medication. She felt better after their talk. He'd be okay, and he'd given his blessing for her to go on with her life. If only the other confusing parts of her could be resolved. Odd how she'd known Bubba Lee all her life and knew she could never marry him, but she'd known Matt a short while and sensed something there that she'd seen in Mom and Dad.

Mule and Bull met her in the hall.

"Can we talk for a minute?" Mule asked. "We spoke to the doctor."

"Sure. Is the report good?"

"We think so. He'll be in the hospital awhile, then laid up at home. We thought you'd want to tell the others."

"I'd be glad to. Thanks. I'm sure your parents are feeling better."

"Did Bubba Lee pop the question?" Mule asked.

A sinking sensation settled in the pit of her stomach.

"What do you mean?"

"We figured he asked you to wait for him to heal so you two could get married."

"No. We didn't talk about anything like that." She wouldn't tell them the contents of their conversation. What made him think they discussed marriage? "I have insurance for Bubba Lee that should help him take care of expenses until he can get back to work."

"Are you selling Bert's Dirts?" Bull seldom spoke, and she was surprised at his question.

"I'd like to before I head off to school."

Bull cleared his throat. "Mule and me would like to buy it—Bubba Lee, too. It's a good living for our families."

She nodded. "We'll work it out. I'd like to see the business go to y'all. You're hard workers, and I'll give you a fair price."

"Bubba Lee talked about it this morning before we came to work. He was going to ask you about it."

"No problem. It's the least I can do with the way you three have helped me build the business."

"Berta, we always figured you and Bubba Lee would get married. He'd wait for you while you went back to school," Bull said. "I mean, he's loved you for as long as I can remember."

Misery inched through her. Were they trying to get her to change her mind because Bubba Lee was hurt?

"I can't marry him. We've talked this through, and we're fine." She smiled and walked down the hall. Back to her friends. Back to Matt, the man who scared her to death—but in a way that was most pleasant.

She raised her shoulders and smiled at her friends. "He's

going to be fine."

"Another prayer answered," Dottie Jean said.

"Did you two get your problems worked out?" Sassy asked.

"Sassy, couldn't that have waited?" Dottie Jean's tone left no doubt about her frustration.

"Well, it's something we all wondered about." Sassy wiggled her shoulders.

"Yes, we did." Berta avoided Matt. She didn't know him well enough to discuss personal affairs. "Everything's worked out, and we came to an agreement."

"Good," Sassy said. "I hated to see you two break off your relationship after all these years."

"Sassy!" This time the scolding came from Sue Ellen.

"It's all for the best. I'm going ahead and selling him and his brothers Bert's Dirts. We'll get all our business taken care of before the end of summer." Berta stole a glance at Matt and read confusion—or was it sadness?—in his eyes.

Matt felt like a fool. Here he'd thought Berta might be the woman God had intended for him, and she had plans to marry Bubba Lee. Thoughts of his stupidity bannered across his mind. He thought she'd showed genuine interest in him, but he'd been so wrong.

"I'm real glad he's pulled through this," he said. "Now that the crisis is over, I'll head back to Biloxi."

"I'd like to take you to a late dinner for all of your trouble tonight."

"No thanks." He forced a smile. "I'm not really hungry."

"How about coffee?"

"I have an early morning." He was one step shy of giving her the brush-off.

She sighed. "I hadn't thought of that. I'll look forward to seeing you on Sunday."

"I'll let you know." He turned to Sassy. "I really appreciate your offer, and I'd like to see your house."

"Whenever you're ready. Glad to help."

"Can I walk you to the elevator?" Berta asked.

He wanted to shout no, that a grown man didn't need a woman to escort him anywhere. But one look at her face, and he felt like mush—instead of grits. "Sure. You ladies drive safely back to Calista, and thanks for helping me out."

He walked with Berta down an entirely too long hallway. He felt as though someone should throw him a banana for making a monkey out of himself.

"What's wrong?" she asked.

"Nothing. I have a lot on my mind."

"You changed from the time I left to see Bubba Lee. Did Sassy insult you again?"

"Not at all. In fact, she offered her house for Grandma's friends."

"I hoped she would. Sue Ellen and I talked about it, but I hadn't had an opportunity to do anything more."

"You have good friends, Berta. They care a great deal about you." The elevator loomed ahead. He needed time to sort out Berta's heading off to school and marrying Bubba Lee.

"Yes, we care about each other. Matt, thank you for driving up here. I'll never forget how kind you've been to me. Your job will be finished in the next day or so, but I hope we stay in contact."

Like inviting me to the wedding? "We can see each other at church."

"I thought—"

"What?" he asked.

"Nothing."

"I'll see you soon." The elevator door opened, and he lunged into its sanctuary. His ruffled feelings had been replaced with anger, especially when he considered that she may have used him to make Bubba Lee jealous. His ability to judge character needed a major adjustment.

Berta didn't understand why Matt had grown so distant in a matter of minutes. She thought they had the beginnings of. . . well, something akin to romance. She pasted on a smile and joined her friends.

"Girlfriend, why haven't you told Matt that you planned to leave Calista?" Sue Ellen planted her hands on her hips and glared. "I thought you liked him."

"I do." Suddenly she felt miserable. "Are you telling me he knows?"

Sue Ellen pressed her lips together. "He does now."

Berta sank into a chair. "This has not been a good day. I planned to tell him on Sunday."

"Looks to me like you were leading him on," Sassy said.

"I thought you didn't like him." Berta wanted to unleash all the frustration of the day—and Sassy was a prime candidate.

"I changed my mind." Sassy stuck her nose in the air.

"This has been a very long day for all of us," Dottie Jean said. "Let's get on the road, and we'll sort this out tomorrow. Berta, I don't think you need to drive back alone. One of us should go with you."

Not Sassy. I'm afraid I'll tear into her even though I know she means well.

"I'll ride with her," Sue Ellen said.

And so it was settled. Berta wanted to cry, and there were a million reasons why she could. Having Sue Ellen along meant they could talk—and cry if that's how it happened.

Once at Berta's truck, Sue Ellen took the keys and slid her long legs into the driver's side. She pulled the truck from the parking lot and onto the street.

"I've made a mess of things," Berta said. "I should have told Matt about leaving at the end of the summer. But. . ."

"But what?"

"I've only known him a short while. It seemed premature to talk about my future when I didn't know how he felt."

"Driving up from Biloxi tonight should have been a clue."

"You're right." Berta leaned back against the headrest. "Sometimes I wish that Mom hadn't wanted so much from me. Her and Dad's expectations have driven me for a lot of years."

Sue Ellen shot her a quick glance. "Are you saying you don't want to go to New York and study for your master's?"

Berta shrugged. "I love singing, and I know it's a gift. And yet I'd rather do something with it other than perform. I'm not recording material, and I can't write a song. Never could."

"What would you like to do?"

"Does it matter when I'd disappoint Dad?"

"I know your dad, and he doesn't come across to me as the type who'd push anyone to do something they didn't want. Tell me, Berta, if given the opportunity, what would you like to do?"

"Teach music to children."

"Wonderful. You'd be perfect. Why, you could easily get your teaching certificate."

Berta swallowed back the tears. "I'm afraid to tell Dad."

"The Berta Dixon I know isn't afraid of anything, especially if she feels God is in it."

She shook her head. "I've often wondered."

"Girlfriend, you need to do some heavy-duty praying. This makes me excited for you. Imagine teaching and marrying Matt—"

"Whoa. Who said anything about getting married?" She remembered Bubba Lee's brothers trying to push her into marrying their brother, but that was private.

"I'm simply thinking about the future." Sue Ellen laughed. "Sounds good, doesn't it?"

Berta nodded and smiled. "I'll pray about it."

"So will I. And you should ask Dottie Jean and Sassy."

She cringed but agreed. Sue Ellen had offered a spark of hope, and the thought of following her own dream sounded better than getting lost in New York and spending her time on a degree and a career she didn't want.

Matt attempted to concentrate on his job. No use. His mind kept drifting back to the night of Bubba Lee's accident. Berta had gotten under his skin in a bad way. Two weeks had passed, and he should be thinking about Sassy's offer and seeing the house in Calista. Except he'd canceled the appointment and discussed Sassy's house over the phone. He should also call Berta and thank her for completing the job on time.

Should. Life was full of all the things a person should do. Couldn't do. Wouldn't do. Refused to do. He felt like a junior high lovesick kid, and he barely knew Berta—the talented owner of Bert's Dirts who sang like a Broadway star. She belonged in New York studying music. And if she truly loved Bubba Lee, then she ought to be married to him.

Matt had looked forward to the move to Calista—the church, the people, his new home. His life had so much order and precision before he met her.

His phone rang, and he answered it on the first ring. Any diversion helped his wounded heart.

"You have a visitor, Matt," the receptionist said.

"Who?" His mind raced with clients and fears he'd missed a scheduled appointment.

"Mrs. Sassy Hatchett."

Chapter 9

S assy, why have you driven all the way to Biloxi to see me?" Matt asked. "I gave my attorney instructions to cut you a check for the rental of your house. It'll work out just fine for my friends, unless you've changed your mind."

Sassy sat back in the chair facing his desk, hugging her purse—or rather a tote bag decorated with fishing lures. She was dressed in her Sunday best. "I came to see you and find out where you lost your brains."

He laughed—the first time in over two weeks. "What did I do now?"

"You're letting Berta get away."

Ouch. She'd hit a touchy spot. "She has her own life. I believe it's all planned out."

Sassy shook her head. "There are some things that only God knows."

"Are you claiming to have a direct line?"

She lifted her chin. "Don't get smart with me. I know your grandma brought you up better than that. But since you asked, we've all been praying about you and Berta. So I came down here to set you straight."

He startled. "What are you talking about?"

"It ain't no surprise to anyone that I can put my foot in my mouth."

He grinned.

"Wipe that smile off your face. I'm serious here."

Sometimes she sounded just like his grandma. "All right. I'm sorry."

"I let on like she and Bubba Lee were going to get married. At the time I couldn't decide if I liked you enough to have you in Berta's life. She doesn't love Bubba Lee, and I'm asking you to forgive me."

"I do, Sassy. But it sure sounded to me like they were going to marry."

"Naw."

"What about her plans to further her education?"

"That's why I'm here. You need to talk to her."

Matt contemplated Sassy's statement. "I'm not standing in the way of her education—and her dreams."

"Of course you're not. That's why you need to talk to her."

"No, I can't interfere."

She leaned in toward his desk. "How bad do you want my house?"

"Oh, you drive one hard bargain." Matt intended to sound light, but the truth was, she had him snagged.

Sassy stood. "I'll expect you in church on Sunday." She turned and stomped out of his office, leaving him somewhere between confused and bewildered.

Berta stared across the kitchen table at her dad. She'd made his favorite chicken-fried steak, mashed potatoes and gravy, and green beans with bacon. None of it good for him, but he loved it all. And she needed him to be in a good mood.

He pushed back his plate and patted his stomach. "Wonderful dinner, Berta. Now that I have a full tummy, what's on your mind?"

She grinned. "You read me pretty well."

"Always have. And it must be mighty important, because you're shaking."

Taking a deep breath, she rubbed her palms together. "It is, Daddy."

He lifted a brow and chuckled. "So now it's 'Daddy.' Best you tell me what's on your mind before you work yourself up into gettin' sick."

She nodded. "It's about going back to school."

"Are you short on money?"

"No. I. . .I don't really want to go. I'd like to stay here."

"All right." He picked up his glass of buttermilk and finished it off.

"You mean you're not going to argue with me?"

"Berta, I want you to be happy. Music was your mother's dream, and when she died, I carried on for her. But if you don't want to leave for New York, then I'm fine—more than fine. Downright happy, in fact." He touched her cheek. "I'm a selfish old man who would like nothing better than to have his only daughter close by."

Tears welled in her eyes. "Thank you, Daddy. This means a lot to me."

"Are you still planning on selling your business to the Crawfords?"

"Yes. I think I'd like to teach music."

"At the school?"

"Yes."

He laughed. "Then get on with it, girl. Time's a-wastin'."

"I was thinking about looking into it tomorrow."

"What about that Matt fellow?"

She sensed her emotions threatening to spill over like boiling milk. "Haven't heard from him."

He wagged a finger at her. "He's a good man. I could tell the moment I met him. And I know you like him."

"I do. I'll call him on Sunday after church."

Sunday morning, Berta sat with her dad. She had plenty of things to talk to God about, but worship came first. Her heavenly Father understood how her heart and mind ached for answers. She had wonderful friends, and they were praying for her just as she did for them.

The piano music started, and she focused on God—not herself. Someone eased down on the pew beside her. She turned. *Matt.*

"Good morning," he whispered and waved at Dad.

His smile made her toes wiggle. "Good morning." She returned the smile, and she was certain her cheeks flushed tomato red.

The service began before she had an opportunity to say another word—if she could have found one to say. Dad chuckled, and she jabbed him in the ribs. How would she ever be able to concentrate on the service this morning? Worse yet, how could she talk to Matt about the problems between them?

The moment the piano sounded the postlude, her heart sped into triple time. She needed to set the pace for. . .friendship, at least.

"How are you?" she asked.

"Much better since I'm here."

Not only did her toes tingle, but the soles of her feet itched. "I'll take that as a compliment. Do you have plans for lunch?"

"Is there a roast in the oven?"

She laughed. "Actually, there is."

"Sounds like a good place to begin."

"Matt."

"Berta."

They laughed together.

"I'd like to apologize for acting like a stupid kid that night at the hospital," he said.

"It was my fault by not being truthful."

Sassy walked by and greeted them. "Sure is nice to see you, Matt. I'll be expecting you at the house about four unless you're too busy." She winked and kept on walking.

What was that all about? "As I said, I wasn't up front with you about leaving Calista."

"I'm sure we'll all see you onstage one day, and I'll be the fan in the front row."

She shook her head. "I'm not going."

"Why not?"

"That was my mother's dream, not mine. It took me a long

time to realize it."

"But aren't you selling your business to Bubba Lee and his brothers?"

"I am." She took a deep breath to still her butterfly-winged heart. "I'm going to teach school—music to elementary children."

"Then you're not leaving Calista?"

"No. The town's stuck with me."

"I'd like to know you're close by." His eyes filled with a special light that she knew matched her own. "In fact, I'd like folks to think we're stuck good."

"Sounds like something Sassy might say."

"I might tell you about Miss Sassy and me one day, but right now I want to spend every spare minute with you." He slipped his hand into hers. "I think we have lunch to fix. I can set the table. Later, let's talk. I have a lot I want to say to you."

"And I have a lot to say to you."

"We're a pair, Miss Berta."

She smiled from the inside out, and from the look on his face, she knew he'd have kissed her if they hadn't been in church. Maybe someday that would happen, too.

DIANN MILLS

Award-winning author DiAnn Mills launched her career in 1998 with the publication of her first book. Currently she has sixteen novels, fourteen novellas, a nonfiction book, and several articles and short stories in print.

DiAnn believes her readers should "expect an adventure." Her desire is to show characters solving real problems of today from a Christian perspective through a compelling story.

Five of her anthologies have appeared on the CBA Best-Seller List. Three of her books have won the distinction of Best Historical of the Year by Heartsong Presents, and she remains a favorite author by Heartsong Presents' readers. Two of her books have won Short Historical of the Year by American Christian Romance Writers 2003 and 2004.

DiAnn is a founding board member of American Christian Fiction Writers and a member of Inspirational Writers Alive, ChiLibris, and Advanced Writers and Speakers Association. She speaks to various groups and teaches writing workshops. She is also a mentor for the Christian Writers Guild.

She lives in sunny Houston, Texas, the home of heat, humidity, and Harleys. In fact, she'd own one, but her legs are too short. DiAnn and her husband have four adult sons and are active members of Metropolitan Baptist Church.

Visit DiAnn's Web site at www.diannmills.com.

Not on the Menu

by Martha Rogers

Dedication

To my husband, Rex,
for letting me attend so many conferences
in lieu of our own vacation.
Also to my critique partners and coauthors in this project.
Thank you for your belief in me.
And thanks to everyone who prayed for me
at ACFW and Mount Hermon.

In his heart a man plans his course,
but the LORD determines his steps.
PROVERBS 16:9

Chapter 1

Dottie Jean Weaver slumped into a chair, thankful the noon crowd had thinned. The older she got, the harder it became to stand on her feet and wait tables for several hours. No matter that she owned the place and could let others do the serving, she'd known most of Calista's citizens for more years than she liked to count and enjoyed seeing them.

She gazed at the two men seated a few tables away. Calista's deputy sheriff, Bud Briggs, and the local mailman, Wendell Meeks, sat enjoying a long lunch break. No doubt they were waiting for two of her friends to join them for a tea break.

Wendell held up his mug. "Dottie Jean, how about some more coffee over here?"

She pushed herself up from her chair. Regardless of how tired she felt, her customers would be served. Dottie Jean retrieved the carafe from the counter and headed for the table.

"I think I'll have a piece of your pecan pie to go with it, if you don't mind."

She poured the hot liquid into his mug, then went back for the pie. When she set the plate on the table, Dottie Jean noted a tiny coffee stain on Wendell's otherwise impeccable mail-carrier shirt. She'd never seen a man more proud of his uniform than Wendell, and if she mentioned the spot now, it would ruin his day. She clamped her mouth shut.

Deputy Briggs held up his cup. "May as well pour some for me while you're here."

Dottie Jean grinned at the two men, the urge to tease a little taking over. "Staying late for lunch today, are you? Didn't realize my pie and company were that good." She glanced at Deputy Briggs's plate. "You're not having any pie?"

The deputy patted his lean frame. "Don't think so. Not that it wouldn't be good, but gotta keep in shape."

Dottie Jean couldn't help but chuckle at that. She set the coffeepot back on the warmer and sauntered back to her place of rest. Truth was, she needed to bake more pecan pies for the dinner crowd. Some days, she couldn't seem to bake enough to satisfy the sweet teeth of Calista's residents. But right now, she intended to enjoy this time of rest in the afternoon. She glanced out the restaurant window and saw Sassy and Sue Ellen heading her way for their afternoon break.

She called over to the two men, "Say, I do believe two ladies are coming this way. Must be the ones you're a-waitin' for."

Wendell's face turned crimson. "Aw, no, Dottie Jean. I just love your pecan pie. Besides, I finished my route for the day. All the mail is safely delivered." He shoveled a bite into his mouth, obviously to prove his point.

She swallowed the laughter threatening to leave her throat.

Neither Wendell nor Deputy Briggs fooled her at all. A clatter at the door announced the arrival of the ladies.

Sassy pushed through the door first and yanked off her fishing cap to let her red hair fall to her shoulders. "Hi, Dottie Jean. We're ready for a cold drink."

Sue Ellen plopped into the nearest chair and stretched out her long legs. "Whew, sure feels good to get off my feet. Friday's a busy day at the salon."

Dottie Jean slid her sore feet back into her work shoes and walked over to the beverage center. One thing for sure, there was nothing fake or put on with these two ladies. What you saw was what you got, which was always best.

She picked up the iced tea pitcher from the counter. Out of the corner of her eye, she watched old Wendell sit up straighter and Bud Briggs suck his stomach up to his chest. Just like Sassy's old rooster strutting before his hens.

Wendell walked over to the ladies' table and greeted them. "Afternoon, Sassy, Sue Ellen."

Dottie Jean chuckled. The way his postal uniform hung from his bony frame reminded her of the scarecrow in Mama's victory garden back during the Big War.

Sassy raised an eyebrow. "What are you still doing here?" She peered in the deputy's direction. "And I could ask the same of you, Bud."

Deputy Briggs almost tipped over the table in his haste to stand. He hurried to Wendell and slapped him on the shoulder, his face as red as the napkins on the table. "We were just leaving. Weren't we, Wendell?"

Perspiration beaded on Wendell's upper lip. He just nodded,

his head looking like one of those bobble head dolls so popular nowadays.

The two men hurried from the restaurant as if a posse were on their tail. Dottie Jean shook her head and poured tea into glasses for Sassy, Sue Ellen, and herself. Wendell's interest in Sassy had only recently surfaced, but she hadn't returned the sentiment.

Dottie Jean eased back into her chair. "Those two. You know they were waiting for you."

Sue Ellen fingered her curly hair. "Of course, but we can't let on we know. Have to let them think we don't care. Right, Sassy?"

Sassy snorted. "Speak for yourself, friend. I don't care what Wendell thinks. I haven't got time for flirtin' with a grown man."

Like she hadn't been seen gazing after him when he visited her bait shop. Dottie Jean poked at Sue Ellen. "And what about you? Deputy Briggs's been eyeing you like a ripe tomato ever since you came back to Calista."

"I know, but I'm not interested in such foolishness."

Sassy leaned forward. "Speaking of food, is that one last piece of pecan pie left over from lunch that I see over yonder?" She pointed to the glass-covered pie server on the counter.

"Believe it is. Just waiting for you." Dottie Jean wrapped her hands around the ice-cold glass of tea.

Sue Ellen shook her head. "Sassy, you need that piece of pie like I need two heads."

"Okay, I'll just eat half." Sassy swatted at her well-padded hip. "Don't need to be putting too many calories on here."

Dottie Jean choked back her mirth. Dear, sweet Sassy.

Rough around the edges and pure cream puff inside.

Sue Ellen raised her hand. "Then bring the rest to me. I'm not worried about my figure."

Sassy laughed and cut the piece in half before returning with it to the table.

Dottie Jean gazed around the now-empty restaurant, thankful for the time each afternoon she could spend with her friends. They always managed to cheer her up and take away the tiredness.

Suddenly she noticed the silence. "What? You two are staring at me like I've grown horns or something."

Sassy ate her last bite of pie. "Just wondering where your mind is."

"Just thinking how nice it is to sit with you two every afternoon."

No sooner had the words left her mouth than another voice called from the back of the restaurant. "Mother!"

Dottie Jean shoved back her chair. "Oh dear. What have I done now? Jen's got that tone in her voice. I feel like a school kid called in to see the principal. Might as well get it over with. With that tone of voice, she won't like to be kept waiting." She scrambled back to the office and peeked through the door to find her daughter seated behind the desk with piles of papers stacked haphazardly across it.

Dottie Jean ran her hands down the sides of her apron. "I'm right here. What's the matter?"

"I can't find the invoice for this month's food bill."

"It's here somewhere." She began flipping through a group of papers.

Jenny stood with arms crossed over her chest and tapped her foot, just like her daddy used to do. "I don't see how you can find anything on this desk." She waved her hand toward the stacks. "Why don't you let me put all these invoices and receipts on the computer? They'd be so much easier to track."

Dottie Jean found the invoice, then began hunting for the checkbook. "You know I don't understand computers. I'd have things in a bigger mess than they're in now."

"Not if you let me handle the business end of the diner. You could devote all your time to the menu, ordering food, and taking care of your customers."

Dottie Jean raised her eyebrows. "That would be nice, but you know how I want to keep involved with the business end, too."

Jenny shook her head. "Mom, don't you understand? Ever since Daddy died and the boys left, I've wanted to help run the diner. I love this place. It reminds me of Daddy and all the good times I had here growing up."

Dottie Jean leaned over and patted her daughter's hand. "I know, I know, and someday I'll give it all to you, but just not yet."

Jenny giggled. "Guess I'll just have to stick around until then."

She hugged her daughter. "I love you, sweetie. I'm heading back out to the dining room. You can organize and make improvements all you want. Buy a computer if you think it'll help. Call your brother and get his advice. That's his job."

When she returned to the main dining area, she found that her friends had gone back to work. She placed the dirty dishes on a tray and headed to the kitchen. Jenny met her in the hallway.

"I talked to Bill, and he's going to take care of getting us a computer. He'll even bring it down and install it." She took the tray of dirty dishes from her mother and handed over a stack of envelopes to mail.

"Good. Maybe you can make sense out of my clutter." Which, to tell the truth, would be a great relief.

Dottie Jean spotted Wendell outside. She clutched the envelopes and ran out to catch him. "Hey, Wendell. I have mail here. Can you take it with you and save me a trip to the post office?"

"Sure thing, Dottie Jean." He hitched up his mailbag on his shoulder. "Be glad to take it for you. Sure enjoyed lunch today. Your pies and Junior Lee's cooking keep Catfish House one of the top restaurants in all of Mississippi."

Dottie Jean laughed and handed him the envelopes. "Thanks. Junior Lee's the best around these parts, and excuse my braggin', but I taught him all he knows."

"Well, you sure did a good job, Miss Dottie Jean."

Once Wendell made his way down the street, Dottie Jean stood on the porch of the Catfish House taking in the sights of Calista's citizens going about their business. A few tourists wended their way down the street, taking a few moments to gaze into the windows of the many gift shops along the way. Soon many of them would be heading here for a good evening meal.

A black luxury sedan pulled up to the curb in front of the antique store. An unusual sight, it caught Dottie Jean's interest immediately. She observed a tall, lean man with graying hair emerge from the car. He turned and gazed toward the diner.

Dottie Jean gasped and darted back inside. *Fletcher Cameron. It can't be.* She hadn't seen anything of him but an occasional picture in the newspaper since their high school days in Jackson—forty-seven years ago now. What was he doing in Calista?

So this was the town his son had praised for its quaintness and good catfish. Fletcher Cameron peered through the window of the antique store and smiled. Barb would have loved this place.

He glanced at his watch. Perhaps some shopping and then a walk through town would take up time before his usual dining hour. He turned and headed north to window-shop.

After visiting several stores, he purchased a toy airplane for his grandson and walked back out to the main street. It lived up to the description given by his son, quaint and low-key. He loved his visits to small towns in his home state more than any others. When Kevin had suggested Calista for its seafood, Fletcher jumped at the chance to try the catfish firsthand.

The Catfish House had opened its doors for evening diners, and Fletcher joined them. Only a few scattered empty tables remained when he entered the diner. An attractive young woman who looked vaguely familiar greeted him, then led him to an empty table for two by the window. She handed him a menu after he was seated.

Fletcher gazed around the room. He had expected paper napkins and plastic cloths, but navy check and red check cotton covers alternated on the tables with matching linen napkins. Photographs of fishing boats and fishermen with their catches adorned the walls. Behind an old-fashioned counter with stools, a large blackboard announced the specials of the day.

Another young woman smiled at him. "Hi, I'm Allie May. What would you like to drink?"

Fletcher returned the smile. The waitress reminded him of his youngest daughter, now in college. "I'll have iced tea, please."

"Coming right up." She scurried off to the kitchen.

He peered around the room until he spied a woman near the cash register. Her profile looked familiar, and he searched his memory for a name. Suddenly she erupted into laughter. The tinkling sound reached his ears, and then she turned toward him and their gazes locked. Her laughter stopped. She gasped.

Fletcher sucked in his breath. He knew that voice but couldn't put a name with it.

Someone called her name—Dottie Jean.

Dottie Jean Miller. Of course, it had to be her.

Chapter 2

There he is. Fletcher Cameron. Dottie Jean choked back her nervous fears. A customer called to her. When he did, the light of recognition dawned on Fletcher's face. He did remember her. *Go over and say hello. Just talk to him.* Her mind gave the instructions, but her feet refused to obey. She took a deep breath, then willed herself to walk his direction.

His face wore the same lopsided smile she remembered from their yearbook. "Fletcher Cameron. What brings you to these parts?"

He stood and grabbed her hand, glancing at the name tag on her blouse. "It is Dottie Jean Miller. Are you with someone? Can you sit down for a few minutes?"

Did she really have the time? Who was she kidding? She hadn't gone home, changed her clothes, and fixed her hair just to stop and say hello to this man. "I'd love to sit and chat."

He grinned. "My son recommended the Catfish House when he returned from a trip along the coast a few weeks ago. It's a nice-looking place."

Allie May set glasses of water and tea on the table. She peered down at them. "Can I get you anything else, Mrs. Weaver?"

"You can bring out a basket of corn bread and hush puppies." From the corner of her eye, she caught Fletcher Cameron looking at her with arched eyebrows and a grin.

"Mrs. Weaver, huh." He snapped his fingers. "If I remember correctly, you and Hank eloped not long after graduation."

Dottie Jean felt the heat rise in her cheeks. "Yes, we did."

Fletcher nodded. "When I came home from camp that summer, you two were the talk of the town. Hank was the best tight end on the football team and absolutely crazy about you. How is he?"

She rolled the napkin with the silverware in it back and forth a few times. "He died several years ago from a heart attack out on his boat."

Fletcher reached across the table and placed his hand over hers. His face revealed true concern. "I'm so sorry. I can't imagine a man as robust and healthy as Hank having a heart attack."

"It was hard to believe, but the doctor said it was coronary disease just like his father. What about you? Did you marry Barbara?"

He took a deep breath. "Yes, but Barbara passed on two years ago. Breast cancer."

Sympathy squeezed her heart. She understood his sorrow. "Oh no. Not gorgeous Barbara. I remember her as the most beautiful homecoming queen our school ever had. I'm so sorry."

Allie May returned at that moment with the breads. She

poised her pencil over her pad. "Would you like to order now?"

Fletcher lifted an eyebrow. "What do you suggest, Dottie Jean?"

Dottie Jean shrugged and peered up at Allie May. "Bring us two catfish dinners." The young woman smiled, then headed to the kitchen.

"I'm taking your word for it that the food is good." He opened his napkin across his lap and reached for a square of corn bread.

"Hank and I came down here to join his grandparents in their fishing business."

Fletcher buttered his bread and nodded toward the wall. "I see the picture of him up there standing by a boat. Was it his?"

"Yes, he had several in his fleet."

After all these years, Fletcher's eyes were still as blue as the sky outside the window. "Hank loved fishing, and I loved cooking. That's how we ended up with the Catfish House."

He almost choked on his corn bread. After a sip of water to get it down, he stared at her. "You mean you own this place?"

"Yes, I do. I didn't mean to startle you, but all of what you see belongs to me."

He just shook his head and grinned as if he couldn't believe she could run a business on her own. Right then, Allie May showed up with two heaping platters of catfish and coleslaw, as well as a bowl of beans and another basket of hush puppies.

"Do you mind if we return thanks?" he asked. At her nod, he bowed his head. "Thank you, Lord, for the food we are about to eat. And in this case, special thanks for the hands that prepared it. Amen."

Dottie Jean toyed with her food and observed Fletcher. He reminded her of how much Hank had loved eating her meals. She bit down on a crunchy fillet of fried catfish. Just the right blend of seasonings. Junior Lee had done himself proud tonight.

Fletcher finally pushed his plate aside and laid his napkin on the table. "My son was right. That's about the best seafood I've had in a good long while. What's your secret?"

She teased, "It wouldn't be a secret anymore if I told you, would it?"

"Guess not." He glanced at his watch. "I hate to break this up, but I have to drive back to Jackson tonight." He signaled Allie May to bring his check.

Where had the time gone? She wished he could stay longer. At least she could take care of dinner. "No, no. The meal's on me. I've really enjoyed talking with you. Please come back sometime. And bring your family with you. I'd love to meet them."

Before he could answer, Jenny joined them. "Are you going to introduce me, Mom?"

"Of course. Fletcher, this is my daughter, Jenny. She just graduated from Ole Miss."

Fletcher stood and greeted Jenny. "Fletcher Cameron, old friend of your mother. No wonder you looked familiar to me when I came in. You're a carbon copy of the Dottie Jean Miller I knew as a teenager."

Jenny's cheeks turned pink. "Thank you. My daddy used to tell me the same thing. Glad you joined us tonight." She glanced toward the door, where another couple had entered. "Duty calls. Very nice to have met you, Mr. Cameron." She hurried back to resume her hostess duties.

"You must be proud of her. She's a lovely young woman, just like her mother."

Dottie Jean's tongue felt glued to the roof of her mouth. She couldn't even say thank you. She simply smiled and accompanied Fletcher to the front door.

"Thanks for the meal. I'll be back sometime soon." He waved and ambled down the block to his waiting car.

She smoothed her hair back from her face and gazed through the window at his departing back. That had been a pleasant encounter, but would she ever see him again? She turned back to her duties of taking care of her patrons and pushed Fletcher Cameron from her mind.

Fletcher turned onto the highway. The food had been just as good as Kevin had said, but the company had been better. Although he sometimes socialized with a number of friends from high school, his visit with Dottie Jean brought back vivid memories of football games, pep rallies, and proms. He chuckled at the image of Dottie Jean at the top of the cheerleaders' pyramid, yelling at the top of her lungs, her ponytail bouncing in the breeze. Perhaps she'd be willing to have dinner with him again soon.

By the time he'd returned home to Jackson, many of the memories of his teen years had returned to be relived. When he turned into the driveway of his expansive home, he again felt the emptiness of his heart without Barbara there to greet him. He let himself into the dark house and locked the door behind him. After a few moments of standing in the silence, he strode across the entryway to the stairs. His footsteps echoed on the polished wood floor.

The house once filled with the love and laughter of a growing family now seemed just an empty shell where he came to sleep. Despite his wealth, loneliness had become his constant companion.

He walked up the stairway to the second floor and made a decision. He would call Dottie Jean tomorrow. At his age, he didn't see any sense in wasting time. The time had come to return to a social life.

Chapter 3

The next day, young Tommy from Patty's Posies plopped a long white box onto the cashier's counter. "Flowers for Mrs. Weaver."

"For me?" Dottie Jean peered over the granny glasses perched on the end of her nose.

"That's what it says. Oh yeah, Miss Patty has a big vase for you if you can't find one."

She handed him a tip.

He grinned. "Thanks, Mrs. Weaver."

"And thank you, Tommy," she called after him. She glanced around the diner to find the five patrons left from lunch all eyes and ears. Even Allie May and Clara stood poised, ready to view the contents of the box.

Dottie Jean's laughter rang out. Well, she didn't mind satisfying their curiosity. She pulled off the ribbon and lifted two dozen yellow roses from their bed of green tissue. Her favorites. Her heart did a little flutter as she inhaled their fragrance.

Oohs and aahs spread around the room. From the office,

Jenny appeared to investigate the noise and stopped in her tracks. "Where. . . Who. . . Mom, they're beautiful. Who sent them?"

Dottie Jean opened the card and read the note silently. *"Thanks for a wonderful evening. Let's do it again soon. My treat this time. Fletch."*

She felt the heat rise in her cheeks and buried her face in the sweet-scented blossoms. "Oh my. What a surprise. They're from Fletcher."

The thought of seeing him again produced another flutter in her heart. Pictures of him in the sports section of the newspaper as a professional football player skittered through her memory, as well as photos of him with Barbara at society fundraisers. What did a man of Fletcher's background see in her?

"Here, Mom. Let me put those in water." Jenny reached for the flowers, but Dottie Jean couldn't part with them just yet. More memories crowded her mind. She shook her head to clear it, then handed the bouquet to Jenny.

"They're so lovely. How nice of him to thank you." She cradled the long-stemmed roses in her arms.

"Patty said she has a vase for them." She knew Jenny wouldn't find one back in the office.

"Good. I'll go get it." Jenny disappeared into the office only to emerge a few moments later, headed for Patty's.

Allie May scurried over to the counter. "Wow, Mrs. Weaver. Those sure were pretty. Were they from that nice man you ate dinner with the other night?"

"Yes, they were. He's an old friend from high school." This would be all over town before sundown, and she'd be answering a million questions, especially from Sassy and Sue Ellen.

After a few moments, the remaining diners resumed their friendly chatter with one another. Then Jenny returned with the vase and disappeared into the office. A few minutes later, she reappeared with the crystal container of yellow beauties.

"Where shall we put them?" Jenny grasped the vase with both hands and gazed around the room. "I know, let's put them near the register. That way everyone can enjoy them."

Dottie Jean bit her lip. Did she really want them out where they'd be in full view of all her customers? *Oh, why not.* "That'll be fine, Jenny. They're really too pretty to sit back in the office." Even if they did cause a few whispers and curious stares.

That afternoon, Sassy and Sue Ellen showed for their usual afternoon tea. The two ladies tumbled through the door like new puppies chasing a toy. Sassy grabbed Dottie Jean by the shoulders and sat her down in a chair.

"Now tell us all about those roses and who they're from." She settled at a table and planted her arms across her chest.

Dottie Jean knew there'd be no moving the two of them until she told them all about it. As she related the previous evening, their eyes lit up with curiosity. Sue Ellen smirked, and Sassy grinned like the Cheshire cat.

Sassy patted Dottie Jean's arm. "Now who has a man after her?"

"Oh, for. . . Sassy, he just came in for dinner. I haven't seen him in over forty years."

Sue Ellen chortled. "Don't give me that, Dottie Jean Weaver. I know how you were laughing and enjoying each other. I was here and saw the whole thing." She sat back smug as a bug.

"You didn't see anything but two old friends talking about their grandkids." Sometimes the girls were a pain, even if she did love them. But how could she have missed Sue Ellen being in the restaurant? Of course, she hadn't seen anything during dinner except Fletcher Cameron or heard much of anything but his words.

Sue Ellen waved her hand. "Don't get your pantyhose in a knot. We're just teasing you like you tease us, and you know it. If you don't want him, I might go after him myself."

"And break Deputy Briggs's heart? I don't think so." Dottie Jean stood. "Now shoo. I still have pies to bake."

After Dottie Jean closed the door behind them, she watched as they marched down the street toward their own homes. Everybody in town probably knew all about Fletcher Cameron and his roses, but for some reason she really didn't mind.

Awhile later, she helped Allie May and Clara set up for dinner. The phone rang in the office, and Jenny poked her head out the door with a knowing grin spread across her face. "Mom, it's for you."

Dottie Jean rushed to the take the call. When she answered, Fletcher greeted her from the other end and asked about the roses.

"Thank you. They're beautiful." She forced her voice to sound steady and eased into the leather chair behind the desk.

"You're welcome, and I meant what I said about wanting to see you. Only this time I want to take you somewhere outside Calista. Can you get away one night this week?"

The sound of his voice turned her knees to jelly. She took

a deep breath and swiped her sweaty palm across her uniform. "I—I think so. We're usually not busy on Thursday nights."

"Great. Thursday it will be. I'll come down around five, and we can drive over to Mobile. I won't presume to offer seafood, so how about steak?"

Dottie Jean swallowed to clear her throat and calm her nerves before answering. "I think that will be fine. I'll be ready."

"Okay, five on Thursday. It'll be good to see you again and catch up on old times."

"Yes, that will be nice. Thank you."

After she hung up, she sat behind the desk for a few minutes staring at a picture of Hank smiling at her. *Oh, Hank. I do want to see Fletcher again. I haven't stopped loving you, but I miss having a man take me places. Forgive me, sweetheart.*

<hr />

Fletcher placed the receiver in its cradle and smiled. He hadn't even thought of taking another woman to dinner until he'd seen Dottie Jean. Being with her brought out a desire to reconnect with that part of his past.

He gazed out the window of his office and remembered how Dottie Jean had always been the top girl on the cheerleader pyramids because of her tiny stature. Even with the bit of gray in her hair, she looked more like a teenager than a grandmother. And her blue-green eyes still sparkled when she smiled.

God, are you bringing us together at this time in our lives? You know I loved Barb with all my heart and soul. I'll never stop loving her, but I'm still young and do want the love of a woman. Guide me, Lord. I want to do what is in Your will.

His son, Kevin, stepped through the door. "Hey, Dad, did you make it to Calista?"

Fletcher nodded. "I sure did, and you were right on the money. Best catfish I've had in a long time."

"That's what I hoped you'd say. Thought I'd check into its finances and ownership. Might be a good investment."

"I know who owns the business. Turns out it's an old friend from my high school days."

Kevin raised an eyebrow. "That so? Think he'd be interested in talking with us?"

"Not a he, a she. Dottie Jean Weaver. And I don't think she'd be interested in anything we have to offer." Indeed, she had seemed entirely content with her responsibility of the restaurant.

Kevin furrowed his brow. "If you say so, but I think you're missing a good bet with this one."

Mrs. Phelps, his longtime secretary, knocked on the door. "I hate to interrupt, Mr. Cameron, but you have a board meeting in fifteen minutes." She placed a folder on his desk. "Here's all the information you requested."

"Thanks." He glanced up at Kevin. "Work calls. Remember what I said and leave Catfish House alone."

"Of course. See you in a few minutes."

Fletcher picked up the folder and scanned the documents inside. Everything looked in order. He leaned back in his chair. Fletcher considered looking up the records for the Catfish House. If Dottie Jean needed any financial help, he could make sure she received it.

Chapter 4

On Thursday, Dottie Jean held a yellow shirt under her chin and tilted her head at her reflection in the closet mirror.

Jenny frowned. "No, Mom, I like the blue one better."

Dottie Jean tossed the offending blouse on the bed and picked up the blue top. "Thanks. I do, too." She pulled it over her shoulders and buttoned it up. She patted her hair, then pulled the pins from the bun at the nape of her neck. The locks fell about her shoulders and down her back. Perhaps she should color it to get rid of the gray, but that decision wouldn't help tonight. "Jenny, what should I do with my hair?"

"I don't know. Let me see if I can fix it." She picked up the brush and ran it through the long strands.

"Maybe I ought to let Sue Ellen cut it short. She's always after me to do it." Dottie Jean wrinkled her nose. "She told me I'd look younger with it off my neck and softer around my face." She couldn't see how it would make a difference, but then, styling hair wasn't her profession.

"I agree, but it's your decision." She swept Dottie Jean's hair back with her fingers. "Let me do a French twist in the back instead of the bun you usually wear."

In a few minutes the magic was done. Jenny stepped back to admire her handiwork. "I like it."

"So do I. Thanks, sweetie." She admired the new do in the mirror before picking up her makeup brush.

Jenny flopped on the bed. "I think your going out with Mr. Cameron is kinda neat. Were he and Dad friends in high school?"

Dottie Jean swept blush across her cheeks. "They were on the football team together, but they didn't socialize. We didn't run in the same crowd as Fletcher and Barbara."

Jenny pulled up her feet to sit cross-legged on the bed. "Mom, you never really told us about your life before you moved to Calista. I don't remember much about Gramma and Granddad or Pawpaw and Memaw Weaver."

Dottie Jean furrowed her brow and pulled a denim skirt up over her hips. "Not a lot to tell, sweetie. Daddy and I fell in love our senior year and eloped the week after graduation. We came to Calista to help Pawpaw with his fishing business."

Jenny sighed. "I know that. It's how you lived and what you did in high school I'm interested in."

"You need to listen more carefully when your aunts and uncles get together instead of running off with your cousins. We talk about that stuff all the time." She grinned at her daughter's exasperation. Of course, the stories told at reunions didn't really reveal the truth of her childhood, but Jenny didn't need to know some of the details of that life.

"Okay, okay. I get the message." Jenny tilted her head. "So where is this relationship going? I mean, do you think you'll go out with Mr. Cameron again after tonight?"

"I don't know. We're old friends, and that's all. This is probably just his way to thank me for the dinner the other night." She buckled a silver and turquoise belt around her waist and considered her appearance. Maybe she needed to look into a diet plan to shed a few pounds around her waist.

Jenny slid off the bed and hugged her mother. "Go on and have a good time, but I'm going to want to hear all about it when you get home." She stopped at the door. "By the way, remember Bill will be here with the new computer this weekend. As soon as it's all hooked up and ready to go, I'll show you how to use it."

"You know I'm not good with machines and electronics and things like that. You use it. That's why you wanted it anyway, isn't it?" Dottie Jean glanced sideways toward Jenny and smiled. Bill and Jenny could worry about the computer. Perhaps she'd learn to use it, perhaps not.

Jenny shook her head and disappeared down the hall. Dottie Jean turned to pick up her purse and caught sight of her 1960 high school yearbook on the bottom shelf of the bookcase. She bent over and reached for it, then sat on the bed. With the book on her lap, she leafed through the pages. Jenny had wanted to know what she and Hank had done as teenagers. Maybe she'd let her see this. Of course, the yearbook told only one part of the story—the fun part.

Fletcher's bold hand had penned across his picture, "Best wishes and good luck to a really cute cheerleader. Keep up the good work." Typical writing for a yearbook, but she had treasured those words from the star football player.

Dottie Jean ran her finger over the picture of Hank Weaver in his football uniform. She considered the irony of her life. She and Hank had run away to Calista after high school to escape the trailer park where they lived. Here she sat now, living in a double-wide. Of course, these days they were called manufactured homes, but it was a trailer just the same. She sighed and placed the yearbook back on the table. Better to let the past stay in the past and deal with the present.

She strolled into the kitchen. Thank goodness Jenny liked things neat and clean. When left to Dottie Jean, everything became cluttered and unorganized. She reached to close the blinds. Her kitchen glistened clean and modern with its shiny appliances and a basket of fresh fruit on the counter. But her mind pictured the trailer park where she and Hank had lived as children. Fletcher's face invaded the memory, and she shivered. Her heart danced in her chest, making her feel like a giddy teenager with a crush on the best-looking guy in school.

A knock sounded on the door. When she answered, he stood smiling on the other side.

***

"Oh, you're early." Her expression reflected her surprise.

"Yes, may I come in?" He stood poised on the stoop. He didn't want to intrude, but he wanted a glimpse into Dottie Jean's life.

Her cheeks turned pink. "Oh. . .uh. . .yes, of course, I'm sorry." She stepped back to allow him to enter.

His gaze took in the neatly kept living room and dining area. The spaciousness surprised him. He had never been in one of these manufactured homes before. The deep green of the carpet and the greens in the upholstered pieces gave him a sense of comfort and peace.

"This is nice. Didn't realize you'd have so much space." He relaxed on one of the chairs. He noted the small details of family photos, unusual figurines, and candles she had added to make the place a home.

Dottie Jean sat on the edge of the sofa, clearly uncomfortable. "Yes, it's fine for Jenny and me."

He stood and walked to the back window. "You have a good view of the river. I can almost see up to the lake from here. Have you had any problems with hurricanes or tropical storms? They can really bring in a lot of water."

"Just the usual." Suddenly she jumped up. "I'm sorry. Would you like something to drink?"

He smiled. "No, nothing. If you're about ready, we can get on the road."

Her cheeks grew pink again, and she stumbled against the coffee table. "Uh, sure. Just a minute. I'll get my purse." She disappeared down a hall.

Fletcher blew out a breath. She looked as nervous as he felt. He'd been out of the dating scene far too long.

She returned. "Okay, I'm ready. Let's go."

Fletcher held the door open for her and followed her out to his car. On the drive over to Mobile, he let her do the talking. Her voice still held the same melodic ring it had so many years ago.

Suddenly she stopped. "I'm babbling on like a river out of control. You must think my brain's out to lunch."

He laughed and shrugged his shoulders. "No, I don't. You sound just like you did when you were talking with your friends back in school." Of course, then he'd thought of it only as chatter and gossip, not real conversation, but she didn't need to know that.

Her eyes opened wide. "Oh dear, I'm not sure if that's any better."

Fletcher laughed. He pulled into the parking lot of the restaurant and found a vacant slot. Inside they were seated and ordered their meals. He noted how she chose only healthy vegetables from the salad bar. No creamy, fat-laden dressings, cheese, or other high-calorie extras on her plate. When they returned to the table, hot bread and their tea waited for them.

He couldn't remember having a better time in a long while and enjoyed watching Dottie Jean savor the tender steak when it arrived. When she declined dessert, he ordered coffee for them both.

He concentrated on how he could offer the invitation he planned to present tonight. True, this was their first date, but he felt he knew her so well. With the charity dinner still a few weeks away, they'd have time to find out more about their present lives. He'd like nothing better than if she'd consent to accompany him. Maybe it was too short notice. Fletcher seemed to remember Barbara saying women needed plenty of notice for a big affair.

After a few minutes, he coughed and cleared his throat. "Um, I have something to ask you, but I'm not sure how to do it."

"Then just ask." Her smile warmed his heart and fortified his courage.

"Okay. I'm on the board of a national foundation, and we're having a fund-raising event in three weeks. I know it's short notice, but I'd love to have you as my date for the evening."

Dottie Jean gulped, and her eyes opened wide. "Three weeks? That *is* soon. I'm not sure. . . I–I've never been to anything like that. Is it formal?"

Fletcher felt like kicking himself. Of course the dinner was formal, and she probably didn't have an evening gown. "Uh, yes. It's black tie. I'll understand if you say no, but I really want you to go with me."

She furrowed her brow, and her blue eyes clouded. "I need to think about this. Can I let you know in a few days?

How could he have been so stupid? Now he'd embarrassed her.

Chapter 5

Dottie Jean flipped the switch to turn on the coffee urn. She had hurried home from the restaurant to prepare for this week's meeting of her Bible study group. Before they became involved in tonight's discussion, she planned to air her concerns about Fletcher's invitation and seek the advice of her friends. Keeping it from them all weekend had been one of the most difficult things she'd done. Especially since Sassy knew her so well.

A rap on the window signaled her friends' arrival, and she scurried to unlock the door for them. Sassy entered, followed by Berta and Sue Ellen.

Sassy plopped her tote bag onto the table. "Well, Dottie Jean, are you going to tell us what's in your craw today?"

She took a deep breath before answering her friend. "What are you talking about?"

Sassy let loose with a whooping laugh. "Don't you think I've seen that distracted look in your eyes all weekend? Why, during the service Sunday night, you looked like you were out in never-never land."

Sue Ellen settled herself at the table. "She's right. I noticed it, too."

Dottie Jean peered at the trio. "Was I that obvious?"

Berta grinned. "Oh yes. Must have to do with that Fletcher fellow."

Dottie Jean felt the heat rising in her cheeks. She busied herself with coffee mugs and the pecan pie on the counter. The air grew thick enough to slice with the large knife she held for cutting the pastry. They sure wouldn't suspect the bombshell she planned to drop on them. After arranging the refreshments on a tray, she steeled herself for their curious stares and pasted a smile on her face. She did want their opinion.

"Okay. Stop your gawking." She set the refreshments on the table. "I was planning on talking to you tonight anyway. I just didn't realize my feelings were so transparent."

Sassy helped herself to a large wedge of pie. "Honey, you haven't been able to hide your feelings from me since we were newlyweds."

"And you've helped me through many rough seas over the years." She poured a cup of coffee and stirred in a packet of artificial sweetener.

Sue Ellen and Berta slipped small slivers of the gooey, nut-laden pastry onto their plates.

Sassy clucked her tongue. "You young'uns don't know how to enjoy life. That's not enough pie to even taste. I know Berta's watching her figure for a wedding, but who are you watching for, Sue Ellen? Don't know of any fellows in this town after you."

"Thanks a lot, Sassy. For that I'll just have more." Sue Ellen slid a generous chunk onto her plate.

Berta raised her hands. "Now, now, ladies, let's quit talking about ourselves so Dottie Jean can tell us about Fletcher."

Dottie Jean wanted to shout, "No! Go ahead." The longer they talked, the more courage she could work up to ask their opinion. She decided to plunge in and let the remarks fall where they may. "I have a dilemma. Fletcher invited me to accompany him to a formal charity dinner in Jackson. I don't know if I should accept."

Sue Ellen and Berta clapped their hands in glee. Both said it was wonderful, but Sassy guffawed. Just the reaction Dottie Jean had expected from her best friend.

When her laughter died down, Sassy leaned forward. "I'm sorry, hon, but that man's ego is big as all outdoors."

"Oh, hush, Sassy. This is a great honor. I'll even do your hair up real fancy for free if you'll go." Sue Ellen grasped Dottie Jean's hands in hers.

"And I'll be glad to go with you to Biloxi or Mobile or wherever to look for a dress," Berta offered. "I found several good places while looking for a wedding gown. Maybe Debbie over at the dress shop could order one for you."

Dottie Jean furrowed her brow. "I haven't seen anything there appropriate for a formal affair." Not that she'd looked recently, but then, nothing fancy ever happened in Calista, so there was no need for dressy clothes.

Berta shook her head. "I'm not sure about that. With those rich folks moving up around the lake, Debbie's taken to buying better-quality clothing."

Sassy shook her head. "Humph. Gonna bring trouble down on your head, mark my words." She stuffed another bite of pie into her mouth.

Dottie Jean's heart sank as she glanced at the older woman. Maybe her friend spoke the truth. Suddenly, despite Sassy, she wanted to go to this affair. She ignored the warning and turned to Sue Ellen and Berta. "What do you two think?"

Berta leaned forward in her chair. "Well, we think you ought to go. Don't we, Sue Ellen?"

"Sure. Give you a chance to hobnob with the rich and famous of Jackson."

Sassy washed her pie down with coffee, then tilted her head. "That's the problem. But go if you like. You know me, I've got no patience with the hoity-toity set in the city."

"I think it's time to get down to Bible study." Dottie Jean retrieved her Bible from a nearby table. She didn't want to discuss the matter any further with them. She'd have to make up her own mind and take whatever consequences resulted.

The next morning, after the diner had cleared of breakfast customers, Dottie Jean followed Jenny into the office. The new computer sat on the desk, hooked up and ready to go. Jenny sat down and punched a few keys, and up came an image on the screen. It looked like a ledger sheet from one of the accounting books Dottie Jean used for bookkeeping.

"I've already set up an account for each of our suppliers and entered all the invoices I could find from last month." She went on to explain how she could track each account and know exactly how much was owed and when it had been paid.

Jenny sounded so proud of her accomplishment, but Dottie

Jean didn't have a clue as to what she rattled on about.

"That's nice, honey. This should make your job much easier. Let me do the ordering, and I'll let you handle the bills and such." If the new computer kept Jenny happy and occupied, then Dottie Jean could handle the change.

"Fine, Mama. You can even order online from our suppliers if you like."

"No thanks. I prefer the good old-fashioned phone, which I need to use right now, but I think I'll go over to the house for this call." No need to publicize what she wanted to say.

Jenny's eyes lit up. "Oh, going to call Mr. Cameron? Oh, Mama, do say yes to his invitation."

Dottie Jean shrugged and scurried out to the double-wide. She did plan to say yes, but she still didn't know if she had made the right decision. Now was the time to think again and change her mind. No, she wouldn't be wishy-washy. She'd made her decision and would stick with it.

When Dottie Jean identified herself and asked the secretary to let Mr. Cameron know she'd called, Mrs. Phelps said, "Oh no, Mrs. Weaver. I'm to put you through right away. One moment."

An instant later, Dottie Jean heard Fletcher's deep voice. "Dottie Jean, I've been waiting for your call."

"Oh, you have? Didn't mean for you to do that, but I'd be delighted to go with you to the dinner." There, it was done.

"Yes. That's the best news I've had today."

She listened as he gave her a few more details about time and place. "I'll call you back and let you know what arrangements I've made for your stay here."

Her stay there? She hadn't considered that, but of course Jackson was too far away to make it a one-day trip. What kind of plans would he be making?

"Better yet, I'll come down there next week, and we can talk more about it then. I could use one of your catfish dinners."

"Hmm, okay. I'll take off, and we can sit down and visit." The dinner patrons would have to do without her for one night.

"Good. I'll see you then."

Dottie Jean said good-bye and placed the phone on the counter. She glanced at her watch. No time to think about Fletcher—or anything else for that matter. It was time to get over to the diner and make pies for the evening crowd.

Jenny met her in the kitchen. "Well, are we going to get you a dress?"

Dottie Jean measured flour into an oversized mixing bowl. "I suppose so."

Her daughter hugged her from behind. "I'm so glad. You deserve to have a good time. You haven't been anywhere but out with Fletcher since Daddy died. Five years is a long time to bury yourself in work."

"Wish your brother felt that way. When he found out I'd been out with Fletcher, he didn't like the idea at all." She reached for shortening.

"That's because he's. . . Oh, never mind. When are we going for your dress?"

"How about next Monday afternoon? Berta said she'd go with us. Sue Ellen and Sassy might go, too, since both their shops are closed on Mondays."

"Sounds good to me. Now I'll leave you to your pies." Jenny kissed her cheek and strolled out to the dining room.

Dottie Jean picked up her rolling pin. Why did she feel so apprehensive about the upcoming event?

———⊶∞⊷———

Fletcher hung up the phone and grinned. She had actually said yes. He couldn't believe his fortune. He pressed a button on his intercom. "Mrs. Phelps, could you come in here, please?"

The elderly woman entered the room. "What do you need, Mr. Cameron?"

"Mrs. Weaver has agreed to attend that fund-raiser with me. I need to be sure she has a place to stay while she's here. See if the hotel where we'll be going has a room available and book it for her."

"Certainly, Mr. Cameron."

Kevin poked his head around the door frame. "A room for who, Dad?"

Fletcher dismissed Mrs. Phelps and motioned for his son to come in. "Dottie Jean Weaver has agreed to attend the dinner with me."

Kevin furrowed his brow. "Isn't she the owner of that restaurant in Calista?"

"Yes, she is." He didn't like the look on his son's face. The clouds there spelled trouble.

"Thought we weren't going to pursue that." Kevin sank into a chair across the desk.

"I'm not pursuing the restaurant, just the owner."

"Oh?" Kevin sat up straighter. "I'm not sure I understand."

"That's what all my trips down to the coast have been about. I've taken her out to dinner, and we've renewed our friendship from our high school days."

Kevin leaned forward, his brow furrowed. "Does anyone else in the family know about her?"

"No, it's really no one's business but my own. I don't know where our friendship will go, but for now, she's a pleasant dinner companion and a good friend." But if his plans succeeded, she'd be more than that.

Kevin stood and shook his head. He blew out a long breath. "Okay, Dad. I just don't want to see you rush into something and be hurt or find you've made a big mistake."

Fletcher grinned. "I'll be fine. Thank you for caring, but don't say anything to the rest of the family just yet."

Kevin opened the door. "If that's the way you want it." He stepped out and closed the door behind him.

Fletcher felt a sense of relief. The big protest he'd expected hadn't appeared. Now if his son did keep his mouth shut, he could proceed with his plans. Time enough later to introduce his old friend to the family. Although his heart felt otherwise, common sense told him to take this relationship slow and easy and see where it would lead. He'd have to slow down to a jog instead of running full steam ahead.

Mrs. Phelps knocked on the door frame. "Mr. Cameron, I have those plans you wanted."

He waved her in. "What do we have?"

"I've booked the hotel where the dinner will be held for Friday night. Mrs. Weaver will have a luxury suite on the tenth floor. It's one of the best rooms in the hotel, and I ordered fresh flowers and a mini refrigerator stocked with water and soft drinks. No liquor. She'll have a full supply of snack items and all the other amenities the hotel offers for VIPs."

"Very good. I'm sure she'll enjoy it." He checked his calendar for a date to head for Calista to enjoy another catfish dinner.

Chapter 6

On the Friday morning of the benefit dinner, Dottie Jean paid the beauty shop a visit. While she sat in the chair, waiting for Sue Ellen to retrieve something from the back room, Sassy showed up and hollered to Sue Ellen, "Get your scissors and stuff. We're going to fix Dottie Jean's hair proper for this shindig tonight."

Dottie Jean yanked the protective smock from around her neck. "What do you mean—scissors?"

Sue Ellen came from the storeroom wiping her hands on a towel. "What's all the commotion?" She glanced from one to the other and then back again.

Sassy pointed at Dottie Jean. "It's time for Dottie Jean to have a new hairstyle. And a good cut will do it."

Dottie Jean's heart leapt. *Cut my hair?* She fingered the long tresses and frowned. "Since when do you care about how a person looks?"

"Since you decided to socialize with the rich and famous of Jackson. Now, let Sue Ellen work her magic."

Sue Ellen grasped Dottie Jean's shoulder. "Is that what you want?"

Dottie Jean slumped in the chair. "Well, I admit I need to do something, but I wasn't planning on doing anything drastic today. Besides, you won't have time. I only reserved time for a shampoo and styling."

She grinned. "I'll make the time if necessary to do whatever you want."

Dottie Jean closed her eyes. Hank had loved her hair long, although she always wore it in a braid or bun. He said he liked the feel of it at night after she brushed it out. It was a lot of trouble now and took so long to dry. Suddenly she sat up in the chair. "Let's do it. Cut it short." If she was going into a new phase of life, she needed a new look to go with it.

Sassy chortled, and Sue Ellen grabbed her scissors and refastened the cape. Before Dottie Jean knew what had hit her, Sue Ellen had woven Dottie Jean's hair into one long braid down her back. Dottie Jean closed her eyes and shuddered.

Sue Ellen rested her hand on Dottie Jean's shoulder. "Are you sure now? After the first cut, there's no turning back."

She squeezed her eyes tight and wrinkled her nose. "Do it while I still have the nerve."

When she heard that first snip of the shears, a tear made its way down her cheek. The cutting didn't hurt, but the memory of all the years with hair halfway down her back did. She didn't open her eyes until Sue Ellen led her to the shampoo bowl. She peeked at the counter and discovered a towel with a long braid lying on it. *What in the world?* She pointed to the hair. "What's that?"

"This is your hair so you'll have it to keep."

Dottie Jean choked back a sob. What a sweet thing for her to do. She had wondered what Sue Ellen would do with all that hair. Dottie Jean avoided looking into the mirror until it was all over.

Sue Ellen stepped back. "Okay, it's done."

Dottie Jean opened her eyes and stared into the face of a woman she barely recognized. Her hair now ended just below her ears and fell softly around her face. "Sue Ellen, I can't believe it. I really do like it."

Sassy slapped her knee. "Honey, you look like a million bucks. We should've done this sooner."

"What's with the 'we'? It's my hair." Then Dottie Jean giggled. "But I'm glad you talked me into it. Wait until Jenny sees me."

She jumped up from the chair. "I'm supposed to be helping Jenny with the food order for the week. Fletcher will be here in less than an hour. I gotta go. How much do I owe you, Sue Ellen?"

She waved her hand. "Not a thing. I've been itching to do that for the longest time. Maybe you can treat me to lunch one day soon."

"That I will." But it'd take more than a lunch to repay her friend for such a transformation. With one last look at herself in the mirror, Dottie Jean hurried out the door.

Jenny didn't see her at first, but Dottie Jean cleared her throat, and Jenny glanced at her mother. She jumped up and grabbed Dottie Jean's shoulders. "Mom! You did it! You cut your hair. I love it." She turned her around so she could see the back. "It looks great."

"Thank you. Now, let's get busy with our order. Fletcher will be here soon. At least all my packing is done."

Twenty minutes later she headed for home. Her bag sat by the door, and her dress hung in its protective bag ready for the trip.

Fletcher arrived promptly. Dottie Jean opened the door, and he stepped back. "Dottie Jean, you cut your lovely hair."

Had she made a mistake? "Um, yes. It was getting to be so much trouble."

His grin lit up her heart like the lights on Broadway. "I like it. Very nice."

Dottie Jean breathed a sigh of relief, then led him to her luggage. He carried her large tote and hanging bag to his car and helped her in. She settled herself against the buttery softness of the leather seats.

His car rode like a dream and was so quiet. The contour seats fit her body to perfection. Fletcher slipped a CD into the player, and the car filled with the magical songs from one of her favorite musicals. Her eyes misted over. How could she be so fortunate? She hoped he didn't expect her to talk, because her tongue felt glued to the roof of her mouth. At this moment she wasn't sure she could say anything even if her life depended on it.

Finally, the tension between her shoulders began to ease, and she relaxed enough to carry on a conversation. Fletcher told her more about the evening. "We'll be at a table for ten. Most of the others at our table will be board members, but I do think you know them. Adele Winston, now Robbins, with her husband, Jack, will be there, and also Liz Greene Barker with her husband, Howard. The other two couples are Ellen and Jim Barstow and Amanda and Sam Goodson."

She recognized the ladies' names from their high school years, but she didn't know the men they'd married. The memory of her experience with them tightened a band around her heart. The girls hadn't even been on speaking terms with Dottie Jean back then. Other than Liz, who had been a cheerleader also, she had no contact with those girls at all.

Dottie Jean breathed deeply. She could handle anything for one night. But that didn't still the tingling of her nerves at the thought.

They finally arrived at the hotel, and Fletcher escorted her to the room he had reserved for her. Dottie Jean felt her mouth drop open at the elegance of the surroundings. She snapped it shut quickly. No need in looking the part of the country bumpkin she felt herself to be at this moment.

Fletcher opened a small refrigerator. "I've had this stocked with your favorite sodas and snacks, so help yourself whenever you feel like it."

She gasped in delight. "How did you know what my favorites are? You've thought of everything."

He laughed. "I have my ways." Then he stepped toward the door. "I'm going to leave you now so you can rest and have plenty of time to get ready. I'll be back for you at six." He grasped her hands in his. "I want this to be an evening you'll never forget." Then he was gone.

She did as Fletcher had suggested and lay down on the bed for a brief nap. Although she didn't think she'd be able to sleep from the excitement building in her chest, she found her eyes closing and her thoughts drifting. Indeed, she felt like the Queen of England.

Dottie Jean awoke suddenly and glanced around the room, not sure where she was. Then she remembered and jumped from the bed. She shook her head in relief. Still plenty of time to dress and be ready for the evening. A few minutes before six, she whirled around for one last glance in the mirror and smiled at her reflection. Sue Ellen had been right—the tiny sparkles of glitter in her hair danced in the light. They looked so glamorous, but she didn't have the nerve to dust them on her shoulders.

She stowed her purse with her billfold in a tote and shoved it into the closet. She checked the contents of the evening bag Jenny had given her. Lipstick, hankie, small comb, room key card, and mirror nestled in the silky lining.

Dottie Jean's fingers trembled as she snapped the bag shut. She closed her eyes. *Lord, I know I'm out of my league tonight. Please help me to have a good time and not make an idiot of myself. I don't want to embarrass You or Fletcher. I've never done anything like this, but I know You will be with me every step of the way. Thank You.*

A knock on the door ended the prayer. Dottie Jean took in a deep breath, then expelled it slowly before opening the door.

Fletcher's smile of admiration bolstered her confidence, as did his words. "Dottie Jean, you look lovely."

What a good way to start the evening. She felt as though she could conquer the world with Fletcher by her side. He slipped her hand into the crook of his elbow and led her to the elevator. When they entered the hotel's grand ballroom, Dottie Jean swallowed her gasp. Never had she seen such decorations and opulence in one room. Her knees shook, and she grasped Fletcher's arm.

She gazed about in awe. The committee for the benefit had chosen an Arabian Nights theme for their décor. Swaths of filmy chiffon in vivid hues were secured with huge floral bouquets. The tables echoed the jewel tones in their sheer fantasy. The whole place appeared twice its size because of the mirrors along one wall.

Fletcher guided her to a table at the front of the room, where they joined several other couples already in place. As he introduced her to the guests, she began to recognize her former classmates.

They welcomed her, but Dottie Jean felt their scrutiny and couldn't mistake the dawning recognition in their eyes. They remembered her, the daughter of the drunk from the trailer park. She smiled and settled into her seat.

Adele leaned toward her. "You were the cheerleader who ran off and married Hank Weaver. I understand he passed away several years ago."

Dottie Jean swallowed hard. "Yes, five to be exact." Maybe this date hadn't been such a good idea after all. Although the ladies smiled and seemed friendly enough, she caught the look of disdain Adele passed to Liz as she reached for her water.

Dottie Jean lowered her gaze to her lap and felt the heat rise in her cheeks. Fletcher reached over and squeezed her hand. She lifted her head to peer at him, and he winked in reassurance.

During the dinner, conversing with nine other people became difficult. Besides, the women made little effort to include her in their conversation. When they did, she answered with her brightest smile and kindest words. This was one night she refused to be intimidated.

After the meal ended, the other guests moved to the silent auction tables. Fletcher covered her hands with his. "We can sit here. I've asked them to bring us coffee."

"Thank you. I'd like that." She slipped her hands from his and reached for her glass of water. Would the evening never end? Why had she allowed herself to be talked into coming tonight? But then, no one had talked her into it. She'd made the decision herself.

"I think the ladies were a little surprised to see you as my date tonight." Fletcher grinned and sat back in his chair.

She shook her head and set her glass back on the table. "Shocked is more like it. This is the last place they expected to see little Dottie Jean Miller from the trailer park." A nervous laugh escaped her lips.

A waiter arrived with their coffee, and Fletcher waited until he had left, then said, "Does it matter what they think? I'm pleased to have you with me."

"I like being with you, Fletcher, but I'm out of my element." She gripped her cup with both hands. Why did Fletcher still have the same effect on her today he'd had back in high school? Hank had been her true love, but Fletcher had been the forbidden fruit that she, like so many of the girls from the trailer park, coveted.

At that moment a photographer stepped up. "Mr. Cameron, may I have a picture of you and your guest?"

Fletcher glanced at her, and when she nodded slightly, he

turned to the cameraman. "Yes, you may." He leaned toward Dottie Jean as the flashbulb lit up the space. When he asked for particulars, Dottie Jean's heart thudded in her chest. A newspaper photographer? Now she wished she'd declined.

"Her name is Dottie Jean Weaver of Calista, Mississippi." Fletcher waited while the reporter made notes.

When the man left, Dottie Jean picked up her handbag. "If you'll excuse me, I'm going to powder my nose." She felt as though she were suffocating. Anywhere would be better than sitting here at the moment.

"Sure. I won't be going anywhere."

Fletcher gazed after the departing figure of Dottie Jean. A smile played at the corners of his mouth. She looked lovely tonight, and he was proud to be with her. Adele and Liz returned to the table with their husbands. Adele glanced around. "Where's Dottie Jean?"

"She's gone to powder her nose, as you ladies say."

"Oh, I see. Tell me, how did you two get together after all these years?"

Fletcher sipped his coffee and peered at Adele. It really wasn't any of her business, but he didn't mind answering. "We ran into each other when I went down to Calista for dinner. We dined together at the Catfish House."

Liz bent forward, her elbows on the table. "I remember her family. Her mother was my mother's seamstress. Dottie Jean had some nice-looking clothes her mother made from remnants of my mother's things."

Fletcher recognized the remark for what it was. He'd never really cared for Liz and had tolerated her only for Barbara's sake. Now he knew exactly why he had steered clear of her as much as possible. He didn't plan to sit here and let them talk about his date. He'd had enough. "Excuse me, please. I'm going over to check out the dessert buffet."

The two women grinned, their dark red lips glistening in the light. "I hear the pastries are really decadent. Full of chocolate, whipped cream, and nuts," Adele said.

He nodded and turned away. True to Adele's words, rich, luscious desserts filled the table. Whipped cream topped many of them, and several, covered with chocolate, also tempted the palate. He could at least kill some time making up his mind as to what he'd choose. He figured Dottie Jean would probably select something chocolate.

He turned his gaze toward the restroom area and searched for her only to see Adele and Liz pushing through its doors. He felt his heart jump, and he shuddered. What were those two up to now?

———— ❦ ————

Dottie Jean's hand reached for the lock on her stall but jerked back when she heard her name mentioned. She stood silently, aware they wouldn't notice her in the end cubicle.

"Can you believe Fletcher actually brought Dottie Jean to an affair like this?" one voice said. She recognized it as belonging to her flame-haired former classmate, Liz.

Another woman laughed. "No, I can't. She's certainly out of place here. Her daddy a drunk and her mother taking in sewing—not exactly the background you'd expect to see with a Cameron." That sounded like Adele.

The bile rose in Dottie Jean's throat, and she felt as though she might be sick. She rested her forehead against the cool steel of the stall door. Why didn't they go away?

"You must admit she looks good. Hasn't lost her figure, and not much gray in her hair," Liz offered.

"Ha. She may look good, but I bet her dress is right off the rack, not more than a hundred dollars or so. Bet she had to save awhile to buy it." The second one snickered.

"Well, I hear she's a waitress at some catfish diner down in Calista. What was Fletcher thinking, bringing her here, where so many remember who she was and who her family was?"

Dottie Jean swallowed hard. This had gone far enough. She didn't have to listen to them. She gathered her courage, unlocked the door, and stepped out. "Good evening, ladies."

The two women spun around at the sound of her voice. They raised their eyebrows, then shrugged. Liz spoke first. "Why, hello, Dottie Jean. We didn't know you were in here." The mirror reflected her smirk.

"Obviously." Dottie Jean strode to the sink and squeezed soap from the dispenser into her hand. She prayed for God to calm her anger.

After washing, Dottie Jean reached for a towel to dry her hands. The other two women busied themselves with applying lipstick and patting their hair.

"I do want to correct one mistake. I'm not a waitress, but I am a cook, a cashier, and whatever else I can do, because I own the diner." She dropped the towel into the bin and opened her purse.

"That's nice. Do you also sew like your mother did?"

Dottie Jean ran gloss over her lips, then pressed them together. She turned and smiled at the women. "No. I haven't had time. In addition to the diner, Hank and I owned a fishing fleet and a seafood company. Perhaps you've heard of Gulf Bay Seafood. They do supply most of the fish for the fine restaurants along the Gulf Coast and in Mississippi."

Their surprised looks and open mouths bolstered Dottie Jean some, but her earlier resolve not to be intimidated disappeared like water down a drain. Oh, how she wanted to swagger out, but instead she grasped her beaded handbag and quickly strode through the door to rejoin Fletcher.

Chapter 7

What could be keeping her? How long did it take to powder a nose? Then he remembered Barbara telling him how women liked to visit and gossip in the ladies' room. That could take awhile. Her voice at his side startled him.

"I see you had the same idea I did. Don't these desserts look delicious?" She reached for a pastry covered with chocolate and topped off with mounds of whipped cream and nuts.

"Just what I thought you'd pick. Looks good. Think I'll have one, too." He made his selection, then grasped her elbow and guided her toward sliding glass doors. "Let's go out on the terrace. It's getting stuffy in here."

Fletcher located an empty table and set his dessert on its glass top surface. "Feels good outside. I love June evenings."

He glanced at Dottie Jean and furrowed his brow. Something had happened. Her face looked as forlorn as a lost kitten. His dessert turned to sawdust.

"Fletcher, when you finish your pastry, I'd like for you to

take me back to my room."

He almost choked on the bite in his mouth. "What? Take you back to your room?"

"Yes, I'm feeling rather tired, like maybe I'm coming down with something."

He noticed the trembling in her hands before she clasped them together in her lap. Her face now looked ashen in the light of the terrace. Clearly something was wrong. Did she really feel sick? "I'm worried about you. I hope you're not getting a virus or something."

She leaned toward him. "I don't mean to spoil your evening. You stay and I'll go on upstairs."

"I should say not!" He pushed his plate away, all interest in the pastry gone. "No gentleman would let a woman go home unescorted, even if it's just up a few floors." He stood and held out his hand to her.

When she finally grasped his, hers felt cold and clammy. She averted her gaze from his and turned toward the exit.

<hr/>

When they arrived at the room, Dottie Jean slid the key into the slot and pushed open the door. "Go on back and enjoy the rest of the dinner. You might even—" She bit her lip, then hurried inside and closed the door before he could react.

She leaned against the door, which shook as Fletcher pounded on it. She strode to the bed, every ounce of her self-confidence and courage gone like the blue sky when storm clouds roll in. She dropped her handbag on the bedside table, then pulled the dress over her head and tossed it in a heap on the bed. She reached for her robe and wrapped it around her body in an attempt to bring warmth to her cold bones.

When the knocking finally ceased, she plopped down beside her dress, pulled a pillow to her chest, and hugged it, then let the sobs escape her throat.

What had happened to her fighting spirit? A few minutes later the phone rang, but Dottie Jean simply stared at it through her tears. Fletcher must have gone down to the house phone and called.

The more she thought about the evening, the more anger replaced the tears and humiliation. She didn't really care about those people. The people she cared about and who cared about her were in Calista. She grabbed the phone book and looked up the number for the bus company. Dottie Jean wanted to go home, sort this all out, and take care of her own business.

Fletcher stared at the house phone. After another attempt with no answer, he resigned himself to the fact that she didn't want to talk to him again tonight.

The evening ruined, he retrieved his car and headed home. Fletcher mulled over the past few hours in his mind, searching for something he had said, or anything that could have made for their early departure. Maybe she'd tell him when he picked her up to take her home in the morning.

He turned his car into the driveway of his spacious home. Instead of going in, he sat in the car. The house would be empty, void of all human life but his. Right now he wasn't very good company, especially with himself. How he had hoped this evening would be the beginning of a long relationship with a lovely woman he had known so many years ago. Maybe she'd feel better in the morning on their drive back to Calista. With the trip ahead, his spirits lifted, and he went into the house anticipating the morning.

Dottie Jean leaned her head against the cool glass of the bus window, thankful to be near Calista, the only place she felt safe. What a disaster last night turned out to be. Maybe she shouldn't have run out on Fletcher as she had, but she didn't feel like facing him this morning—and perhaps never again.

The memories, suppressed for so many years, came roaring to the surface. Why couldn't she get over the shame of her family and where she'd grown up?

Tears rolled down her cheeks as she remembered the shabby trailer they called home. She and her sister had worn clothes made from scraps and hand-me-downs from her mother's customers. At least Liz hadn't mentioned the day Dottie Jean showed up at school in one of Liz's discarded dresses.

The city limits sign of Calista welcomed her home. She stepped down from the bus at the depot and trudged the few blocks to her place behind the restaurant. The deserted streets offered a little comfort. She crept into the house and into her room undetected. She crawled into bed, hoping she could sleep and forget about Fletcher. Why hadn't she listened to Sassy?

Fletcher stared at the desk clerk in disbelief. "What do you mean, she's checked out?"

The young man shrugged. "Just what I said. The file here says she left her key here at two this morning. Is there a problem?"

"No, I'm just surprised. Thank you."

He strode outside to his car and shook his head. Why had she left like that? The only thing he could do was drive down to Calista anyway and confront her. The ring of his cell phone interrupted his thought. He punched it on. "Fletcher Cameron."

"Dad. I have to see you now. In your office or at home, either one, but it has to be now." The sound of his son's anger crackled over the phone connection.

"Hold on, Kevin. What's so urgent? I was just leaving town for the day."

"Cancel it, because we need to talk. I'm sorry, Dad. It's just that I really need to discuss something with you, and I didn't want to wait until tonight."

His son's apologetic tone softened his own anger. From the sound of things, Fletcher wouldn't be going anywhere until the issue was resolved. He could go down to Calista after he talked with Kevin.

"Okay. I'll drive over to your place. Be there soon." He ended the connection and headed for his son's home. A short time later he greeted his grandsons, gave them a hug, then followed his son into the family room.

Kevin handed him a newspaper with his picture and Dottie Jean's displayed in the center. "Dad, I don't know what to make of this."

Fletcher sighed and held the paper in his hand. "That's

Dottie Jean Weaver. I told you I invited her to the charity dinner. What difference does it make?"

His son slumped into an oversized leather easy chair. "A lot." Kevin leaned forward. "What do you really know about her? A man in your position, with your money, and with your reputation can't go out with just anybody. How do you know she's not. . ." He stopped abruptly and pressed his lips together.

Fletcher frowned. "After my money, you mean? Well, let me tell you a thing or two. It wouldn't matter if she was—I'd gladly give it to her. I was in love with Dottie Jean in high school, but she and Hank Weaver were planning to be married. I wasn't about to ruin it for either of them."

Kevin's face twisted in grief. "But what about Mom? You married her."

He tried to soothe his son's anguish. "I loved your mother with all my heart. We had a good marriage and a good life. My heart broke when she died, and I've been terribly alone these past few years."

Kevin rose and paced across the room again. "But you've had me and Brooke and the children, as well as Holly and her family and Kristen. You haven't been alone."

Fletcher sighed. "Yes, I have. I've missed having a woman to talk to about my day. Someone to rub my shoulders, kiss my neck, and just listen. I've missed the companionship that comes with a good relationship."

"I see." He stopped his pacing and peered at his father. "I think I understand what you mean."

Fletcher smiled. "Thank you. Dottie Jean is fun, has a

wonderful sense of humor, and makes me feel good inside. I've fallen in love with her all over again."

Kevin's mouth gaped open. "Dad! Are you saying you want to marry her?"

"Possibly, if she'll have me. Before you go worrying about the money bit, Dottie Jean and Hank Weaver had a highly successful fishing fleet and wholesale seafood company. She sold it all last year for a very tidy sum. In other words, she doesn't need my money."

"But what about the diner and life in Calista? Will she want to come up to Jackson to live?"

"I doubt it, but I'm not worried about that. I don't need to be here for the business to carry on. You and our partners can handle the everyday stuff, so I've already inquired about a piece of property in Calista and will move down there as soon as a house can be built."

"I wasn't expecting this." He slumped into the chair again. "You're really sure this is what you want to do?"

"I am, but I need to take care of a few matters first." He stood and offered Kevin his hand. "I need your support, Kev. It's important to me."

His son stood and shook his hand, then wrapped an arm around him. "I need time to think and pray about it. I just want you to be happy and not hurt or disappointed."

"Thanks. Now I've got some errands to run." Fletcher hurried out to his car. He had to get her to talk to him and tell him what had happened.

Chapter 8

Dottie Jean awakened, feeling somewhat better, but still disappointed at the way last night had turned out. She needed to be busy, and Saturdays were always that way. Jenny could use her help in the restaurant.

Before leaving for the duties of the day, she stopped to gaze at Hank's picture. *Well, my love, I made an idiot of myself last night.* Then she smiled. *Oh, Hank, if you were here, we'd have a good laugh about this and the hoity-toity set, as Sassy calls them.* That's who she needed to see—Sassy.

A short drive brought her to Sassy's. A few customers lingered in the bait shop, and her friend greeted her. "Hey there, Dottie Jean. Be with you in a minute." She turned to a customer, but a sudden realization came into her eyes, and she peered with furrowed brow at Dottie Jean.

A few minutes later the customer departed. Sassy turned the sign on the door over to CLOSED and spun around. "Okay. Let's have it. What happened last night to give you that hang-dog look? And what are you doing home so early?"

Dottie Jean sighed as her friend pulled up two chairs and motioned for her to sit. "Oh, Sassy, I should have listened to you. Last night was awful—well, at least some of it was nice, but not all."

Sassy clicked her tongue. "I knew it. What did those biddies in Jackson say to upset you? No, wait until I get Berta and Sue Ellen here, too. No need to tell it more than once."

Sassy made her calls, then turned to Dottie Jean. "They'll be here in a minute. I'm putting on a fresh pot of coffee."

In no time, the other two women joined them in the bait shop. Sue Ellen burst through the door. "What in the world is going on? Lucky I'm between appointments for a bit." Then she spotted Dottie Jean. "What are you doing here? Shouldn't you still be in Jackson?"

Berta held the morning edition of the Jackson newspaper in her hand. "I could ask the same question. This looks like you had a good time." She handed the paper to Dottie Jean.

The picture of Fletcher and her at the dinner stared back from the page. "Oh my. I had no idea they'd use this."

Sassy looked over Dottie Jean's shoulder. "Well, it doesn't do you justice. You're prettier than that."

Sue Ellen and Berta nodded in agreement. Dottie Jean sighed and laid the paper on the counter. "The picture's not so bad, but what happened after is."

The questions in their eyes led her into her tale of the events of the previous evening.

At the end of Dottie Jean's story, Sassy pressed her lips together and shook her head. Berta and Sue Ellen stared in disbelief.

Then all three began talking at once.

"How could they?"

"How rude."

"The nerve!"

Dottie Jean held up her hands. "Slow down. I can't hear all of you at once.

Sassy stomped off to pour mugs of coffee. "I don't care if it is hot outside. Steaming coffee suits how I feel."

Finally, Berta asked, "But how did Fletcher react, and what did he do?"

Dottie Jean sighed. "He doesn't know about it. He was a perfect gentleman all evening and tried to make me feel comfortable. I ran off with no explanation, but I just couldn't tell him last night or face him this morning. I'm nothing but a coward."

Sassy returned with a tray of mugs filled with hot coffee. "Smart, if you ask me. Get out of this as soon as you can. You don't need a man in your life right now."

Berta shook her head. "No, I don't think so. Maybe let things ride for a while. Then talk to Fletcher and let him know how you feel."

Sue Ellen set her mug hard on the table. "Men! Now I know why I don't care about finding me one."

Sassy laughed and slapped her knee. "I know what you mean. I had me a good one. There's not another one like him, so why bother?"

Dottie Jean relaxed. Talking with her friends proved what she should have known all along. She didn't need to see Fletcher again. She belonged right here in Calista.

Fletcher parked his car along the main street of Calista and headed for the restaurant. He knew it would be open for lunch, and he prayed Dottie Jean would talk to him.

He entered and spotted Jenny. She came toward him. "Mr. Cameron. Good to see you. Where's Mom?"

"I was hoping you could tell me. She left without saying good-bye or anything."

Jenny bit her lip. "I haven't seen her, but she may be down at Sassy's."

That wasn't a good sign. From the looks Sassy had given him the few times they had seen each other, he could tell that lady didn't like him. No telling what she'd be saying about him to Dottie Jean. He hurried back outside, into the heat. Sassy's bait shop was up near the river. He jumped back into his car and sped that way. Just after he parked, Dottie Jean and another woman stepped through the door. Neither of the women looked happy.

"Dottie Jean, wait up. I need to speak to you."

To his dismay, she took one look at him and ran toward her car. The other woman shook her head at him. He drove after Dottie Jean. Instead of going into the restaurant, she headed for her home.

When he caught up, she was already inside. He knocked on the door. "Dottie Jean, please come out and talk to me. I don't understand what happened or why you left in such a hurry."

No sound came from the other side. He tried the doorknob, but the door was locked. He rapped on the door again. "I just need to talk with you. Please come out. Please."

She must have been near the door, because he heard her quivering voice plain as day. "Please go away. I'm not ready to talk to you right now. I'm a little confused at the moment. I'll. . . I'll have to get back to you later."

What? He stepped back. Despite her faltering voice, her determined tone unnerved him. The previous evening rolled through his mind. Everything had run smooth as silk until she'd gone to the ladies' room. Then he remembered seeing Adele and Liz headed there. The truth dawned on him. The women had said something to Dottie Jean.

His heart ached for the hurt she must feel. He had to think of something to ease the pain and let her know he didn't care what the others thought—although at the moment, he cared very much and wanted to strangle the two snobs.

He sat down on the step and cradled his head in his hands. He figured Dottie Jean wouldn't listen to anything he had to say for the moment. No amount of apology could change whatever had happened.

Fletcher swiped his hands along his thighs and stood. Might as well walk around town a little. But he'd steer clear of Sassy's bait shop. That was one woman he didn't care to have on his back today. All his plans and dreams for a future with Dottie Jean seemed destined for the trash heap. No. He wouldn't give up. Suddenly he knew just what he had to do to win back Dottie Jean's trust.

July stretched toward August, but Dottie Jean avoided Fletcher's calls for several weeks. She didn't know how much longer she'd be able to ignore him, especially when he visited the diner this morning searching for her. When he came in for a hot lunch, she stayed in the kitchen until he left.

She stretched her arms and rotated her head slowly. Lunch hour had been exceptionally busy today, and her body ached from being on her feet. She sank into a chair and poured artificial sweetener into a glass of tea. She stirred the cold liquid and gazed out the front window. Suddenly she sat up and leaned forward. Fletcher was walking along Main Street with Berta again. This was the third time she'd seen them together. What was going on? Berta was engaged to Matt, who was building a new house in Calista where he and his elderly friends could live.

She continued to stare until Berta's red truck bearing the Bert's Dirts logo turned a corner. Her eyes misted over. Fletcher refused to leave her thoughts. She missed his company but had decided he was better off without her.

Rising from the table, she wiped off the water ring with a napkin, then carried her glass to the kitchen. Junior Lee glanced up from peeling potatoes. Dottie Jean nodded and said, "I'm going out for a bit. I'll be back to get my pies done for the dinner crowd. Tell Jenny for me if she asks."

"Sure thing, Miz Weaver." He inclined his head toward the back. "I think Miss Jenny's in the office."

Dottie Jean waved and headed out. She hurried the few blocks down to the church and Pastor Jordan's office. Once inside, the reverend stood and indicated a chair. "Have a seat, Dottie Jean. What brings you here in the middle of the day?"

She sat on the edge of the straight-back chair and folded her hands in her lap. After a moment she moistened her lips and said, "I have something I need to discuss with you."

He leaned back in his chair, pressed his fingertips together, and waited for her to continue.

After a deep breath, she told him of her predicament with Fletcher. At the end, her gaze lowered to her hands, now damp with perspiration. "I don't know what to do. I care about him, but I'm not in his league, so to speak."

Pastor Jordan moved forward and clasped his hands on the top of his desk. "Dottie Jean, how do you really feel about him?"

"I'm not sure. I enjoy being with him. He makes me feel special, and I miss that since Hank died." She picked at a hangnail and avoided his gaze.

"Now isn't that what's important? You don't have to be 'in his league,' as you say. Those women in Jackson have nothing over you. If he's trying to talk with you and see you, then he doesn't care about things like that. He's a good Christian man from what I gather."

She peered into his face. "Yes, he is."

"And you haven't told him the reason for your hasty departure after the dinner?" He rested his elbows on his desk.

Dottie shook her head. "No. I think I was too embarrassed by it all."

"Then I think it's time to talk it over with him." He came around the desk. "Your birthday party is this weekend. Why not invite him to it?"

"I don't know. I'll have to think about that. I'm not sure I want to see him that soon." She extended her hand. "Thank you, though. I'm really going to consider your advice."

The pastor held her hand in his. "I'll be praying for you to make the right decision. In fact, let's do it now."

She bowed her head and listened to Pastor Jordan's soothing tones. "Dear Father, our sister has a dilemma and needs Your guidance. Show her the way she should go, what should be said, and when. Thank you for Your love and care for us. Amen."

"Thank you. I do feel better now." She glanced at her watch. "Oh dear. It's time to get my pies made for tonight. Thank you again for your prayers." She smiled and waved good-bye to the secretary, then headed back to the diner. A block from the Catfish House, she spotted Sassy coming from the bank.

"Hi, Sassy. Come on by the diner and have a glass of lemonade with me."

Her friend stopped abruptly. "Don't have time, Dottie Jean. See you later." She turned on her heel and made a beeline back into the building.

Dottie Jean shook her head. What had gotten into her? This was the second time she'd avoided Dottie Jean this week. Maybe it had something to do with the birthday party on Saturday. She shrugged and shook her head. What had started out to be a secret party for her sixty-fifth birthday had turned into a celebration for the whole town. No time to think about that now. She had cooking to do.

A few minutes later, she donned her apron and assembled the supplies to make the pie filling. The crusts, rolled out earlier in the day, sat ready and waiting in the refrigerator for her luscious concoction of eggs, butter, sugar, syrup, and pecans.

As she poured the mixture into the pastry, she again thought about the curious behavior of her friends. She had to get to the bottom of it one way or the other. As she made pies, she prayed. Pies and prayer, two things she could do quite well.

⚬⚬⚬

Fletcher helped Berta secure a set of blueprints on a tree stump with two stones. He peered over her shoulder at the plans.

Berta shoved her cap back on her head. "Well, Fletcher, what do you think?"

He glanced from the paper to the framework now going up, then back to the plans. "Looks good, Berta. I know you didn't want to do this at first, but I really appreciate it. Having you to oversee the plans for me takes a load off my mind. The contractors say you're a big help."

Berta grinned and rolled up the plans. "Dottie Jean deserves something grand, and this will do it. I'm sure she suspects something, and I'm hoping she thinks it concerns her birthday party."

"Berta, Fletcher," a familiar voice called out.

He spun around to find Sassy stumbling across the lot wearing her fishing overalls and hat. Oh no. What could she want? When the older woman stopped, she bent over at the waist and panted to catch her breath.

"What in the world brings you out here, Sassy?" Berta scurried to her friend's side.

The older woman straightened up and pointed a finger at him. "You, Mr. Fletcher Cameron. You're getting me into trouble with my best friend."

Berta patted her arm. "Now, Sassy, what happened?"

"Dottie Jean, that's what!" She planted her hands on her hips. "I had to lie to her again today and avoid being with her."

Oh no. Sassy could ruin everything. How could he convince her to keep quiet? "I'm sorry, but you can't tell her about this. Please don't say anything."

"Humph. You and your secrets. What makes you think she'll even want this place, or you, for that matter?"

He shook his head. "I'm praying she will, but it has to be a surprise for her birthday." And if she didn't like it, he'd still have the place for himself, but surely God would consider his prayer and soften Dottie Jean's heart.

Sassy narrowed her eyes at him. "Well, I just learned from a friend at the bank that you made inquiries about her and the diner. Looks to me like you're putting your nose in where it doesn't belong."

"I'm sorry about that. Ever since what happened in Jackson, I've tried. . ."

Sassy exploded. "Say what? How do you know what happened in Jackson?" She turned a fire-filled gaze to Berta. "You! You told him. And after we promised Dottie Jean. Why, I oughta go up there and spill the whole thing to her."

Fletcher tried to soothe her by placing a hand on her arm, but Sassy jerked away. "Leave me alone. I'm madder than one of those hens in the rain."

"And I don't blame you, but when I explained to Berta how I felt and what I wanted to do, she did tell me. But I had already guessed."

Sassy peered at Berta again. "I don't know what to think

about this now. Are you sure we're doing the right thing?"

Berta shrugged. "I don't know."

Fletcher placed his cap back on his head. "Come on back to the truck. We need to get out of this sun."

Sassy stood her ground. "No. If we go anywhere, I want to go up to the house." Without waiting for a reply, she strode toward the construction.

He shrugged, raised an eyebrow, then followed with Berta behind him.

Once on the foundation, Sassy inspected the expanse of the concrete slab and the few framing walls now in place, with Berta calling warnings to be careful. She finally returned to where they waited by the entrance.

Sassy waved her hand toward the structure. "It's going to be a fine house. Dottie Jean certainly deserves a place like this."

"That's what I told him. Now will you keep quiet?" Berta tapped a foot on the concrete floor.

"I suppose so, but I might bust a gusset in the meantime." She narrowed her eyes at him. "What I want to know is what you're going to do if she doesn't want it."

Fletcher patted her shoulder. "If she doesn't want this house, then I plan to move in myself. After that, I'll start courting her proper-like."

"Humph. Seems to be a waste of money, but I'll keep quiet."

"Thanks, Sassy. Like I told Berta, I loved Dottie Jean back in high school, and I believe God brought us back together again. I only pray I can get her to talk with me. So far, I haven't made any headway in that department."

Sassy shook her head. "Well, I don't think I can help much right now. If I start suggesting she talk to you, she'll jump all over me like a hound dog after a coon. Then I'll spill the beans for sure."

Berta wrapped an arm around her friend's shoulder. "That's okay, dear. I'll take care of that. You steer clear of anything to do with Fletcher."

He folded his arms across his chest. "I'm sure glad you ladies are on my side. Don't know what I'd do if you were against me." Indeed, talking to Berta in the first place and winning Sassy over had been two of the smartest things he could have done. He really didn't know what he'd do if the plan failed.

He escorted them back to Berta's truck and Sassy's car. After driving back to town, Berta let him out. Fletcher jumped down. "Thank you again, Berta. Everything looks great. I'll see you Saturday. Pray she doesn't throw me out of the party." Before getting into his own car, he glanced again at Sassy, who had followed them. She sat with arms crossed, staring straight ahead. He prayed she would keep her word and not betray him before then.

As he backed out onto the road, Berta stood by Sassy's car window, and the two women were deep in discussion. Passing by the diner without stopping took all the strength he could muster, but after the extremes Dottie Jean went to in order to avoid him this morning, he didn't want to risk another rejection today. Saturday would be soon enough. *Dear Lord, please let her listen to me, and please help me to make her understand how much I love her and want this house for her. . .for us.*

Chapter 9

Dottie Jean gazed around the noisy dining room. The lunch crowd buzzed with conversation as Allie May and Mary Beth scurried around taking care of the customers. Sassy and Berta finished their lunch and beckoned for Dottie Jean to join them.

She plopped down in the empty seat at their table. "What's up, ladies?"

Berta set down her iced tea glass. "We were just thinking about your party Saturday. Have you invited Fletcher Cameron yet?"

Dottie Jean shook her head. "No, and I'm not sure I'm going to."

Sassy slapped her hand on the table. "And why not?"

Dottie Jean frowned. That didn't sound like Sassy. "I haven't spoken to him in weeks. I'd look kinda silly calling him now when I've avoided him like the plague." Why were they talking about Fletcher? He was the last person in the world she wanted to discuss.

Berta toyed with her napkin. "I just thought it'd be nice to have him here."

And why should that matter to them? At that moment, Fanny from the supermarket lumbered into the diner and eased into a chair behind Sassy. Her ample body spilled over the edges.

"I need some service here. I'm so hungry I could eat the horns off a billy goat." Fanny's whining voice rang above all the others.

Sassy muttered under breath, "More than likely, the whole billy goat, too."

Dottie Jean threw Sassy a warning look as she signaled to Allie May. The young waitress hurried to Fanny's table with a tumbler of ice water. She scribbled down the order and headed back to the kitchen.

Fanny cocked her head toward Berta. "Whose fancy house are they building on that land you cleared near that man's with the fancy name?"

Sassy reached over and smacked Fanny's arm. "Shush your mouth, girl."

"What house?" Dottie Jean's gaze darted back and forth between the two women.

Berta cleared her throat, then swallowed. "Um, I'm clearing land for a new client. Thought I'd take care of one last customer before selling out to the Crawford boys."

Dottie Jean narrowed her eyes to peer at Berta. "Is that what you and Fletcher have been up to these past few weeks?"

The young owner of Bert's Dirts averted her attention and raised her hand as though to call the waitress. "I don't know what you're talking about."

At that moment, Jenny arrived at the table. "What can I do for you, Berta?"

"We were just discussing your mom's party. How's it coming along?"

Dottie Jean didn't hear Jenny's reply as her mind filled with questions Berta needed to answer. From the corner of her eye, she observed Sassy holding Fanny's arm in a death grip. The older woman yanked her arm, trying to loosen the hold, and glared at Sassy, but Sassy's strong fingers merely tightened around the flesh.

Berta rose from her seat and followed Jenny to the office, and Sassy leaned over to whisper something into Fanny's ear.

"That does it! You girls are up to something, and I aim to find out what it is. Sassy, let go of Fanny's arm. You're going to squeeze the blood out of it." Dottie Jean pushed back from the table and marched to the back of the diner. The sound of Fanny's anger as she complained to Sassy followed her.

She stormed into the office, where Berta and Jenny huddled over the desk. "I'd like to know just what y'all are cooking up. I've never seen so many secrets and furtive glances since Tilly Hatchett came back to town."

The two younger women exchanged glances. Jenny shrugged her shoulders. "You may as well know, Mom. I invited Fletcher and his family to your party."

"You what?"

Jenny held up her hands as if to fend off Dottie Jean's anger. "Just wait a minute. Now I've seen you moping around the past month. I don't care what happened in Jackson—you still care about Mr. Cameron."

"Who says so, and what does it matter if I do?"

"Look, we're simply trying to help you patch things up. He's been prowling around this town waiting for you to speak to him two or three times a week." Berta extended her hand to touch Dottie Jean's arm.

"And that's why you've been hanging around with him so much?"

"Yes and no. Honey, I've never seen two more miserable people than you two. We only want you to be happy, and that's why we thought the birthday party would be a good time to get you together." Berta wrapped her arm around Dottie Jean's shoulders.

Her friend's soothing voice calmed some of her anger, but she still peered at them suspiciously. Jenny reached out to hug her. Then the anger began to dissolve. Hadn't she decided just this morning to ask him to come anyway? Her friends and her family loved her and wanted only what was best.

"Mom, we just want you to be happy like you were when you and Mr. Cameron first started going out. He's really a nice man. We all like him."

Berta nodded. "Yes, and he isn't like those ladies in Jackson. They're snobs with their noses so high in the air they can't see what Fletcher sees in you."

Dottie Jean felt her mouth quivering. She had been miserable these past weeks, and evidently everyone else had recognized it, too. "Okay. Let him come to the party. I guess it's time we had a little talk. I'll call and do the inviting myself. . . . No, if you've already done it, I'll just leave it at that."

Jenny grinned and embraced her mother again. "Thanks,

Mom. It'll be a grand time. Just you wait."

"Maybe so. Now I'm going back out there to make sure Sassy and Fanny don't kill each other." She headed for the dining room, but Sassy and Fanny were nowhere to be found. Dottie Jean shook her head. More was going on around here than any of them were letting on. She'd let them have their little fun and games now, but come Saturday, she'd get some answers.

Fletcher decided he'd get an answer from Dottie Jean one way or the other on Saturday. He punched the intercom button. "Mrs. Phelps, call Kevin and tell him I need to see him."

He swiveled his chair to gaze out at the buildings of downtown Jackson. Jenny's invitation both surprised and delighted him. At first, he'd planned to crash the party, but then he'd decided not to ruin Dottie Jean's day. Now he could attend without worry.

He spun back around when Kevin entered the office.

"Hey, Dad, what's up?" His son relaxed in one of the chairs by the desk.

"I'm going down to Calista for Mrs. Weaver's birthday, and I'd like for you and Brooke to go with me."

Kevin furrowed his brow. "Are you sure, Dad? I didn't think she was speaking to you."

Fletcher fingered some papers on the desktop. "She isn't, but her daughter called earlier and thinks I ought to come."

"But Mrs. Weaver doesn't know about the house or your plans to move to Calista?" His son shook his head.

"No, and her birthday will be the perfect time to tell her. I've prayed about this, and it's what God wants me to do."

Kevin shrugged. "I'm not one to argue with God. I'll talk to Brooke about going with you." He smiled. "You know she thinks this is all so romantic, and I'll bet she'll be happy to tag along and not hear it all secondhand."

Fletcher chuckled. "Yes, she will be." He pushed away from the desk. "I'm glad that's settled. To be honest, I'm a little nervous about all this, but I do have her friends and Jenny on my side." Then he remembered Sassy. That one he couldn't be sure of, but he counted on Berta and Sue Ellen to keep her in line.

His son rose and headed for the door. "I'll talk more about this with you later. I'm going to call Brooke so she can arrange a sitter for the boys."

"Wait. Don't do that. I'd like it if you brought them with you. I want her to meet your family. I only wish Holly and Kristen could be there, too. Kristen won't be back from her mission trip with the church until next week, and with the new baby coming any day, I know Holly doesn't want to travel."

"If you're sure about the boys, I'll tell Brooke we're all invited." He hesitated a moment, then blurted out, "Dad, I'm sorry for my attitude a few weeks ago. I really hope this works out for you. I want you to be happy."

"Thanks, son. Your support means a lot to me." He stared at the door after Kevin closed it, then slumped back into his leather chair. He checked his calendar for afternoon appointments. Only one needed his attention; the others he quickly canceled. After his one o'clock meeting, he'd take a quick trip down to Calista to consult with the contractors.

By two thirty he headed for his destination. When he arrived, Berta glanced up from her work, then smiled when she recognized him. "Hi, Mr. Cameron. I wasn't expecting to see you again until Saturday. You *are* coming to the party, aren't you?"

Fletcher laughed. "Yes, Jenny talked me into it. I asked my son and his family to come with me. I thought it was time for them to meet Dottie Jean."

"Oh? Well, the more the merrier. By the way, Jenny told her mother about inviting you, and she didn't object." Berta sat back in her chair and twirled her pencil.

"Hmm. That's a good sign. I hope. I don't know what I'll do if she decides to ignore me." He rubbed the back of his neck. "Guess I'll cross that bridge when I get to it."

Berta handed him some sketches. "Just came back from the site. Here are a few ideas I had as I talked with the contractor. We're going to make this a place Dottie Jean won't be able to resist."

Fletcher settled into a chair. "How are things going with you and her friends keeping this secret?"

Berta raised her eyebrows and shrugged. "As well as can be expected, I guess. Fanny almost got us into trouble at lunch today." She told him about the incident between Sassy and Fanny at the diner.

Fletcher chuckled. "Good ol' Sassy. She came through for us after all. I only pray you all won't regret this."

"We won't. Without Sassy, you'd be dead in the water, so her response today is a good sign."

He knew that for sure. "I'm going to run out to the house and see what's been done since the other day. You don't need to go with me. I'll then be heading on back to Jackson."

Berta tilted her head. "You're not going by the diner this visit?"

"No, I'll wait until Saturday to see her. Thanks again for all your help." He shook hands with his young cohort and ambled back to his car. Amazing what Berta's friends had accomplished in such a short time.

After a visit to the house under construction, Fletcher's heart filled with love for Dottie Jean. Satisfied with the progress, he meandered through the debris and back to where he'd parked. Before turning the key, he bowed his head on the steering wheel.

Lord, I commit this house, my relationship with Dottie Jean, and my future into Your hands.

A few minutes later, he turned onto the highway leading to Jackson, his thoughts filled with the surprise for Dottie Jean.

Chapter 10

Dottie Jean pulled the red top over her head and flung it toward the bed, adding it to the pile already there. She frowned at her reflection in the mirror before finally reaching into the closet for her favorite denim skirt and vest. She might as well wear something comfortable. This was worse than her first date with Fletcher.

So far, plans were going right today. Jenny, Berta, Sue Ellen, and Sassy had outdone themselves. She smiled at the sight they had made earlier, hanging streamers and blowing up balloons.

She shrugged her arms into the vest. Nothing looked right. The idea of meeting Fletcher's family sent her heart into a tailspin. How should she dress? She turned in front of the mirror and sighed. She looked like a small-town matron. But then, isn't that what she was? She raised her shoulders. Banish those thoughts. Nothing would spoil her day.

At that moment, Jenny popped in. "Hey, Mom, you about ready? This is going to be the greatest day. Wait and see."

Dottie Jean sighed. "I hope you're right." With her head

held high and her shoulders squared, Dottie Jean felt ready to face anybody's family as she strode across to the restaurant.

Friends had already begun to assemble in the dining room when she and Jenny made their entrance. Wendell Meeks gave her a hug.

Sassy kissed her cheek. "You look great. Go get 'em, girl." She winked and headed for the buffet table.

All through the congratulations and best wishes of her friends, Dottie Jean's gaze roamed the room and darted to the plate glass window for a glimpse of Fletcher. *Lord, I'm so nervous. Control my tongue and help me to say and do the right things.* Her heart pounded so loudly she was sure everyone could hear it.

Her grandson drew her attention to the balloons. "Grammy, can I have a red one?"

She lifted the three-year-old boy to her hip. "Sure, Jason. We'll tie it around your wrist."

The dark-haired tot grinned as she set him in a chair and secured the string. The big red balloon bounced as he waved his hand and giggled. "Thanks, Grammy." He scooted from the chair and ran to his mother.

A hand touched her shoulder. "Dottie Jean, happy birthday."

The voice set her heart to singing and her knees to trembling. She turned to face Fletcher. Her voice squeaked out a thank you while their gazes locked. Suddenly they were the only two in the room.

"I'm—I'm so happy you're here." She felt the heat rising in her cheeks.

"I'm pleased we were invited." Fletcher's dark eyes searched her face. Then he stepped back and wrapped an arm around a young man just behind him.

"I'd like you to meet my son, Kevin. Kevin, this is Mrs. Weaver."

She smiled at the handsome younger version of Fletcher. "I'm pleased to meet you. Call me Dottie Jean; everyone else does."

Kevin placed a hand on his wife's shoulder. She held a young boy in her arms. "This is my wife, Brooke, and our son Taylor."

Dottie Jean shook the woman's hand. "I've heard so many nice things about all of you. It's truly a pleasure to meet you."

Then Kevin ruffled the hair of the boy standing next to him. "And this is Scott."

"How do you do, Scott? You're a fine-looking young man."

The lad grinned and exposed two gaps from missing teeth. "I'm six years old."

The familiar lisp brought a broad smile to her face. "Well now, that means you'll be in first grade this year. How about a balloon for you and your brother?"

"Can we have one, Mom, please?" He tugged on his mother's hand.

"Sure. Daddy and I will get it for you. A pleasure meeting you, Mrs. Weaver. . .I mean, Dottie Jean." She set the younger boy down, and he headed for the balloons. Kevin followed them.

"Nice family, Fletcher. The boys are adorable. Jenny and Bill are over there with the rest of the family. Come, I want everyone to meet you." Her heart still thudding, she didn't want to be alone to talk just yet.

She led him to the table where Bill and Jenny sat with her other son, Henry, and their spouses and children. After making introductions all around, Bill spoke to Fletcher.

"I'm in Jackson with Computers Plus, and I've heard a great deal about your electronics firm. In fact, I use quite a few of your software programs in some of the work I do."

Fletcher smiled. "Thank you. Firms like yours help keep us in business." He turned to Henry. "You do resemble your namesake, Henry. Did you play ball in school?"

The bulky young man laughed. "Sure did. Played on defense. Went to Ole Miss, too. Followed your career while I was growing up. Dad talked about you being the best quarterback around."

Dottie Jean smiled at the flush rising in Fletcher's cheeks. "Well, he caught enough of my passes to make me one." He grasped Dottie Jean's arm. "Mind if I steal your mother away a minute?"

She turned from the table with him, and he whispered, "Is there somewhere private we can talk?"

"In my office." She felt the tightening in her chest, dreading the conversation she had postponed for so many weeks. After closing the office door, she scurried to a chair, uncertain whether her legs would hold her much longer. She waved her hand to indicate the other chair for him.

He nodded and then pulled it closer to her before seating himself. "We have a few things we need to clear up. First is an apology for what happened at the benefit dinner. I had no idea what you had heard until later, and I'm truly sorry."

The sincerity in his eyes warmed Dottie Jean. "I should've

explained my abrupt departure, and I should've known you'd understand."

A dimple flashed in his left cheek. "Looks like we both made a mistake or two." He moistened his lips, and the smile disappeared. "Something else I need to tell you before you find out from someone else and get the wrong idea."

She clasped her hands in her lap and waited, fearing what he might say.

"When we first saw each other again, I was elated. I could see you had a fine diner, and I wanted to make sure you have what you need." He hesitated and peered at the floor before gazing into her eyes again.

"Forgive me, but I did a check on the diner to see if you needed any help with the financing and keeping it in the black."

She sucked in her breath. "What?" Then her eyes narrowed to slits as she waited for him to continue.

"I'm sorry. I just wanted to help in any way I could, but I discovered you didn't need my help. You've done a great job here. Hank would be proud."

At first, anger rose in her throat, but she swallowed it and closed her eyes. She needed help understanding his motives, but he was only thinking of her best interests. Pleasure over his concern replaced the anger that had filled her at first.

He waited until she opened her eyes to speak. Then he breathed a sigh of relief when he realized the anger had disappeared and her eyes reflected forgiveness and understanding.

"I should be so mad at you, Fletcher Cameron, but my heart tells me you were only doing it out of concern. I'm glad you told me. If I had heard it from Sassy or Berta, I might never have spoken to you again." A faint smile touched her lips.

"Whew, that's a relief. Thank you." Now if only she felt that way about his big surprise. He could hardly contain his joy and slapped his knee. "Now let's go enjoy the party."

Later, after the cake had been served and the gifts opened, Fletcher called the crowd to attention. "Please, I have a request."

Conversation halted, and all eyes concentrated on him. "If you don't mind, I'm taking Dottie Jean to get her birthday present from me. We'll be back shortly. Y'all go ahead and have fun."

He almost choked with laughter at the sight of Berta, Sassy, and Sue Ellen nudging each other and grinning. Sassy even winked at him. Bless her heart, he sensed her loyalty and knew she'd be a great friend to have. With his elbow extended to Dottie Jean, he held his breath until she hooked her hand on his arm and followed him to his car.

When they arrived at the house site, the sun still shone in the west far enough above the horizon to give plenty of light for him to present his gift in grand fashion. His heart tightened at the thought of how she might react. If it went as planned, he wouldn't be able to contain his joy. If it didn't, he shuddered at the thought.

He parked the car, then helped Dottie Jean from her side. She furrowed her brow and glanced up at him, then back to the rising framework.

"What is this, Fletcher?"

His excitement bubbled to the surface and exploded in a

broad grin. "It's your birthday gift from me." He held his breath waiting for her reaction.

Her mouth dropped open, and she stared at him with a stunned expression. In a moment she recovered and sputtered, "My—my gift? What on earth do you mean?"

He blew out his breath and grasped her hands. "I mean it's your house. I know how you love the river, and now you can be near it again."

She gasped and blinked her eyes. "Fletcher, I can't accept something like this. It's too much."

Now for the main part. "Even if I come along with it?"

Her cheeks turned pink, and he pulled her hands to his lips. "If you say no, then I'm just going to move in and live here until you decide to come live with me as my wife."

Her bottom lip trembled. "Fletcher, I don't know what to say. I hadn't. . . Well, I. . . Oh my."

"I don't need an answer right away." His heart felt as squeezed as it had so many years ago when he learned of her marriage to Hank. "I loved you in high school, but you were Hank Weaver's girl, and I liked him too much to hurt him. When I came home from college and learned you two had eloped, I felt I had lost it all."

"But what about you and Barbara?" Dottie Jean furrowed her brow and peered at him. "You two were the perfect couple."

"I cared for Barbara and loved her dearly for all those years until God called her home."

She slipped her hands from his and wrapped her arms around her body. He had to lean toward her to hear her soft words.

"I had such a crush on you. You were the quarterback and a

senior. Barbara was the homecoming queen, and I decided you were the perfect pair. Hank and I had known each other forever, and it was natural for us to be together. When you went off to college, I fell in love with Hank even more than I could imagine."

"I think God is giving us a second chance at love. We've both had good marriages, and I think we can have our own." His soul sang at the prospect of spending the rest of his days with this wonderful woman.

※

Another marriage? Did she want one? Her heart thumped, and her stomach felt like it was in a vise. She turned to face the framework of the house. What could she say? Was God truly giving them a second chance for love? She felt Fletcher's hands on her shoulders.

He whispered in her ear, "You don't have to answer me yet. All I ask is for you to consider it. I'll wait as long as it takes."

Suddenly the sun sent forth brilliant shafts of orange, purple, and pale gold, as if God Himself were giving His blessing. A peaceful calm settled on her soul. She lifted her hands to Fletcher's, still at her shoulders.

A place to begin a new life and a new future as Mrs. Fletcher Cameron. Dottie Jean Cameron. Yes, she liked the sound of it. "I think this would be a beautiful place to live the rest of our lives."

He tilted her chin toward him and leaned forward. "I came to Calista for a catfish dinner and found the best thing not on the menu." Then his lips met hers with a kiss filled with the promise of more to come.

MARTHA ROGERS

Native Texan Martha Rogers' published works include articles, Bible studies, devotionals, and stories in compilations. This is her first fiction release. Martha enjoys writing about older women because she believes they can have just as much fun and romance in their lives as younger ladies do. Through her stories she hopes to touch the hearts of her readers and encourage them in their faith. Martha is a retired teacher at both high school and college levels and is active as a volunteer worker at her church, where she sings in the choir. She and her husband, Rex, live in Houston and are the parents of three sons and their wives who have blessed them with nine grandchildren.

Gone Fishing

by Janice Thompson

Dedication

To Rebecca Germany:
Thanks for pulling Sassy from the slush pile.
She was starting to smell a little fishy.

Above all else, guard your heart,
for it is the wellspring of life.
PROVERBS 4:23

Chapter 1

Sassy Hatchett slipped her legs over the edge of the rickety wooden pier and dipped her toes into the warm waters of the Biloxi River. She twisted a fishhook from her hat, then reached into the front pocket of her overalls to pull out a plastic bag filled with ice-cold shrimp. She yanked out a large one and ran the clean silver hook straight through it.

"Why can't everything be this easy?"

Sassy spoke to no one but herself. Certainly none of the other residents of Calista, Mississippi, could hear her from out here at the water's edge.

A host of irritating mosquitoes swarmed down upon her. She swatted them away with a wild swing of her right arm. "Pesky critters. Get on out of here." They refused to budge, though she slapped the air in a frantic attempt to shoo them away. Sassy pulled a can of mosquito repellent from the tackle box and sprayed it in every conceivable direction. They disappeared on sight. "Serves you right."

Reaching for the comfort of a familiar wooden fishing pole,

she tried to settle down, though an unexplained frustration still gripped her. Troubling thoughts rolled madly through her head. She forced herself to turn her attention to the skies.

"Well, here I am again, Lord. Just You, me, and a mess of catfish I ain't caught yet." She lifted up a small, empty ice chest toward heaven—a sign she half expected to see it filled before the conversation ended. "I don't know what's wrong with me today. Nothing seems to be going right. Seems like everything gets me madder than a hornet, and this heat isn't helping a thing, either."

The warmth of the late August morning enveloped her like a shroud. She paused to lift her hat and wipe the ring of sweat from her brow. *Everything was so much easier when Joe was here to help me.*

Sassy's thoughts drifted to her husband, and she swallowed back the lump in her throat. Not a day went by she didn't think of him, wish she could have just one more moment with the love of her life. The day she'd pulled the *'n' Joe's* from the sign out in front of their bait and tackle shop had been the saddest day of her life.

"It's just too much, Lord. Running the store by myself sure ain't no fun. Everything's falling apart at the seams. I know I complain about this a lot, but every day it just gets worse. The lock's broken on the front door, and the roof needs to be patched. I can't get up there to do it myself. And the nerve of those vendors—trying to talk me into selling my bait recipes to the big names. I won't do it, Lord. I won't!"

Sassy added a couple of sinkers and a floater to her line and cast it out into the water as far as it would go. With the release of the line, she felt the weight of her problems lift a little.

I'm sorry, Lord. I know I whine a lot. I do thank You for the friends You've given me. And for Wendell.

Wendell. For weeks now, Joe's oldest and dearest friend had ventured in and out of the shop on a regular basis. Seemed every time Sassy turned around, he came by again—to look at the latest in custom rods, to buy magazines, knives, bait, fishing line—anything and everything to fill his tackle box. Wendell seemed anxious to learn all he could about fishing before retiring.

Not that she minded. He had always been so kind, so tolerant. . .finding something pleasant to say with each visit. Somehow, just the thought of him brought an unexpected smile to her lips.

Sassy felt a sudden tug on her line. "Oooh, I've got something." She clasped the reel and began to work it in her favor. "Well, lookee there." She pulled in a large catfish, a fine catch. He looked up at her with woeful eyes.

"Looks like I'm not the only one having a bad day," she observed as she pulled him loose. She tossed him into the ice chest, then turned to bait her hook once again.

"Wendell Meeks, have you lost your mind?"

" 'Course not." Wendell leaned his elbows onto the small table at the Calista Catfish House and grinned at his best friend, Gus, who sat across from him looking stunned.

"Well, what's gotten into you, then? There are plenty of good women in the great state of Mississippi without setting your sights on an ornery old thing like Sassy Hatchett. Sassy Hatchett, of all people!" Gus erupted in laughter, causing others in the diner to turn their heads in curiosity.

Wendell lifted his glass of sweet tea and struggled to look casual and confident as he took a small sip. His hand trembled, causing the cold liquid to tumble out of the glass and slosh across the bottom half of his face. He carefully dabbed at his mouth and chin with a cloth napkin. "Sassy is a great woman," he said finally. "I can't think of anyone I'd rather spend my time with." He folded the napkin neatly and laid it in his lap.

Dottie Jean chose that moment to appear with two plates full of steaming crabs, fries, and hush puppies. Placing one down in front of Wendell, she added her thoughts on the matter. "You've got your eye on Sassy? You're a brave soul, Wendell Meeks! She's a real pistol, that's for sure. 'Course, I love her. I always have. Gotta love Sassy." As she giggled, Dottie Jean's grip on Gus's plate slipped. It hit the table with a soft thud, sending the pepper shaker into a tailspin. Wendell grabbed it just as it hit the edge of the table.

"Go ahead and laugh, both of you." He unfolded his napkin and tucked it into the collar of his starched blue postal shirt. "It won't do you any good. I know what I'm doing." His elbow bumped up against the glass of tea, knocking it off balance. He managed to catch it before too much could spill out onto the blue-and-white-checkered tablecloth.

"Uh-huh." Dottie Jean left the table with a sure-you-do nod and the most aggravating grin Wendell had ever seen on a woman's face. He mopped up the mess with his napkin.

Gus continued to laugh until his cheeks turned crimson. "When was the last time you even thought about trying to snag a woman's heart?" he asked. "Thirty years ago? Forty? And why in the world would you start with a piece of work like Sassy Hatchett? She's always as mad as an old wet hen!"

Wendell didn't answer for a moment. He shook his head in silence as he continued to dab at the tablecloth. "I'm not sure you'd understand, Gus," he explained.

"Try me."

Wendell fought to formulate the words. None seemed to come. Truth be known, he hadn't deliberately avoided married life. In fact, he'd always wished for a loving wife. But the good Lord hadn't seen fit to give him one, at least not yet. In the early days, asking a woman out on a date had been a nerve-racking ordeal. His own shyness and insecurities caused him to put off the matter for years. But now, at sixty, Wendell just couldn't seem to get the idea out of his mind. He still had a number of good years left after retirement, and he didn't want to spend them alone.

"I don't expect you to make any sense of this, Gus," he said quietly. "You were married for nearly thirty years before you lost Nettie—even had a houseful of kids and grandkids. But when a man gets to be my age and he's shut up all alone in the house, he gets to wishing he had someone to share it with, that's all. I'll be retiring from the post office in a couple of years, and I'd like to spend my retirement years with—"

"Sassy Hatchett?" Gus shook his head in mock despair. "Everyone in town knows she's got a bite worse than any shark out there in the Gulf. Talk about a temper. Why, she could kill a man with just a look. Is that the sort of woman you want to spend your retirement years with?"

"Absolutely." Wendell's heart began to beat a little harder

just thinking about the possibility. "I know she has a quick tongue." A smile crept across his lips. "I sort of like that side of her. But she's got a soft side, too. I've seen her in church on Sunday mornings. She really loves the Lord. Spends a lot of time up at the altar in prayer."

"My point exactly." Gus nodded emphatically. "She's repenting."

"Come on, now." Wendell popped a piece of crab into his mouth and swallowed it whole.

"I could understand all of this—the temper, the sharp tongue, the nasty disposition—if we were talking about a knockout here." Gus dumped ketchup all over his hush puppies as he spoke his mind. "But she's no beauty queen. In fact, I'd be willing to bet she hasn't been over to the Rhonda-Vous to have her hair done in years." He gestured toward the beauty shop down the street. "That carrot red hair of hers is messier than a chicken's nest. And that crazy getup she wears out on the pier wouldn't attract much of anything but the flies."

Wendell bit his lip to keep from responding. Sassy Hatchett had a beauty that ran far deeper than the physical, although Gus had apparently never noticed it. Her gray-blue eyes glistened merrily when she got riled up. Lately they seemed to glisten a lot. Her skin, tanned from years in the sun, seemed firmer than that of most women her age. Her thick, curly hair glistened with a sunset-rivaling shimmer. Even her worn fishing hat with its dangling fishhooks held a certain unexplainable charm.

"I don't know how ol' Joe Hatchett did it," Gus rambled on. "Thirty-five years with Sassy. Gotta give a man like that a lot of credit."

"Joe Hatchett was a good friend of mine," Wendell said thoughtfully, "and a great man. He loved Sassy from the time he was a kid in school. Loved her till the day he died."

"Always felt a little sorry for him," Gus mumbled, his mouth full of food. "Poor guy."

"Don't be ridiculous."

" 'Course, Sassy was always a pill. Even before she married Joe."

Wendell swallowed a couple of french fries, then took a long, cool drink of the tea. He had heard the tale for years. According to legend, Sassy, who had been born and raised just outside of town, had come out of the womb swinging and swearing. Her parents had given her a good Christian name—though, for the life of them, no one in Calista seemed to be able to remember it. Her own mother had taken to calling her Sassy as a little bitty thing, and the name had stuck.

As the story went, Sassy's temper would flare up to the boiling point pretty regularly. Her father, being a good Christian man, would hand her a fishing pole and send her out to the pier at the edge of their property for a time of good old-fashioned repenting. Young Sassy spent many a day at the edge of the Biloxi River fishing and praying, praying and fishing. As her temper grew, so did her ability to catch fish. Day after day, she reeled them in.

Once Sassy and Joe Hatchett married, she spent more time than ever with a pole in her hand. After their twins, Tucker and Tilly, came along, she practically set up house on the pier. Rumor was, Joe Hatchett spent so much money on bait that he finally gave in and opened up Sassy 'n' Joe's Bait and Tackle just to keep his head above water financially.

The whole thing made for a great story.

"You can't believe everything you hear." Wendell turned his attention back to Gus. "Besides, I think it's nice that Sassy has a way to vent her frustrations. Fishing's a good thing."

"She purt-near keeps my restaurant supplied with catfish." Dottie Jean reappeared with more napkins. "That's quite a temper, if you ask me. 'Course, I'm not complaining. Saves me having to buy from a distributor. I figure it's true what the Bible says—"

"What's that?" Wendell asked.

" 'What Satan meant for evil, God will use for good.' " Dottie Jean smiled with a playful wink as she turned her attention to other customers.

Wendell shook his head in defeat.

"Just answer this one thing." Gus suddenly grew serious. "Is this why you bought that new boat last month—why you've spent so much time fishing? To get close to Sassy?"

Wendell shrugged. "I like to fish. What can I say?"

"Right, right." Gus nodded. "Well, don't say I didn't warn you. If you're looking to hook Sassy Hatchett, you'd better have a good piece of stink bait in your back pocket. Nothing else will work on an old snapper like her."

He burst into laughter again, this time drawing the attention of nearly everyone in the restaurant. People began to murmur among themselves from table to table.

"Sassy Hatchett? Wendell's taken a liking to that persnickety old thing? Pretty fishy, if you ask me." The story went around the room and bounced back again, reverberating in his ears.

He stood impulsively. "Now listen here," he announced to all curious onlookers, "I may be old, but I'm not deaf. You all just mind your own business now, you hear? You leave my love life to me."

Their laughter nearly deafened him.

Chapter 2

Sassy took small sips from her colorful mug and tried not to make a face. "What did you call this stuff again?" she asked her daughter, Tilly.

"White Chocolate Mocha Frappuccino, Mom. It's what everyone drinks nowadays."

"Uh-huh." Sassy took another small sip, wishing for a real cup of coffee. Regular. Black. But she didn't want to hurt her daughter's feelings. She gazed into Tilly's beautiful young face. Her daughter's pierced eyebrow and tongue distracted her slightly, along with six or seven earrings lining each ear. Tilly had a flair for the dramatic, though most found her quirky side a little too much to take.

Ever since she opened the Café Latte across the street from the church, the defiant young woman had done everything in her power to prove her individuality to the Calista community. If the prominently placed piercings didn't get the necessary attention, the catfish tattoo on her ankle did. And if, by some odd happenstance, folks managed to overlook that, she got them with her décor at the coffee shop.

An eclectic collection of colorful plastic fish heads and skeletons hung on the walls, and black fishnet hung from the ceiling above with shimmering iridescent shells dangling below. Bright coffee mugs lined the lengthy front counter, which Tucker, Tilly's twin brother, had painted in blue and white ocean wave patterns. The mugs she had designed herself, shaping them like fish, their fins serving as handles. They seemed to swim above the Technicolor waves in a dizzying array.

"So, Mom, I hear Wendell Meeks has been hanging around your place a lot these days. What's up with that?"

"Up with that?" Sassy asked. Something in her daughter's tone sparked her curiosity. "What makes you think something's up?"

"Come on now, Mom. Get real."

"I'm very real, thank you—and I don't have a clue what you're talking about," Sassy said, totally taken aback. "He just came out to fix the seal on the freezer a couple of weeks back, that's all."

Tilly shook her head. "I thought Tucker was supposed to take care of those kinds of things for you."

"He is," Sassy said with a shrug. "But you know your brother."

Tucker had always been a little on the irresponsible side—putting his own needs above those of others. Tilly had risen above her twin brother in many ways, graduating from high school first in her class and finishing her business degree at the college in only three years instead of four. Unfortunately, many in Calista couldn't see past her artistic appearance to notice her good features. *She's such a wonderful girl at heart, Lord. If only people could see that side of her.*

To be honest, most were too irritated at her for buying out Harry's barbershop and putting the Café Latte in its place to consider the possibilities. Others pointed fingers because she kept the coffee shop open on Sundays. It had become a haven for Calista's troubled teens. Tilly subtly enticed them with her wacky personality, her warm muffins, and ceramic fish-fuls of hot coffee. Many hadn't been back to church since the shop opened.

"Call Tucker again," Tilly said, jolting her back to reality. "He'll come out and fix whatever you need. I'll make sure of it."

Sassy smiled as she remembered the look on Wendell's face as he'd worked on the freezer.

Tilly's voice interrupted her thoughts. "Mom, be honest with me here. Do you like him?"

"Like him?" How should she go about answering such a crazy question? Wendell Meeks had been Joe's best friend. Of course she liked him. She had always liked him. "He's a nice man," Sassy said with a shrug. "What's not to like?"

"You just be careful." Tilly turned to wipe the countertop.

" 'Be careful'? What in the world are you talking about? Don't go making mountains out of molehills, Tilly Mae," she admonished.

"But, Mom, everyone in town is talking."

Sassy's anger rose immediately, squeezing the breath out of her. "Who's everyone?"

"Fanny, for one. I went over to pick up some creamer this morning, and she told me you and Wendell were an item. 'Two for One Special.' That's what she called you."

"Don't you know any better than to listen to Fanny?" Sassy asked heatedly. "That woman's mouth is so big, she could sing a duet all by herself." Sassy paused to calm down a bit, allowing the shame to wash over her. "And for your information, if I ever felt like I needed a man, which I won't, I'd pick out one on my own. I wouldn't need you to do it for me."

Tilly shook her head in defeat. "I just thought you'd like to know what everyone's been saying."

Sue Ellen chose that moment to enter the shop, bags in hand. "I just came from Fanny's." She dropped the bags onto the floor and sat at the counter with a deep sigh. "I thought I'd never get out of there alive. She's got a special on honey buns this week. Two for one. Get it? Two for one!" She began to rock back and forth with laughter.

Sassy slapped herself in the head.

"So I hear Wendell Meeks has been turning up at your place a lot these days." Sue Ellen sounded more than a little interested.

"What are you—the *Calista Courier?*"

Sue Ellen looked startled. "Well, I just—"

"Why don't you all just mind your own business?" Sassy's voice rose, along with her temper.

"Why, Sassy Hatchett. I do declare! I think you're protesting just a bit too much."

Lord, I'm halfway to the pier already. If You can just get me out of here, I'll do my best to repent for the things I'm wanting to say.

Sassy stood, forcing her lips together—begging the words to stay put. "I've got to go, ladies. I have a sudden urge to go fishing."

Wendell studied his reflection in the mirror, gauging his expression as he spoke to himself—"Say, Sassy, I was wondering if you'd like to go to dinner with me this Friday night." *Nah, that won't work.* "Sassy, how would you like to be my date at the fall festival?" *Nope. She'll never buy it. Besides, the festival is weeks away.* "Sassy, I was thinking you might need some help around the shop. Would you mind if I came over and had a look at that broken lock on the front door?" *Ah. Definitely a winner. Not exactly a date, but an opportunity to see her, nonetheless.*

Wendell picked up the phone, hesitantly dialing the number. A trip out to Crab Cove might be just the ticket on a beautiful day like today.

"Sassy's Bait and Tackle." *The machine.* "If you need me, pick up a pole and meet me out at the pier. Or leave a message. Whatever." He waited for the tone, then spoke nervously. "Uh, Sassy. This is Wendell. Wendell Meeks. I was thinking maybe I'd come around sometime this afternoon and have a look at that broken lock you've been talking about. I'll try to be by around three." He hung up the phone and wiped the sweat from his forehead with a handkerchief. "It's hotter than blue blazes in here."

For the first time in quite a while, he thought about his property out off of Calista Avenue—just on the outskirts of town. For years, Wendell had held on to the large piece of land, hoping to someday build a home for his own family. As the years had come and gone, the value of the property had dropped. So had his prospects of ever finding a wife or having children. But lately something seemed to have come over him, something nearly miraculous.

For some unexplained reason, Wendell suddenly had the tenacity of a bulldog, and Sassy Hatchett was tugging at his leash. The opinions of others made no difference anymore. *What matters is what I think—and I like her. A lot.* His heart suddenly swelled within him. Sassy might not be everyone else's ideal, but she was looking a little more like his every day.

The more Gus debated her looks and personality, the more Wendell felt himself drawn to her. "She's no spring chicken," he said, staring at his own reflection. "But then again, neither am I." He scrutinized himself, running his fingers through his thinning gray hair. "Hmm. I need a haircut." He glanced at his watch. One fifteen—just enough time to stop off at the hair salon for a cut before heading out to Sassy's place.

Moments later, Wendell pulled his truck up to the front of the beauty salon feeling as nervous as a long-tailed cat in a room full of rocking chairs. Things were a sure sight easier before Sassy's daughter, Tilly, bought out Harry's barbershop and turned it into the Café Latte. That left only one place in town for a man to get a haircut. Of course, it couldn't really be blamed on Tilly. Harry had up and left Calista when his wife got an itch to move to Kansas City to be near their children.

Must be nice to have children.

A chemical smell, strong enough to knock a man down, greeted Wendell as he entered the shop. *Never had to deal with that at Harry's.*

"Well, hello, Wendell," Sue Ellen's cheery voice rang out as he entered. She turned her attention from Dottie Jean, who sat in the chair with plastic rods in her hair and smelly goo all over her head. "How's my grandpa Gus's best friend today?"

"Fine, and you?"

"Busier than a one-armed paper hanger." She rolled Dottie Jean's hair at lightning speed. "What can I do for you?"

"Just a cut," he mumbled nervously. "But if you're too busy, I understand."

"Never too busy for you, handsome. You're as welcome as the sunshine anytime. Have yourself a seat."

Handsome? Wendell felt his ears heat up. He rubbed at them frantically.

"Just give me a minute, hon," Sue Ellen said. "I'll be with you in two shakes of a lamb's tail—just as soon as I get these last few rods in, she'll have to sit and cook awhile anyway."

"Cook?"

"Sure. Perm solutions have to stay in for twenty minutes. That'll give me plenty of time to give you a nice cut. In the meantime, you sit right down there and look through those magazines for a style you like."

A style? I never had to tell Harry how to cut my hair.

Wendell sat and pretended to look through a magazine. He stared, mesmerized, at Dottie Jean, who chattered incessantly about her life as an engaged woman. She droned on and on about Fletcher, her husband-to-be. It was "Fletcher this" and "Fletcher that" until Wendell felt sure he would snap a twig.

He took a quick look at his watch: 1:54. *Come on now. I don't have all day.* Harry wouldn't have made him wait this long. And he would have offered him a cup of coffee, too—hot and strong.

"I've got peach tea, if you'd like a glass," Sue Ellen said, as if reading his mind.

"Uh, no thanks."

"Well, are you ready, then?" She gestured toward an empty chair.

"Sure." He stood with a bit of hesitation, then made his way across the room. *Let's just get this over with.*

Sue Ellen pulled a leopard print cape around his neck and then stood back to observe him. "You know, Wendell, you're a real looker."

"Well, thank you very much." He felt a smile creep across his lips. Not many people complimented him on his looks, though he had always felt they suited him. At five foot ten, he weighed in at 158, just twenty pounds more than the day he graduated from Calista High. Not too bad. Of course, his postal route kept him on his feet much of the time. That might have something to do with it. *See, Wendell, you've still got it.*

"You're a real looker," she repeated, running her fingers through his hair. "But you've got to do something about all of this gray."

"Excuse me?" He spoke to her reflection in the mirror.

"Tell you what. . ." She elevated the chair with a mischievous grin on her face. "I'm going to make your day. I'm going to turn you into a new man."

A new man? She would do no such thing. He instinctively reached up to unsnap the cape, ready to make his getaway.

"Oh, relax." Dottie Jean looked up from her magazine. "She's never ruined me yet, has she?"

"Well, no, but—"

"Just you sit still and let me think," Sue Ellen said thoughtfully. She studied his head, picking up strands of hair and examining them as a doctor might inspect a specimen under the microscope. "A different cut would be nice," she said. "Something a little more contemporary. And just a little color to take a few years off."

He sat frozen with fear as she made her way to the back of the shop, unable to speak or voice any sort of opinion at all. *Are you a man or a mouse?* Wendell asked himself as she disappeared into the back room. *Squeak up!* But no words seemed to come.

Sue Ellen returned moments later with a small glass bottle in her hand. "This should just do the trick," she said with a grin. "Chestnut brown."

"What in the world happened to your head?" Sassy stared dumbfounded at Wendell. His fine gray hair had disappeared. In its place a dark brown mop of something—she wasn't quite sure what—had taken its place. A few select hairs stood perched atop his head, stiff as a poker; the rest lay obediently at their side.

"I, uh. . . Well, I. . ." He fidgeted with the fishing hat in his hands. "I just went over to Sue Ellen for a cut, and the next thing you know—"

"She tied you to the chair and ran shoe polish all over your head?"

"Well—"

"Where's your own hair?"

"This *is* my own hair." He pressed the hat back on. "Sue Ellen and Dottie Jean talked me into putting a little color on it—said it'd make me look like a new man."

"Well, I'll give 'em that," Sassy said, then laughed again. "I hardly recognized you. What'd you say your name was again?" She stuck out her hand for a shake.

Wendell shook his head in defeat, clearly refusing to play along.

A little sensitive, eh? Better ease off. "Well now, don't you get your knickers tied up in a knot over this, Wendell," she said, trying to sound matter-of-fact. "It'll grow out soon enough, and maybe that color'll fade into something halfway decent in the meantime. Besides, every dog has to have a few fleas—gives him character—and something to complain about. We all need something to complain about. I know I do."

Wendell groaned loudly. "Sassy, please."

"What can I do for you today?" she asked, quickly changing the subject. "Need some bait? Sinkers? Hair gel?"

"Very funny. Didn't you get my message?"

"Message? Nope. Just got in from the pier. Haven't checked the machine yet." She reached over to push the button, wading her way through a couple of messages before she got to his. She listened to it thoughtfully. *Aha. So that's why he's here. To help. Well, thank You, Lord, for answering my prayer.* "So you think this place needs a man's touch, huh?"

He shrugged. "I just thought maybe. . ."

"Well, I don't know the first thing about fixing that confounded lock." She pointed to the door. "I called Tucker a week ago, but he's slow as molasses. Can't get out here till Thursday, and I can't wait that long."

"I'd be happy to take a look at it," Wendell said with a smile.

"I brought some tools, just in case."

"Whatever." She waved her hand in the air haphazardly.

The bell on the door rang out. Sassy looked up as her friend Dottie Jean stepped into the shop, a large bag in her arms and an undeniable smirk on her face. "Dottie Jean, what in the world brings you out here in the middle of the day? Restaurant shut down after that last episode of food poisoning?"

"Very funny. I was just, uh, in the neighborhood and thought I'd stop by and drop off these crafts for the festival." Dottie Jean set the bag down on the counter and turned her gaze to Wendell. "Well, hello there. I didn't know you'd be out here. Wendell, I do declare—with that new hairdo, you're as handsome as a movie star. I almost didn't recognize you."

"You're not the only one," Sassy mumbled as she placed the bag under the counter. "He had to introduce himself when he came in." She couldn't help but notice the look of chagrin on Wendell's face as he turned toward the door.

"I'll just be getting the tools out of my truck," he mumbled. "You two ladies don't mind me."

"Fine, fine." Sassy swatted at the air with her hand. He could come and go all he wanted. What did she care?

Chapter 3

Wendell stared long and hard at the checkerboard before making a move. His mind wasn't really on the game, anyway. It had drifted nearly a dozen miles away—to a certain scenic spot on Crab Cove.

"What's wrong with you?" Gus leaned back in his chair. "Cat got your tongue?"

"Nah."

"Well, what, then? You ain't been yourself for days now. Are you sick?"

"Nope."

"Is it the hairdo? People still giving you a hard time? I had a long talk with that granddaughter of mine. Told her she turned you into the laughingstock of Calista."

Wendell shrugged, trying not to think about his hair. For two long weeks he had agonized over it, finally opting to have it cut shorter than he'd ever worn it. The new roots were beginning to peek through, their soft gray streaks providing him some sense of comfort and hope.

"Something wrong up at the post office, then?" Gus glanced up as a car pulled into the station's only self-service pump.

"Nope. Fine, fine." A little too fine, possibly—nothing there to distract him from the one thing that really held his mind captive.

Sassy. Day and night he thought of little else. He had grown to admire her amazing wit and uncanny sense of humor. The day he'd spent out at her place had lit a fire in him like nothing he had ever felt before. "Sassy's just fine," he said with a nod.

"Sassy? Who said anything about Sassy?" Gus looked at him with a worried expression.

"Oh, I meant to say work's fine." Wendell shifted his gaze back to the checkerboard, hoping Gus would let the moment pass.

He didn't.

"Sure don't know what any man would see in a woman like Sassy Hatchett," Gus said with a wicked grin. "That girl fell out of the ugly tree when she was just a kid and hit every branch on the way down. And that temper of hers. . ."

Just one more word and I'm leaving.

"You can't argue with a cantankerous woman like Sassy." Gus shook his head sadly. "She'd try to have the last word with an echo."

That's it. Wendell stood suddenly, knocking over the checkerboard. The red and black pieces scattered all over the parking lot, spinning madly. *I'm not putting up with this anymore.* He turned to walk away, not even offering so much as a word of explanation to his friend.

"Hey, where ya goin'?" Gus hollered.

Wendell never had time to answer. Just as he stepped out onto Main Street, Sassy raced by in her work truck, nearly running him down.

≈≈≈

Sassy pondered her latest dilemma as she made her way toward home. A simple trip into town had stirred up more unwanted gossip. Apparently the comment about Fanny's "Two-for-One Special" had made its way around town, all the way from the grocery store to the coffee shop to the Catfish House. Dottie Jean, usually not one to chide, had given her a hard time today. Dottie Jean!

Though she tried to push troubling thoughts aside, Sassy found her temper mounting as she approached the familiar pier. Moments later, she sat at the water's edge, a prayer on her lips.

Lord, here I am again. Sassy stared up at the sky, basking a moment in the mesmerizing red and gold sunset. *Looks like we've got some talking to do. Again.* She slowly baited her hook and cast her line far out into the water. *What am I going to do? Maybe I just worry too much about what people think. Guess that's wrong.* Sassy felt something begin to tug at her line. She squinted, the sun playing tricks on her eyes. *People round here sure have a way of driving me to the edge of my sanity. And what's all this talk about Wendell Meeks? Do they, for one cotton-pickin' minute, think I've got some kind of feelings for him? Have I ever let on like that?*

She fought to reel in the catch, but something felt wrong, very wrong. Sassy struggled to see past the dizzying colors to what held her line taut. She took a step toward the edge of the pier, shielding her eyes from the glare. *What in the world?* She appeared to have snagged a large branch. She pulled with all her might, trying to free the hook, but it didn't seem to want to let go. She struggled, refusing to give up her hold.

Taking another small step forward, Sassy Hatchett suddenly found herself plummeting facefirst into the gray-brown waters of the Biloxi River.

⚬⚬⚬⚬

Wendell exited his car, anxiously making his way toward the pier. *If I don't do it now, I'll never do it.* He couldn't wait one moment longer to tell Sassy what his heart had been longing for weeks to say. *Sassy Hatchett, I'm crazy about you. I just want to know if there's any chance in the world you could ever feel the same way about me.*

Just as he stepped onto the pier, he heard a thunderous splash. Off in the distance he saw it. Someone had just fallen into the water. Someone dressed in old blue overalls and a dingy fishing hat. He heard the frantic, "Help me—help!" just as he recognized the familiar carrottop. An arm shot up out of the water, waving like crazy.

"Sassy? Sassy, is that you?" He ran along the edge of the pier.

Her head emerged from the water, covered in a mesh of twigs, leaves, and fish bait. "Confound it! Can you help me, Wendell? I'm caught up in this fishing line." She sounded more exasperated than frightened.

Wendell reached for the pole, which had lodged itself between the wooden slats of the pier. The line had wrapped itself around Sassy several times. *You're a feisty one, Sassy Hatchett!* He fought to free her, finally cutting the nylon with a fishing knife.

She grabbed hold of the edge of the wooden pier, looking up at him like a drowned cat.

"I lost my hat." Her eyes had a frantic look.

"It's just a hat, Sassy." He extended his hand to help her up. "You can always get another one."

She took hold of his hand, nearly pulling him in. He fought to maintain his balance as he pulled her up—out of the water and onto the safety of the pier.

Sassy, you're so beautiful.

"You don't understand," she said, water rolling down her cheeks. "Joe gave me that hat. If I've lost it, I don't know what I'll do."

Wendell squinted against the glare of the colorful September sunset, trying to focus on the water. Nothing. He glanced along the pier. There, just yards away, sat the missing hat—perched atop Sassy's tackle box. "Looks like you're in luck." He picked it up and handed it to her.

She placed it atop her wet head, looking flushed and irritated as she reached for her tackle box and pole. Then Sassy sighed as she looked at the cut line. "Nothing's ever easy."

As she turned away, Wendell tried to get her attention. "Sassy, don't you want me to come with you?" He trudged along behind her, dejected. "At least let me drive you up to the house. It's nearly half a mile, and you're soaked to the bone."

"Nope."

"But—"

"No buts, Wendell. Just go on home now, okay? I need a chance to dry out on my own. Thank you very much for saving my neck, but if it's all the same to you, I need to be alone right now."

Wendell shrugged, defeated. "Fine." He never had a chance to say what he had come to say in the first place. Now, watching her standing here in soggy clothing with the sun going down behind him, he felt he never would.

Chapter 4

The sun rose on a beautiful Sunday morning. Sassy walked out onto the front porch of her tiny wood-framed home with a cup of black coffee in her hand, breathing in the scent of the fresh morning dew and listening to the birds in the oak tree to her right. "I haven't missed a church service for nearly six years, Lord. But I just can't make myself go today after being so humiliated. I can't face Wendell. I just can't."

She took a sip of the hot brew, then settled down into the chipped metal chair, deep in thought. "I'd watch church on the television, but those TV preachers make me so mad—all they want is my money. Back in my day, a preacher lived a life of poverty, and I reckon that's the way it oughta be."

Staring out onto her new property, Sassy's thoughts shifted slightly. She'd scarcely had time to fall in love with her new home. Selling off the big house to Matthew Van-what's-his-name had been a hard task, indeed. On the other hand. . .

She looked around, content settling in—until her gaze fell

on Tucker's belongings off to the side of the house.

"That boy." She stared in disbelief at her son's broken-down car, tires missing and paint peeling. It, along with the hodgepodge collection of tires piled up behind it, was a grim reminder of Tucker's years as a wannabe mechanic. *He's a wannabe son, too.*

Sassy shifted her gaze to the tall sprawling oak tree with leaves as green as emeralds. It provided her with some sense of relief. And hope.

A loud noise from the street distracted her as a large van raced by, music blaring loudly. "You're driving too fast!" Sassy hollered toward the road. Crazy kids. They needed something to motivate them, to keep them out of trouble. They should be in church on a Sunday morning.

I should be in church on a Sunday morning.

Sassy turned her attention back to the house, sipping her coffee. The home, though new to her, was still in need of painting, and years of weathering had weakened the front porch steps. The large courting porch should be draped with flowers but instead stood barren, waiting for attention. Not that it had been used much for courting, anyway.

"I hope you can forgive me ahead of time, Lord." Sassy looked at her watch: 10:25 a.m. The service would be starting any minute now. "I hate missing church. I wanted to hear Pastor Jordan's sermon on forgiveness—I really did. But I'm so embarrassed. They already think I'm just a big joke, anyway. When everyone gets word I fell in the river. . ." She shuddered, just thinking about the jokes that would make their way from the gas station to the Catfish House. She leaned back in the chair and took another swallow of her coffee, which had cooled down.

The leg on the chair shifted suddenly, and Sassy found herself sprawled across the front porch, her head striking the back of the metal chair with a hard thud. The cup of coffee leapt from her hand, covering her bathrobe and slippers in the warm liquid. Staring dizzily at the front porch steps, her head began to swim. "Well, cut off my legs and call me Shorty," she muttered. Everything after that faded to gray.

<hr />

Wendell Meeks reached over to shake hands with Dottie Jean and Fletcher before sitting down in the fourth pew of Calista Community Church. "Mornin'," he said with a smile.

"Mornin', Wendell." Dottie Jean placed her Bible on the pew as she spoke. "Seen much of Sassy lately?"

He hesitated before answering. "Yeah. Saw her for a few minutes last night, as a matter of fact."

Dottie Jean gave him a sly grin, and Fletcher reached to give him a firm pat on the back. "Atta boy," he whispered.

Wendell nodded lamely, then glanced back to the rear of the sanctuary, hoping to catch a glimpse of Sassy. She had been noticeably absent from Sunday school—a real rarity. *I hope she's not sick.* His mind drifted back to the evening before. What a sight she had been. She arose from the river—so wet, so frustrated, and yet so beautiful. Her damp hair had curled into amber ringlets at the edges of her face, and her crazy hat had only accentuated her beautiful features. *Don't they all see how pretty she is?* He looked back and forth from the pulpit, where

Pastor Jordan now stood, to the back of the auditorium, where Sassy should make her entrance.

"Where are you?" he whispered.

He only half heard the pastor's welcome and found himself facing backward through much of the first song. Finally, about midway through the offering, he had to conclude, *She's not coming. She's actually not coming.* He sat in solitude as the pastor spoke on forgiveness—a good sermon, though a little on the long side. Maybe his patience had just worn thin, Wendell couldn't be quite sure, but he felt a sudden urge to drive out to Crab Cove.

<hr>

"Mother, could you explain again exactly what happened?" Tilly's words were filled with concern as she raced her sports car down the highway toward Biloxi.

"I don't rightly know." Sassy pressed a damp washcloth to her right eye and leaned groggily against the window of her daughter's vehicle. "I was just sitting there, happy as you please, when the chair gave way. Next thing you know, I was staring up at the heavens, hearing the angels sing. Or maybe it was the birds, I'm not quite sure. But I don't know what all the fuss is about." She pulled the washcloth away from her face, examining it carefully. "See? I'm hardly bleeding anymore. There's nothing wrong with me."

"That's for the doctors to decide," Tilly said firmly. "And I, for one, will feel much better after they take a look at you in the emergency room. You'll need some X-rays, if nothing else."

"I'll be fine," Sassy mumbled, feeling her head begin to

swim again. "Just as soon as this headache clears."

"Mother, I want to talk about your living situation," Tilly said firmly. "You really need someone up at the house with you at all times. At your age—"

"My age?" Sassy's anger flared immediately. "Hogwash! I'm barely fifty."

"Mom, you've been pressing fifty so long now, it's pleated. You're going to be sixty next month and everyone knows it."

"What's that got to do with anything?"

"Nothing. Only I think you're reaching the age when you need someone to stay with you. If Tucker won't come, maybe I should—"

"No." Sassy used her strongest possible tone. "I like living alone. No offense, honey, but I enjoy my privacy. Besides, I know you like living over there in that trailer of yours."

"It's a manufactured home, Mom. They don't call them trailers anymore."

"Well, great." Sassy rubbed her aching brow. "The next time a twister picks one up and flies it over my house, I'll know what to call it." She leaned her head against the back of the seat as Tilly sighed deeply.

"Honestly, Mother. What are we going to do with you?"

"Do with me? Just let me be, Tilly Mae," she said finally. "I do believe that's your answer."

———— ∞ ————

Wendell pulled up to Sassy's house, working up the courage to face her once again. *Sassy, where were you this morning? Are you okay?* He glanced at her truck in the driveway. *Needs a good washing. I'll have to remember to do that for her.* Making his way out of his vehicle, he walked across the frazzled lawn and up the rickety front porch steps. He carefully stepped over a broken chair and knocked on the door.

Wendell waited for what seemed like an eternity before deciding to press the bell. Maybe she was sleeping. His hands were trembling as he reached to press the button, formulating words in his mind.

I miss you when you're not there, Sassy.

Several moments passed, and no one answered the door. Wendell looked at her truck once again. "She has to be home," he muttered. He made his way down the steps and around to the side yard. "Must be working out back," he said. The backyard sat empty—unless you counted the broken barbecue pit, a scattered pile of lumber, and a bunch of old tires thrown around.

"Where in the world is she?" He scratched his head, then ran his fingers through the short stubble of brown-gray hair. "Surely she's not back at the pier. Not this soon."

He walked back to his car, where he sat for a moment, head in his hands. *Lord, am I crazy? Maybe everyone else is right.* He turned the key in the ignition. *Then again, if they're right, why do I feel the way I do about her? Why can't I get her off my mind?* He put the car into reverse and pulled out of her driveway.

Wendell drove a block or so, just past the bait and tackle shop, and turned off toward the pier. *I've got to tell her soon, Lord, or I'm not going to be able to go through with this.* He climbed from the car, walking toward the familiar pier.

Empty.

But not half as empty as his heart.

Sassy sat in the diner, twiddling her thumbs as her friends worked diligently on crafts to sell at the upcoming church bazaar. "I don't know why you won't help us, Sassy," Dottie Jean said with a grimace. "Is your head still hurting?"

"Not too bad," she said with a sigh. "I'm not a crafts sort of person. You know that. Besides, I'm just thinking. . ." *When are they going to mention it? Surely the whole town knows by now.*

"Thinking about what?" Berta asked with a sly grin. "Wendell Meeks?"

Sassy slapped herself in the head, completely forgetting about the stitches above her right eyebrow. "Confound it! If you all don't stop harassing me about Wendell Meeks, I'm going to. . . I'm going to. . ." She stopped midsentence, rubbing her aching brow. "It's bad enough I've got to sit down here every Tuesday night and watch you three piece together these ridiculous craft items, but all this gossip about Wendell is enough to make me question my salvation. Besides, I know that's not really what you want to talk about—"

Let's just get this over with, Lord. I can only take so much ridicule. If someone doesn't mention my tumble in the river soon, I'm going to do it myself.

"Let's change the subject, then," Berta said hurriedly. "Pastor Jordan asked me to come up with an appropriate name for the fall festival this year. I was thinking about something unique, something different from anything we've done in the past.

"What about Fall Fiesta?" Sue Ellen said, her eyes widening. "We could do a Latin theme. Lots of bright colors and piñatas for the kids."

"Oooh! I have an idea. What about Autumn in the Orchard?" Dottie Jean suggested excitedly. "We could make centerpieces out of fresh fruit. That would be fun."

"Actually, I was thinking about Fall in the Old South—sort of a *Gone with the Wind* theme," Berta said. "What do you think about that?"

"Fall Fiesta, Fall in the South, Fall in the River," Sassy mumbled to herself.

"What was that you said, honey?" Berta asked. "Fall at the River. . . ?"

"No, I—"

"What a great idea!" Berta interrupted. "We could do a whole river theme. . .work it around Pastor Jordan's name! People are always teasing him anyway."

"I didn't say 'Fall *at* the River,' " Sassy said impatiently. "I said 'Fall *in* the river.' "

"I'm not sure I get it," Dottie Jean said, looking at her oddly. "What sort of decorations did you have in mind?"

Why are they making this so difficult? "Oh, come on now," Sassy said, standing. "You know you've been wanting to talk about it all night."

"Talk about what?" Sue Ellen asked, giving her a funny look.

"My accident." *Are they just plain cruel?*

"We know all about your accident, Sassy," Dottie Jean responded. "You told us when you got here, remember? You fell out of the chair and hit your head, right?" She looked at the other ladies with a concerned expression.

"Not *that* accident," Sassy spouted. "I'm talking about what happened to me last Saturday. Didn't Wendell tell you?"

"You're not making any sense," Sue Ellen argued. "Are you sure you're feeling okay?"

"I'm feeling just fine, but I'd feel a whole lot better if you ladies would just up and confess that you know I fell in the river the other day."

"You what?" All three spoke in unison, then erupted in laughter.

They don't know. Wendell didn't tell them. Suddenly that put a whole new spin on things. "Well, shut my mouth." She sat with a thud.

They all stared at her curiously, waiting for an explanation.

"I, uh. . .I fell in the Biloxi, and Wendell Meeks fished me out."

"Oh my." Dottie Jean grinned. "Well, that would explain why you weren't in church Sunday morning, I guess."

Sassy shrugged. "Too humiliating. I couldn't look him in the eye. Not sure I ever can again." *This just gets worse by the minute.*

"Of course you can, honey." Dottie Jean patted her hand. "Besides, men love it when they get to play hero. It brings out their macho side."

"Wendell Meeks has a macho side?" Sue Ellen nudged Berta. "That I'd like to see. He's such an old marshmallow. Talk about a softy."

"Ooh! Speaking of which, I have an announcement to make." Berta spoke excitedly. All eyes turned to the younger woman. "Since Matt and I got engaged, I've been thinking a lot about men and women—about how they relate to each other and all that. . ."

Sassy rolled her eyes impatiently. "Does your train of thought have a caboose?"

"Now, stop it, Sassy. I'm being serious here. I've had an idea in mind—thought maybe you ladies could help me with it."

"Do go on."

"I was wondering if you all would be interested in doing a new Bible study. Something along the lines of. . .oh, I don't know. Something to get me ready for marriage."

"Great idea," Dottie Jean chimed in. "You know, it'll be no time until Fletcher and I tie the knot. I could use a refresher course, too."

Berta nodded as she spoke. "That's what I was thinking. I even have a topic in mind. What about submission? You all know how strong-willed I am."

Submission? She wants to do a Bible study on submission? "Are you kidding?" Sassy asked angrily.

"Well, no. I'm not," Berta said quietly. "I'm very serious, in fact."

Sassy stood to her feet abruptly, reaching for her purse. *They're just doing this to get to me, Lord—and I don't like it one little bit.*

Berta looked flushed as she spoke. "I just thought it might be a good idea for all of us to learn how to submit ourselves to the husbands God is placing in our lives, and ultimately to the authority of Christ." She glanced nervously down at her hands, then at the other ladies. They all looked back and forth, from one to the other, obviously confused.

214

"Well, you go right ahead and get married and be as submissive as you please." Sassy headed for the door. "If you need me, I'll be the one telling all the fish how to swim out on Crab Cove."

Chapter 5

Sassy stood in line at Fanny's Fancy Foods with cherry gelatin, frozen chicken livers, a large box of oatmeal, and five cans of dog food in her small handbasket.

"Come on," she mumbled. "This is supposed to be the express lane." With only two people in line ahead of her, she should have reached the register in record time, but Fanny was managing the "10 Items or Less" lane today—and everyone in Calista knew what that meant.

Waiting.

Fanny had a way of turning "Good morning" into a full-blown discussion.

"That's not the only thing full-blown about her." Sassy gave the clerk a thoughtful once-over. Fanny was practically as broad as the lane itself. Her parents had built the grocery store when she was just a little girl and had proudly placed her name on the marquee outside. Of course, they had no idea how prophetic that name would turn out to be.

At a younger age, Fanny had manned the register on foot

like the other clerks, but these days found her seated in a special swivel chair in the widened aisle of the express lane, portions of her anatomy loping over each side in defeat. Her body, like her conversation, tended to linger a bit, so you could always count on standing awhile.

Sassy shifted the basket to the other arm, growing more frustrated. Out of the corner of her eye, she saw the store's front door swing open. Wendell stepped through, his eyes darting in her direction. She quickly grabbed a magazine from the rack to her right and held it up in front of her face. *Please, God, don't let him see me.* She had managed to avoid him for days now and didn't want to spoil her clean record. She tipped the magazine a bit to the left, trying to see where he had gone. At that moment, someone tapped her on her shoulder, startling her. She turned around, finding herself face-to-face with Wendell Meeks.

"Hey, Sassy. How're you feeling?" He looked genuinely concerned.

"Fine," she said. "Why?"

"Well, I heard you had to go to the hospital." His gaze landed on the bandage above her right eye.

"Oh, this little thing?" She reached to touch it. "It's nothing."

"Still," he said, "I've been worried about you. I've tried to call out to your place a couple of times but always seem to get the machine."

Sassy flinched, remembering all too well the calls she had deliberately avoided. Ironically, his voice had brought her comfort, even over the machine, though she never would have admitted it to anyone. *Why am I avoiding him, Lord? He's such a good man.*

"Thank you for calling." She closed the magazine and put it back on the rack. "I've been really busy the last few days."

"You need to be taking things easy, Sassy." His soft voice, laced with compassion, made her feel better.

She shrugged. "Too much going on."

His gaze traveled to the items in her hand, a look of curiosity settling in them as they landed on the dog food. She shuffled it under her arm, trying to hide it.

"Did you get a dog?"

"Nope." No point explaining what she used the crazy stuff for. He'd probably just laugh at her, anyway.

Fanny cleared her throat loudly, and Sassy realized she had worked her way up to the register without knowing it.

"How are you today, Sassy?" Fanny asked, her eyes locked firmly on Wendell.

Look at me and I'll tell you.

There was a momentary lull in the conversation until Fanny turned to look at her. "I'm fine, thank you."

"Quite an accident you had." Fanny scanned the chicken livers. "Or so I hear. How wonderful that Wendell came to your rescue. Lucky for you he showed up when he did. Amazing coincidence."

Wendell looked sheepishly down at the floor. Sassy couldn't help but notice a peculiar look on Fanny's face. *Is that jealousy?*

"Wendell's one of my favorite customers," Fanny said with a broad grin. "I always look forward to our visits together." She thrust out her hand. "That will be $10.67."

Sassy pressed eleven dollars into the woman's robust hand and waited for her change.

"Yes, Wendell's one of my very favorite customers." Fanny clutched the money in her fist and gazed tenderly at Wendell.

I'm still here.

After what seemed like an eternity, Fanny finally handed Sassy thirty-three cents. "Have a nice day," she muttered, her eyes still on Wendell. Sassy made her way to the door, ready for a quick exit.

Wendell followed silently behind her, waiting until they were outside before he spoke. "Sassy, are you headed home?"

"Yes, why?"

"Well. . ." He suddenly looked frightened, like a kid facing a school principal. "I'm, uh. . ."

"You're what?"

"I'm going to be having a Chickenfoot party at my place this Saturday night and I thought maybe you might like to come."

"Is it a Sunday school party?" *That's what I get for missing church last week. I'm always the last to hear everything.*

"No. Just a get-together for a few friends."

Sounds suspicious. "Like who?"

"Oh, Gus'll be there, of course. And Fletcher and Dottie Jean. You could ask several of your younger gal friends, if you like. That Sue Ellen's a sweet thing—even if she did try to turn me into a new man."

Sassy laughed long and loud before responding. "Yep. She like to have ruined you. Glad to see you've forgiven her."

"I have. And why don't you go ahead and invite Berta and that guy she's gonna marry—the one with all them names. . ."

"Matthew Jordan VanMichael."

"Yeah. Well, if you think he'd like to come."

Sassy looked at Wendell intently. In all the years she had known him, she had only been inside his home three or four times—and always with Joe. Did she dare go alone?

"Give me a couple of days to decide, Wendell." She inched her way toward the truck. "Right now I've got so much work to do I can't think straight."

"I understand." He offered up a sad shrug.

She nodded a polite good-bye as she got in her truck and pulled away.

The phone rang repeatedly as Sassy fought to balance the bags and open the front door of the bait and tackle shop simultaneously. She reached it by the fifth ring. "Sassy's Bait and Tackle."

"Mom?" *Tilly. She sounds upset.*

"Yeah. What's up, honey?" She dropped the bag onto the counter, leaning against it to catch her breath.

"That's just what I started to ask."

"What do you mean?" Sassy began to unload the groceries, the phone pressed between her ear and her shoulder.

"I mean I saw you and Wendell Meeks together a little while ago when I drove past Fanny's."

"He is a good friend, Tilly."

"Aw, come on, Mom. Everyone in town knows he likes you. Might as well admit you like him, too."

Sassy's heart began to pound in her ears, making it difficult to hear. "I think you've got the wrong number," she said and then slammed the phone down, disconnecting the call.

That'll teach her.

She pulled the chicken livers from the bag, unwrapping them as she mumbled, "If she knows what's good for her, she'll leave me alone." Still angry, she reached for the box of oatmeal and a large mixing bowl. "I do declare—she's got a lot of nerve."

Sassy quickly mixed the cherry gelatin, then poured it over the oatmeal, shaking her head in disbelief. *People round here have too much time on their hands. They need to get busy taking care of their own lives and leaving mine to me.* She dumped a large can of dog food into the mix, stirring it with all her might. Pulling out a large butcher knife, she began to chop up the chicken livers into bite-sized pieces. She tossed them into the bowl with the gelatin, oatmeal, and dog food, mashing the whole thing into a thick paste. Pinching off pieces of the mixture, she began to work them into small round balls.

"Those big city fellas think they're gonna one-up me with their bait recipes," she mumbled. "Well, I'll show them a thing or two." She rolled with a vengeance, laying the finished balls out on a tray to harden. "They've met their match in Sassy Hatchett."

Her thoughts began to wander as she continued to work. *"Everyone in town knows he likes you, Mother."* She could hear Tilly's words now—words she fought to ignore. But perhaps her daughter knew more about Wendell Meeks than she did.

But how do I feel about him, Lord? Sassy reflected on Wendell a moment. *He is awfully nice, and so generous. He'd be a prize catch for some great lady. But me? Surely you're not thinking of hooking me up with Wendell Meeks, are You? 'Cause if You are, I sure would like to know it ahead of time.*

She reached for more chicken livers, dicing them into oblivion as her thoughts wandered. *He really does seem to like me, although I can't, for the life of me, figure out why.* She stared down at the meat on the counter, recognizing the mess she had made of it. Scraping it off into a trash can, she muttered, "Chicken-foot party. Sounds suspicious."

Sassy paused, looking at the door—the door he had so recently fixed. Suddenly she knew exactly what she must do. "Wendell Meeks is a good man," she said to the door. "I don't care what Tilly or anyone else thinks. I believe I'll go to his party."

With his nerves a jumbled mess, Wendell sat at the Catfish House and relayed his story to Bud, who seemed more interested than most of Calista's residents in hearing his thoughts on Sassy. "I don't know if she'll come or not," Wendell said, "but I invited her."

"Good for you," the young deputy sheriff said with a smile. "I always knew you had it in you."

"Well, just don't go making a big deal out of it in front of Gus or Fletcher. They'll never let me hear the end of it."

"Thought they were coming."

"They are. I'm just not going to mention Sassy until they get there and see her for themselves."

Bud laughed. "Sounds like quite an evening."

"I'd like it if you'd come, too." Wendell grew serious. "I could use someone on my side. Besides, that pretty, young Sue

Ellen Caldwell's back in town, and she's gonna be there. If memory serves me, you two were sort of an item back in high school, weren't you?"

Bud suddenly choked on his tea, turning all shades of red. He had barely begun to recover when his beeper went off. "I've gotta go," he said, looking down at it. "Maybe we could finish this conversation another time."

"Fine, fine," Wendell said, grinning at him. *Looks like I struck a nerve. Maybe I'm not the only one with my hook baited here.*

Chapter 6

A storm blew into the Gulf of Mexico just as Biloxi's best weather forecasters predicted this year's hurricane season would be mild.

Sassy fought her way home from town—the back of her truck loaded down with enough lumber to board up the Bait and Tackle—just as the skies darkened. Though she tried not to, she couldn't help but think back to that horrible day when Katrina had come ashore.

A shiver of fear ran down her spine. *At times like this, I realize how safe Joe always made me feel.* Sassy longed for that safety now, though she wondered if she could ever know such comfort again.

Her thoughts immediately shifted to Tilly and Tucker, and she prayed for their protection. *Lord, help Tilly at the Café Latte. Keep her safe, and guard the store. Oh, and, Lord—give Tucker the good sense to come in out of the rain.*

She drove past her house and on around the bend to the bait and tackle shop. The wind whipped at the old truck, causing the lumber to jolt. A large sheet of plywood shot up, nearly coming through the back window. As if on cue, it settled once again into the bed of the truck.

She rounded the final corner, breathing a huge sigh of relief as she spotted a familiar car in front of the shop.

Wendell. Thank God.

Wendell hammered a large sheet of plywood over the front window of Sassy's Bait and Tackle, fighting high winds as he worked. A sudden gust picked up his hat, dancing it across the open field in the direction of the river. *No point in trying to get it. I'd never make it back alive.* He picked up the small container of nails and the large hammer, struggling to make his way back into the shop.

"Everything okay out there?" Sassy asked, filling two cups with coffee.

He closed the door tightly, pausing to catch his breath, and then placed the hammer and nails into his toolbox. "It is now."

She smiled warmly as she handed him the cup. "I can't thank you enough." Their fingers touched briefly as the cup exchanged hands. Wendell used the opportunity to gaze into her eyes for a response. Sassy's cheeks turned pink, and she shifted her attention to the floor. "I'm sorry about your party." She gestured for him to sit at the small table at the back of the shop.

"Aw, that's okay." *After all, I'm still spending time with you. That's all I really wanted, anyway.* "There'll be plenty of opportunity for parties after all this dies down." He gave her a wistful look.

"Coffee okay?" she asked.

I'm too distracted by those incredible eyes to notice.

"Wendell?"

He took a careful sip. "Great. Better than your daughter's, if you don't mind my saying so."

Sassy's raucous laughter rang out. "Thanks. I think I can say without too much pride that you're right. I don't think I could ever get used to those fancy names, anyway. Mocha Cappa Whatchamacallit. Cinnamon Streusel Delight. Caramel Mocha Something-or-other. Good grief."

"Whoever heard of putting whipped cream in coffee?" He shook his head in disbelief.

"Or chocolate," she added, making a face. "That's just sinful."

"Crazy." They both spoke in unison. Sassy laughed again, taking another drink.

"Just give me good old-fashioned black coffee." He pointed to his mug. "Like this."

"Me, too," Sassy said. "But this is my third cup since you got here. If I drink one more, I'll be able to thread the sewing machine with it running."

What an amazing sense of humor. Does she have any idea how clever she is? He reached to touch her hand as he spoke. "You're so funny, Sassy." He pulled it away instinctively, worried about what she might think.

"Some people don't think so," she said with a shrug.

"They just don't know you like I do."

She gave him a curious look and then took another swig of coffee. "I was hoping to make it back up to the house before the storm passed over." Her brow wrinkled. "But it doesn't look like that's going to happen." As if to accentuate her words, a blast of rain suddenly battered the roof.

The noise continued as they talked. "We should be just fine here." Wendell spoke loudly, trying to sound as confident as he could, though his own nerves were more than a little rattled.

Just then a booming peal of thunder shook the building. Sassy let out a scream and dropped her cup onto the floor. It broke into pieces, splattering coffee all over Wendell's feet. At that very moment, the room went dark. The hum of the fan overhead slowly died down as reality set in. *We've lost power.* He reached across the table for her hands. "Are you okay?"

"I—I'm fine." She clutched his fingers, but he didn't mind a bit.

They sat quietly for a moment, hands securely clasped, listening to the driving rain. The building shook with the rumble of thunder on occasion, and Sassy trembled in fear. Wendell held on tighter during those moments.

In spite of the storm's fury, he suddenly felt a peace and contentment he had never known. His heart pounded in his ears, drowning out the sounds above. The whole place could crumble to the ground around him and he would die a happy man. He held Sassy Hatchett's hands in his own.

<hr />

"Mother, are you okay?" Sassy could barely make out Tilly's voice over the static on the line.

"I'm fine, honey." She looked out of the corner of her eye at Wendell, who sat quietly on the sofa in her living room, eating a ham sandwich and homemade cookies and drinking a large glass of milk.

"Did the storm do much damage to the house?"

"I've only been home a few minutes, honey," she said, looking around. "I haven't really had time to take inventory."

"You were at the shop when the storm hit?" Tilly sounded more nervous than ever.

"I was."

"Are you all right? Is the shop okay?"

"I'm fine." Sassy smiled in Wendell's direction. "And the shop is, too, thanks to Wendell."

"Wendell?" Tilly's voice suddenly reflected an undeniable degree of irritation.

"He showed up just in time to board up the windows for me. Wasn't that nice of him?"

"Well, I suppose, but. . ."

"No buts, Tilly," Sassy said, her heart surging. "And I never want to hear another thing about it, do you hear me?"

The silence on the other end of the line lasted a little too long before her daughter finally responded. "Whatever you say, Mom."

They went on to talk about the storm, Tilly giving her take on the damage in town. With only a couple of minor exceptions, the storm had passed over causing little destruction. Fanny's store had lost a front window when strong winds blew a wayward shopping cart through it from the parking lot side, and the church had lost a few tiles from the roof over the fellowship hall, but these were small calamities, considering what could have happened.

"I'd imagine half the women in town will show up at the

hair salon tomorrow to have the storm combed out of their hair." Sassy ran her fingers through her own messy mop of hair, conscious of the fact that Wendell's eyes were fixed on her.

"I just hope people stop in for a cup of coffee while they're in town," Tilly said wistfully. "To be honest, business has really been down lately. If the kids didn't come in after school, I don't know what I'd do."

"Yes, well. . ." Sassy decided it would be better to end the conversation here. She glanced once again at Wendell, who sat quietly on the sofa. As her daughter rambled on about the Café Latte, she fought to pay attention. For some reason, her thoughts continually drifted back to what had happened back at the Bait and Tackle. When Wendell reached for her hand, she couldn't seem to control the emotions that followed—the overwhelming sense of peace and security his touch had brought.

"Are you there, Mother?" Tilly's voice startled her back to the present.

"Uh, yeah, honey. I'm just a little tired."

"Well, get some sleep, then. I'll be out to see you in the morning."

"All right. Good night, Tilly." She hung the phone up, catching Wendell's eye. He moved in her direction, empty plate in hand.

"Thanks for the sandwich, Sassy." She took the plate from his hand, carrying it into the kitchen. He followed closely behind. "Tasted great."

"I can't thank you enough for being there for me tonight." She placed the plate in the sink and turned to look at him. *I never noticed how blue his eyes were before.* They held her captive, tugging at her heart and twisting it unexpectedly.

"You're more than welcome," he said, his eyes never leaving hers. "I'm just glad I was in the right place at the right time."

He's such a great man. Why do people give me such a hard time about our friendship? Even as the words crossed her mind, Sassy realized. . .

She and Wendell Meeks were more than just friends. Far more.

—◦∞◦—

Wendell grinned all the way home. *Thank You, Lord, for the storm.* An odd prayer, he had to admit, but he meant every word. *Thank You for giving me the opportunity to be there for Sassy. Thank You for the woman of God that she is.*

His heart swelled suddenly as he relived that moment when his hand reached for hers. "I'm not imagining it," he said aloud. "I know I'm not." She could have let go, but she chose to hold tightly to him. For nearly an hour they had sat in the dark, clutching hands. It felt so comfortable, so right.

A perfect fit.

Chapter 7

October arrived, and the Mississippi coastline quickly recovered from the storm's assault. However, the unexpected storm had blown in more than high winds. On the heels of this tropical tempest, the truth had swept into town. This truth, in its awful beauty, had torn the blinders from Sassy Hatchett's eyes, allowing her to see clearly for the first time in years. With her new vision came a startling revelation.

She liked Wendell Meeks. She really liked him.

And as the cooler days of October slipped by, she began to realize exactly why. He captivated her with his everyday goodness. In the little things. In the big things. This man had no pretense, and Sassy could pretend no longer, either. For the past three weeks she had been quite candid with herself, though she had shared her thoughts with no one else, not even Wendell. *When the time is right, we'll tell each other.*

In the meantime, they enjoyed cups of strong, black coffee on her front porch as the crisp autumn season wrapped them in its cool embrace. They strolled along the edges of the Biloxi River, watching the sunset over gentle golden waters. Each occasionally reached out to grasp the hand of the other, neither saying a word in response.

They didn't have to.

And now, just one week away from the fall festival, Sassy felt a longing to be with him more than ever. She felt it as she crossed over the Biloxi Bridge each morning and saw the local fishermen cast their lines out into the water. She felt it as she waved to vendors selling their fresh fruits and vegetables along the side of Calista Avenue. She felt it every time she turned the key in the newly repaired lock at the Bait and Tackle.

Even the weekly chore of meeting with her friends to work on crafts didn't bother Sassy much anymore, as long as her thoughts remained on Wendell. Their Bible study on submission had turned out to be quite different than she'd anticipated, and she found herself intrigued by what the scriptures really had to say on the subject. Turns out, women weren't the only ones called to be submissive. The Bible was clear that all believers were to submit to one another in love.

As Sassy drove to the Catfish House the third Tuesday night in October, she hummed all the way, unable to wipe the smile from her face. She reflected on the way recent frustrations had lifted. Whether she had wanted to admit it or not, her anger over the past few years had stemmed from Joe's death. And the Lord had finally revealed it, in all its ugliness. How wonderful to be rid of such a weight. And how good of the Lord to give second chances—at life and at love.

Thank You for the changes in my life and my attitude. Thank You that in spite of everything, I haven't lost my love for fishing. After all these years, Sassy finally had to admit the truth. She loved to fish—angry or not. In fact, quiet hours with a pole in her hand had become even more enjoyable with Wendell at her side.

Her joy remained as she made her way inside, where the other ladies finished up craft items for the festival. "Sassy?" Berta looked at her curiously. "You're mighty happy tonight. What's up?"

"What makes you think something's up?" She smiled as she placed a large bag of supplies on the table.

"Mighty suspicious, that's all," Dottie Jean said with a wink. "That look on your face."

Sassy shrugged but felt the same silly grin turn her lips upward. She fought against it.

"So tell us, Sassy. How are you—really?" Sue Ellen pulled pieces of orange poster board from the bag and placed them on the table.

"Fine, fine. If things get any better, I'll have to hire someone to help me enjoy it."

"Very curious." Dottie Jean pointed a pair of scissors at her. "But I'm going to get to the bottom of this if it's the last thing I do."

"It's Wendell, isn't it?" Berta asked. "You and Wendell are—"

"What we are—or aren't—is nobody's business. Now, could we talk about something else, please?"

"To be honest, I'm getting a little tired of all this talk about men, anyway," Sue Ellen mumbled. "There's got to be something else worth discussing."

"Whatever you say." Dottie Jean turned back to her work. "We could talk about my wedding, if you like. Fletcher and I have settled on a date—Saturday, December seventeenth. You're all invited."

"No!" Berta nearly dropped an armload of baskets.

"What, honey?"

"That's the same date Matt and I have chosen. We're getting married right here in Calista—at the church."

Dottie Jean looked dejected. "Have you rented it yet?"

"Nope. We were gonna do it tomorrow." Berta looked up with knitted brow.

"So were we."

"Looks like we'll just have to put the two of you into the ring and let you fight it out." Sassy chuckled. "Let the best man—uh, woman—win."

"That's not funny, Sassy," Berta said with a pout. "This is serious."

"It's awful is what it is," Dottie Jean agreed.

"I'm sure you'll work something out." Sassy attempted to change the conversation. "Say, did any of you hear about that new department store out on Highway 19?"

Sue Ellen chimed in. "Looks like we won't have to drive all the way to Biloxi to shop for clothes anymore."

"I feel bad for Debbie Peterson." Sassy tried to draw the others into the conversation. "She opened her dress shop here in Calista less than a year ago, and already she might have to shut down. Seems like it's happening to so many. . ."

"Our small town shops are quaint, but they sure don't stay long enough," Sue Ellen noted. "Just since I've been back, the barbershop and the dry cleaner's have gone under. What's next?"

"I heard a rumor," Dottie Jean said, shaking her head. "Fanny's thinking of taking over the bakery."

"No!" Berta looked stunned.

Sue Ellen shook her head in disbelief. "You're kidding me."

"Honestly," Sassy said, "that woman's getting just a little too big for her britches."

Wendell drove by Dottie Jean's and saw Sassy and the others in their Tuesday night meeting through the window. *I wonder what they do in there.* He drove on past, fighting the urge to pull in.

You need to tell Sassy how you feel about her. He slowed his car. *The longer you wait, the harder it's going to be. Just go in there and tell her you'd like to talk with her outside. That's not so difficult.* He yanked the steering column to the left, then pulled his car to a stop next to the curb. His hands trembled as he turned off the engine.

"There's no turning back now." Wendell tried to assure himself. Stepping from the car, he glanced across the way toward the light inside. He slowly made his way to the front door, stopping just a few yards short of it.

What will I say? I have to get this right.

Wendell began to pace slowly back and forth in front of the door, feeling a chill cross over him as he moved under the blanket of the evening's shadows. For what seemed like an eternity, he paced in circles, trying to formulate just the right words. He mumbled aloud, phrasing and rephrasing, using his hands to emphasize each statement.

"You sound like a crazy man," he muttered, sticking his hands in his pockets. He moved toward the door, then back away again. "Come on, old man." Wendell turned one final time to face the door, completely lost in his thoughts.

He raised his hand, reaching for the front door as a booming voice rang out. "Put your hands up in the air and turn around. Slowly."

Wendell's hands, now vibrating uncontrollably, shot up in the air, no questions asked. He turned nervously in the direction of the familiar voice. "Bud?"

"Wendell? Is that you?" The deputy pulled out his powerful flashlight, shining it in his face. "For the love of Pete! Dottie Jean thought she had a burglar out here."

"A burglar. . . ?" Wendell's hands fell to his side in disbelief.

"She and the other ladies called the station about five minutes ago—said they saw a prowler outside making his way toward the front door. Scared them half to death."

"Oh, good grief." Wendell gripped his forehead with his hand, overcome with confusion. Everything he had hoped to say suddenly slipped from his mind.

At that moment, the front door swung open, and all of the ladies emerged, jabbering at once. Wendell squinted to make them out in the shadows.

"Bud, thank God you're here!" Dottie Jean spoke excitedly.

Sue Ellen nervously gripped Berta's arm. "We were so scared."

Berta sounded a little more confident. "Did you get 'em?"

"Let us at him. We'll take care of him!" Sassy's words rang out above the others. Wendell's heart twisted inside him at the sound of her voice. *Now what do I do?*

"Yeah. I caught the monster," Bud said with a laugh. He turned his light on Wendell once again, and the ladies broke into laughter.

"Wendell?" Dottie Jean stared at him. "What in the world were you doing out here? Why didn't you just come on in?"

"I, uh. . ."

"Where's your car?" Berta looked out at the road, curiosity etching her face.

He pointed lamely.

"Why'd you park all the way over there, anyway?" Bud asked. "Something wrong with the car?"

"Nope."

"Well, is something wrong with you, then?" Berta asked, approaching him.

"Nope."

Dottie Jean looked at him nervously. "Do you need to use the telephone?"

"Nope."

"Well, you must have needed something, Wendell."

He stared at Sassy, trying to express himself with his eyes. She gazed back at him, her silence speaking volumes. "I, uh. . . I. . ." *Come on, man!* "I need to get on home now. It's getting late."

He began to move in the direction of his car, shaking like a leaf. Just as he reached the door, he felt someone touch his arm. He turned, facing Sassy.

"You came to talk to me, didn't you?" She spoke quietly.

He nodded lamely. "Yes."

"What did you want to say, Wendell?"

His heart began to race, pounding so loudly in his ears he could hardly hear himself think. He reached for her hand, squeezing it. "Sassy, I need to tell you something."

"Go on."

"I need to tell you that I—" His palms suddenly felt sweaty.

"Be careful driving home, Wendell!" Bud's voice rang out from across the yard. Wendell squinted as the flashlight hit him in the face once again. He dropped Sassy's hand immediately.

"You what, Wendell?" Sassy looked at him nervously.

"I, uh. . .I need to borrow your popcorn machine for the festival next week."

"What?"

His mind began to race, trying to come up with a workable story. "I need to borrow that old popcorn machine you used to keep at the shop when the kids were small. Do you still have it? I want to make popcorn balls for the kids at the festival this year." *Good cover.*

"Well, yes. It's packed away in the storage room some-where, but you're welcome to it, of course." She suddenly looked hurt.

"That's fine, fine," he stammered. She turned back toward the house. He reached out to grab her hand one last time. "Oh, and, Sassy. . ."

238

She glanced back at him with a look of impatience. "Yes, Wendell?"

"Sassy, I love you."

Chapter 8

Sassy made her way across the small cemetery to the now-familiar place on the southeast corner. It had become her custom to visit this spot every October twenty-seventh—her wedding anniversary.

Sassy carried daisies purchased from Patty's Posies, another tradition dating back to her first date with Joe Hatchett. He had arrived at her home nervously clutching a fistful of fresh daisies picked from his mother's garden. From that day on, they had remained her favorite. And now, as she had so many times before, Sassy found herself face-to-face with the memory of the man who had filled her life with joy for thirty-five years.

This place is a mess. She reached down to pull weeds from around his tombstone, laying the flowers at her feet. She wiped the dirt from her hands, then ran her finger across the familiar words on the tombstone: JOE HATCHETT, A MAN AFTER GOD'S OWN HEART.

"Sassy, I love you." The words she heard now were Wendell's. They had startled her down to the core of her being. She hadn't

responded. In fact, when Wendell had appeared at her door on Tuesday afternoon to pick up the popcorn machine, she had treated him as if it had never happened at all.

How would Joe feel about this? Sassy's heart began to pound in her ears, and tears slipped down her cheeks. *Am I betraying him, Lord? Wendell Meeks is a good man, but...* "There will never be a man like Joe Hatchett." She spoke the words aloud.

Brushing the tears from her cheeks, she reached down to plant the daisies.

Wendell loaded the backseat of his car with goodies for the festival. *Cake, pie, card table, and four chairs. I'm forgetting something. What is it?*

Gus pulled up. "Need any help?"

Ah! I remember now. "I was just trying to figure out how to get this popcorn machine in the car. Think you've got room to carry it over in the back of your truck?"

"Sure, sure." Gus hopped out, then came around to the front of the vehicle. Between the two of them, they maneuvered the large, bulky contraption into the bed of the truck. "This machine's as old as dirt," he continued. "Where'd you get it, anyway?"

"Sassy. She used to keep it up at the Bait and Tackle when the twins were knee-high to a tadpole, remember? I used it to make popcorn balls."

"Speaking of old. . ."

Wendell's blood began to stir, anticipating his friend's next comment. "What?"

"Sassy's so old, when she was born the Dead Sea was just getting sick."

"Very funny."

"Now me," Gus said with a wink, "I'm looking for a younger woman, myself. I've been thinking about asking my granddaughter to hook me up with one of her friends. Someone like. . ."

At that moment a horn honked, startling them. Wendell looked up to see Fanny, waving from the front seat of her luxury sedan as she drove by.

"What a wonderful idea," Wendell said with a grin. "You and Fanny would make a terrific couple."

"Come on now." Gus got back in his truck with a sour look on his face.

"No, I'm serious," Wendell said with a grin. "Fanny's a good fifteen years younger than you, and she's certainly available. Oh, that reminds me. I believe I told her you'd help her out at the cakewalk tonight."

"You didn't."

"I did."

"Wendell Meeks, I'm going to. . ."

Wendell found it difficult to understand what Gus said over the sound of squealing tires as his truck pulled away.

❧

Sassy crossed the churchyard, marveling at the sights and sounds that greeted her. There were pony rides for the kids, who should be arriving any moment now. A petting zoo would also keep little ones amused, along with booths of every sort—everything from face painting and a ring toss to bobbing for apples and a cakewalk. The teens had erected some sort of a coffee shop area, where most of them would probably be content to hang out and chat. The festivities would begin shortly, if everything went according to plan.

And speaking of plans—Pastor Jordan had readily accepted "Fall at the River" as the appropriate theme for the festival, even agreeing to be "baptized" in the dunking booth. The ladies had worked diligently to prepare. Sue Ellen had concocted a river out of a wide bolt of shimmering blue fabric, winding it across the lawn and through the booths and finishing it off at the street's edge. Sassy had placed paper fish in the river, and Gus and Wendell had worked with Fletcher to build up the edges with rocks and dirt. All in all, they had created a pretty impressive replica of the Biloxi.

Sassy grinned as she crossed a tiny bridge over the makeshift river. She turned her sights to the food counter, where she had agreed to work with Sue Ellen and Fanny dishing out hot dogs, cotton candy, popcorn balls, and caramel apples. Fanny gestured frantically. "Hurry, Sassy! We need you over here."

"I'm coming," she said, picking up the pace.

"Hey, Sassy." She looked up at Wendell, who struggled to carry a large container of popcorn balls. He placed them on the counter, breathing a sigh of relief as they landed safely.

"Finished them, eh?" she teased.

"Yeah," he said, stifling a yawn. "Stayed up half the night, but they're done. I've got your popcorn machine in Gus's truck. We'll make the transfer to your vehicle before the night is over."

"Great." She shivered in the cool night air. "It's chilly out tonight," she said. "I should have worn my coat."

"Here. Wear my sweater." He yanked off his simple gray button-up and slipped it over her shoulders.

"Thanks," she said, avoiding eye contact. *He's such a good man.*

"I passed the pie toss on the way over," Wendell said with a grin. "You should have seen Matthew Van-what's-his-name getting set up—looks like a deer caught in the headlights."

"I'll have to get over there before the night's over." Sassy giggled. "That fella's got so many names, he could stand to have one or two of them knocked off with a lemon meringue pie."

They burst into laughter just as Sue Ellen appeared with an armload of hot dog buns. "Have you been over to the craft area yet?"

"Stopped by on the way here," Sassy said as she helped her unload. "Looks like Dottie Jean and Berta have their work cut out for them. People are already standing in line to get in."

"Speaking of which. . ." Wendell gestured to the line of children forming at the food booth.

Sassy glanced at her watch: 5:45. "Oh my goodness." She pulled items from bags in a rush. "We're running late."

Sue Ellen rapidly spun cotton candy and rolled it onto long paper funnels. Sassy and Wendell worked side by side until the popcorn balls were unloaded and apples were pressed onto sticks in readiness for dipping, then they turned their attention to the hot dogs, which they feverishly placed into warmed buns.

"Sassy, I love you."

"What did you say?" She looked up at Wendell, astonished.

"I said, I've got to get over to the dunking booth to see how Pastor Jordan is doing."

"Oh, okay." Sassy took a few deep breaths, trying to slow the rhythm of her heart as he walked away.

"Are the caramel apples ready?" Sue Ellen looked at her curiously.

"Not quite."

"It's nearly six, and I've got some very anxious kids over here. How much longer?"

"The caramel is melted, and I've got the apples on sticks," Sassy explained, wringing her hands. "But I've run into a hitch. Fanny was supposed to bring chopped pecans, and she brought whole ones instead. I'm doing the best I can to mash them, but it's taking awhile."

"Just hurry, honey," Sue Ellen said, turning back to the crowd. "I'll try to pitch Wendell's popcorn balls in the meantime."

She glanced to her right as she heard a youngster's voice. "Tilly needs you, Miss Sassy."

"What for? I'm really busy."

"I don't know, but she said it's important."

"Okay. Tell her I'll just be a minute." Sassy quickly finished up the apples, selling one to Gus before taking off. "I've got to leave, Sue Ellen," she said. "But I'll be right back."

She made her way through the maze of kids to the kissing booth, where Tilly and Dottie Jean's daughter, Jenny, worked. "What's wrong, honey?"

"Oh, Mom. I'm glad you're here. The teens are out of coffee, and I've got to go across the street to the shop to get some.

I need someone to stay here with Jenny for a few minutes till I get back, okay?"

"What?"

"She needs someone to help with the money. See how long the line is?"

"But. . ."

"Please, Mom." Tilly sprinted off toward the parking lot. Sassy watched helplessly.

Gus walked up, nibbling on his nutty caramel apple. "So are you here doling out kisses for real?"

" 'Course not. I'm just. . ."

Wendell approached with a silly grin on his face.

Oh, dear Lord, no. Please don't let him think. . .

"Sassy. . ."

"Yes?" Her heart began to race as he laid a dollar on the counter and then looked teasingly into her eyes.

———

I'm going to do this. I'm going to kiss Sassy Hatchett. I'm going to let the whole world know how I feel about her—right here, right now. Wendell pressed his lips together in preparation.

"What are you doing? Are you crazy?" she asked, looking stunned. He closed his eyes and leaned in for the long-awaited moment. His lips very nearly brushed hers when Gus suddenly began to choke.

"Gus?" Wendell pulled away and stared as his friend turned several shades of red. Gus's choking spell dissolving into shallow gasps for breath. He shook his head frantically, pointing to his chest.

"What does he want?"

"The Heimlich," Sassy explained. "Does anyone know how to do it?"

Wendell's hands began to shake. "I don't have a clue. Never learned. Any of you?"

"I don't rightly know what I'm doing, but I've seen it on television." Sassy raced around the booth and wrapped her arms tightly around Gus's chest. She pressed her hands in a repetitive motion, but nothing happened. "He's too big. My arms won't reach all the way around."

Bud raced over just at that moment. "Here, Sassy. Let me take over." Wendell breathed a huge sigh of relief as the deputy sheriff gave a few sharp thrusts before a large pecan shot out of Gus's mouth.

Gus doubled over, gasping for breath. "I. . .I. . ."

"Gus, are you okay?" Wendell asked nervously.

"I am now." He looked up, stunned.

Pastor Jordan arrived, wet and breathless. "Everything okay here?"

"Yes, Pastor," Sue Ellen said, arriving. "Bud just saved my grandpa's life."

No one spoke for a moment as Gus regained his composure. "Someone had to do it," he said finally. "Sassy Hatchett tried to kill me."

Chapter 9

Sassy took a sip from the fish mug, finding it difficult to swallow. *This stuff is terrible.* "What do you call this one, again?"

Tilly grinned from across the counter. "Swiss Chocolate Surprise."

"It's a surprise, all right. Does it come with yodeling instructions?

"Mom."

"If you don't mind, could I have a real cup of coffee?" She pushed the mug across the counter.

Tilly's face fell immediately. "Whatever you say." She filled a new cup with coffee and handed it to her. "Now, if you don't mind, I have other customers to wait on."

I know I must sound agitated, but I just can't seem to help myself today. Sassy looked around at the room full of teens. Their heads were buried in books. Every once in a while, one would lift a head to make a comment to someone, then dive right back into the book. "What are they doing?"

"Homework."

"At a coffee shop?"

"Sure." Tilly picked up a rag. "It's like this every afternoon. If you came in more often, you'd see for yourself."

"What's Ginny Peterson doing over there?" She pointed to a girl in the corner who seemed to be directing a group activity.

"She leads a Bible study in here every week."

"You're kidding."

"No, I'm not. I'd never kid about anything like that. She's even been working on me."

"Meaning. . . ?"

"Meaning I've been giving some thought to what I've read. If this whole God-thing wasn't so confining, I might consider it. But there are too many hypocrites in this town for that. That's why I hang out with the kids. What you see is what you get with them."

"I suppose." Sassy looked them over a bit more carefully.

"They're good kids, Mom."

You're a good kid, Tilly. Sassy watched out of the corner of her eye as her daughter made the rounds, laughing and talking with each customer. *She's really great at this, isn't she, Lord? I should say something nice to her, something encouraging.*

But she couldn't. Not today. In fact, Sassy hadn't been able to say much of anything nice in the three weeks since the festival. She had avoided nearly everyone in town, nodding silently at them in church and avoiding the express lane at Fanny's like the plague.

"I guess you saw they've shut down the hair salon for a few

weeks," Tilly said, approaching the counter once again. "I hear Sue Ellen's got some great plans for renovating the shop."

"Makes no difference to me," Sassy said with a smirk. "I never get my hair done anyhow."

"It wouldn't hurt, Mom."

The bell on the door rang out as more teens entered. Tilly smiled in their direction, waving.

"What's the update on all the wedding plans? Wasn't there some sort of conflict or something?" Tilly asked.

"Well, from what I hear, Dottie Jean and Fletcher have settled on a morning service, and Berta and Matthew Van-what's-his-name are taking the evening. Pastor Jordan's going to have his hands full that day. I'm so tired of hearing about weddings. Berta's having a big fancy affair. I tell ya, since she met that fella with all them names, she's so stuck up she'd drown in a rainstorm."

"Mother."

"I'm not kidding. And I've really gotta wonder about marrying someone you hardly know. I mean, he's got the money, but they've hardly had a decent courting time. And you know what I always say. Marriage is no way to get acquainted."

"That's none of our business."

"They're making it my business. Every time I turn around, someone wants me to go shopping with them. Or worse! Can you believe Dottie Jean actually asked me to be her matron of honor—at my age?"

"Are you going to do it?"

"I'd feel like a goofball standing up there in a pink satin dress with a handful of wilted roses in my hand. Wouldn't I look a sight? Besides, I've already given everyone enough to talk about. I'd like some privacy, if no one minds."

"You've certainly had little of that since the festival," Tilly said with a sigh. "Seems everywhere I go in town, someone's talking about you. Especially Gus. Every time he tells his story, it grows a little."

"That man," Sassy said, feeling her anger mount. "He's a legend in his own mirror. Someone needs to put him in his place."

Tilly shrugged, then reached to refill Sassy's cup. "I suppose we should show him a little grace. After all, the man faced death just three weeks ago."

"I saw him over at Fanny's just this morning—looking as fit as a fiddle," Sassy argued. "There's nothing wrong with him that a few swift kicks wouldn't cure."

"Mom, you've been in a really bad mood lately. Are you okay?"

She shrugged. *I'm not okay, to be perfectly honest. I miss Wendell. That's what's wrong with me, if you'd really like to know.* Sassy's heart twisted inside her just thinking about him. Every night as she rested her head on the pillow, his words were the last thing to go through her mind. *"Sassy, I love you."* He had really said it, and from everything she could tell, he meant it. She had twisted the sheets into knots night after night fighting the notion that she might feel the same.

But she could fight it no longer. *I love him, Lord. But I'm no good for him. I'm no good for anyone. That's why I've avoided him. That's why I can't return his calls.*

Tilly rambled on. "Are you just upset about what happened

at the festival, or is more going on that I should know about?"

Sassy shrugged. Her daughter sat down next to her, then reached to grab her hand. "We haven't been close lately, I know, but. . ."

Sassy immediately felt tears well up in her eyes. She dabbed at them with a napkin already stained with coffee, causing them to sting even more. "I'm okay."

"You're not. And I wish you'd talk to me."

Just tell her. She'll understand. A lump rose in Sassy's throat, one far too large to speak over. She just shook her head back and forth until it finally began to dissolve.

"Well, could we at least talk about Thanksgiving?" Tilly asked, standing. "I need to decide what to bring this year—and who to bring."

Sassy looked up at her curiously. "Are you dating someone?"

"Maybe."

"Someone in town?" Sassy racked her brain, trying to imagine who he might be.

"No, he's a vendor from Biloxi. Came out to the shop with coffee samples awhile back. We're not really dating. We're just. . ."

"Interested in each other?"

"I guess you could put it that way. I was wondering if I could bring him to Thanksgiving at your place."

"Sure. Of course."

"I figured Wendell would be there."

Sassy smiled just thinking about it. "Hadn't really thought about it," she said with a shrug.

"Well, that's exactly what I've been wanting to talk to you about." Tilly looked nervous.

"Wendell?"

"Yes."

"What about him?" Sassy's temper began to rise in anticipation.

"I, uh. . ."

"Go on."

"I just wanted to say how sorry I am that I've given you such a hard time about him, Mom. He's a great man, and I can see how happy you are when you're with him." She looked at the ground sheepishly. "I know I've been a real pain in the neck."

"Yep."

"But you haven't exactly been a piece of cake, either," Tilly interjected.

Sassy shrugged. "Nope."

"Can we just call a truce and try to get along during the holidays? I'd really like to bring Fred."

"Fred? His name is Fred?"

"Yes, Mother. But no wisecracks, okay?"

Sassy shrugged again. "Bring him. I'll be an angel. And who knows. . .maybe I'll even break down and invite Gus Caldwell to Thanksgiving dinner. Wouldn't that be a hoot?"

Chapter 10

Sassy pulled the turkey from the oven with a shake of her head. "Not a very pretty one, are you?" she mumbled, looking it over carefully. "And not very big, either." *Might be an issue, considering the guest list.*

For the past week she had stewed over her situation, finally spending a chilly November afternoon at the pier, setting things right with the Lord. Her anger had truly dissipated once she'd placed her issues into the Lord's hands.

But how to make peace with Gus—now that was another question. She had finally settled on doing so in her own way—with good homemade food. Gus would be her guest of honor today. She glanced at the table, covered in a new tablecloth and spread with her best dishes.

"You've done a nice job, Mom," Tilly said, filling glasses with ice. "When do you think everyone will be here?"

"Oh, ten or fifteen minutes." She glanced at the clock.

"Who all did you end up inviting? Looks like quite a spread."

"Well, since Tucker couldn't come, I decided to ask a couple of extra people. Dottie Jean and Fletcher already had plans but said they'd stop by for dessert. Berta and Matthew might come by a little later, too. But Gus was free."

"You actually invited him? I'm so proud of you, Mom."

"Yep. I invited Sue Ellen, too. He is her grandfather, after all."

"Who else?" Tilly asked, smiling at her as she placed glasses on the table.

"Bud Briggs. If anyone could use a good meal, that man could."

Tilly began to fold napkins as she spoke. "Anyone else?"

"Well, yes," Sassy said with a smile. "I invited Fanny."

"Fanny? Are you kidding?"

"Nope. I felt a little sorry for her. Now that her parents have passed away, she's got no place to go for the holidays. No one needs to spend the holidays alone. Oh, and I've set a place for Fred. He's still coming, right?"

Tilly nodded and smiled. "Yep. But you haven't mentioned Wendell. Will he be here?" She spoke with a hint of a sparkle in her eye.

"Wendell." Sassy's lips turned up as she spoke his name. "He's coming." His voice on the phone had reflected his joy at the invitation. She had looked forward to his visit just as much. Today, somehow, some way, she would let him know—in either word or deed. *I love you, too, Wendell.* She had rehearsed the words for days, ever since her encounter on the pier. No more debating whether or not he deserved better. He loved her. She loved him. Nothing else mattered.

"That's great, Mom." Her daughter returned to readying the table.

Sassy busied herself with the side dishes, leaving the turkey till last. *I'll ask Wendell to carve it. That will make him feel good.*

Minutes later, her home filled with guests, and Sassy called everyone to the table.

"Before we start, I'd like to go around the table and have everyone tell what they're thankful for this year," she said, taking a seat. "If you don't mind, let's start with you, Sue Ellen."

Sue Ellen nodded. "That's fine. I'm just so happy to be back, and I'm thankful the renovations are going well at the shop. I never dreamed I'd own my own place, but God has brought it to pass. He's been so good to me."

"Gus, your turn." Sassy gave him a nervous glance.

Instead of his usual sarcasm, Gus spoke politely. "I'm thankful for good friends and looking forward to good food." He patted his belly and grinned like a schoolkid.

"Bud. You go next."

He looked nervously around the table. "Well, I'm happy to be in Calista, at least for now. And I'm thankful for good friends to share this special day with." Sassy couldn't help but notice his gaze turn toward Sue Ellen, who pretended not to notice.

"Fanny, your turn."

Everyone looked at the woman, quietly seated at the end of the table. She opened her mouth to speak, but tears tumbled down her cheeks instead.

"Are you okay, honey?" Sassy stood and moved toward her.

"I'm—I'm fine."

"Are you sure?" Tilly asked nervously.

"I'm just so blessed to be here," Fanny whispered. "Thank you all so much for inviting me."

The lump in Sassy's throat grew as she reached out to squeeze Fanny's hand. "You're welcome anytime." She sat back down, smiling at Tilly. "Now, what about you, honey? Anything special you're thankful for today?"

"As a matter of fact," Tilly said, her eyes growing misty, "I do have something. In fact, I have a bit of an announcement to make."

Sassy looked nervously between Tilly and Fred, who sat at her daughter's side. *Not yet, Lord! It's too soon for this.*

"Fred has been a wonderful addition to my life," Tilly began, "and I've learned so much from him. But he's given me one thing that's extra special." A lone tear trickled down her cheek. She reached to brush it away. "He's told me that he loves me. . ."

Sassy's heart began to twist inside her. *They hardly know each other, Lord.*

". . .but he's convinced me that God loves me even more."

"What?" Sassy's heart leapt into her throat. "Are you telling me. . . ?"

"I've given my heart to the Lord, Mom," Tilly whispered. "Just last night, in fact. And I have more to be thankful for this Thanksgiving than any other."

Sassy's emotions suddenly took over. She began to weep, leaning her face down into open palms.

Tilly stood, rushing to her side. "I didn't mean to upset you."

"I—I'm not upset." She squeezed her daughter's hand. "I'm

just so happy, I don't know what to do."

"I've decided something else, too," Tilly said with a grin.

"I don't know if my heart can take anymore," Sassy said, shaking her head.

"I think you'll like this. I've decided to close the shop on Sundays—or at least offer it to Pastor Jordan for the church's use. It's time the kids and I came back home."

Sassy threw her arms around Tilly's neck and held her until she heard Wendell clear his throat.

"My turn," he said with a sly smile. All eyes turned to him.

⸺∞⸺

Wendell sat at the head of the table, surveying the group. He looked across at all of the smiling faces, his gaze finally resting on Sassy. *This feels so good, Lord. So right. I belong here—with her. With them.* "I have a lot to be thankful for this year," he said quietly. "But one thing above all."

He looked Sassy in the eye, feeling Gus's eyes on him but not caring. The opinions of others didn't matter anymore. Only one thing mattered. "I've come to know myself a lot better this year," he said. "I know what I've been missing in my life. I believe I've found it. In fact, I'm sure I've found it."

He reached out to take Sassy by the hand and squeezed tightly. She squeezed back, dissolving into tears once again. Wendell's heart filled with emotion, and he felt the sting of tears in his own eyes. *Could this day get any better, Lord?*

After a moment or two, she lifted her head, looking around the table. "Look at me," she said, sniffling. "Getting all emotional."

"It's okay, Mom." Tilly took Fred's outstretched hand.

"Well, don't mind me," Sassy continued, passing the stuffing. "Let's say the blessing. Otherwise, this food's going to get cold."

She nodded Wendell's direction, and with a full heart, he thanked God for the food. Inwardly, he thanked the Almighty for Sassy Hatchett.

"Eat up, everyone," Sassy said when he finished. "Food's getting cold."

Her guests began to fill their plates, and the clinking of silverware filled the room, along with the laughter of those present as they enjoyed one another's company. Wendell drank it all in, enjoying every delicious moment.

"Sassy, this is gooder'n grits," Fanny said as she pressed a hefty spoonful of mashed potatoes into her mouth.

"Thank you," Sassy responded with a smile. Under the table, she reached for Wendell's hand. He took it willingly.

Chapter 11

"Well, what did you think of the wedding this morning?" Sassy rolled up her pants to the knee and kicked her legs over the edge of the pier.

"Beautiful," Tilly said with a nod. "Dottie Jean looked amazing. Fletcher didn't look half bad, either."

"Well, I looked ridiculous in that satin dress, if you ask me." Sassy pulled out her fishing pole. "But it's over now. Thank goodness, Berta only wants me to serve cake at her reception tonight. No telling what sort of getup she and Van-what's-his-name would have dressed me in."

"It's going to be quite a show, from what I hear," Tilly said. "A full-blown Christmas theme. Berta's got half the town working to decorate the church this afternoon. How'd you get off the hook, anyway?"

Sassy smiled at her daughter's attempted pun. "Told her the only way I could come tonight was if she would give me the afternoon off. Besides, everyone knows I'm no good at decorating."

"You don't give yourself enough credit, Mom," Tilly argued. "I'd be willing to bet there are a lot of things you're good at."

Sassy shrugged. "Could you hand me that container of bait?" She worked to straighten out the line, finally freeing it to her satisfaction. "Tilly?"

She turned to find Wendell standing where her daughter had been. He had a funny look on his face. Something inside Sassy immediately began to stir. "What are you doing here?" she asked, squinting up at him.

"Thought you could use some help baiting your hook," he said, reaching for her pole.

"That's plum crazy. I've been baiting my own hook since I was a kid." She shivered against the cold, pulling her jacket tighter.

"Just the same, I'd be grateful if you'd let me handle it for you this time," he said. He grabbed the pole, hands trembling.

She turned to open her coffee thermos. "Do as you please." Sassy poured a cup of coffee and then settled back to look at the murky waters of the Biloxi. The reflection of bare tree limbs in the water held her gaze, bringing tranquility. After what seemed like an eternity, she turned to face Wendell once again. "It's taking you a mighty long time to do that," she whined. "Either fish or cut bait."

"I think I'll fish," he said, handing her the pole. "But you'd better take a closer look at the bait."

She reached for the line, pulling until she reached the hook on the end. The sparkle of a diamond caught her off guard, leaving her breathless. A silver ring, petite and exquisite, hung precariously from the hook.

Wendell's hands trembled as he pulled the ring from the fishhook and gripped it in his hand. *Help me, Lord.* He carefully dropped to one knee, looking Sassy in the eye. *Lord, is she terrified or horrified? It's hard to tell. . . .* Tears trickled down her cheeks as he placed the ring on her finger.

"Sassy," he said quietly. "I don't exactly know when I first started loving you, but I do know why."

She leaned her head down, burying her face in her hands. He carefully lifted her chin with trembling fingers. "You're the most beautiful thing I've ever laid eyes on, Sassy Hatchett," Wendell said. "Beautiful inside and out. You've got enough electricity inside you to keep the whole town lit, and as good as you are at fishing, I know we'll never go hungry."

She stifled a laugh, then looked up at him with tearstained cheeks. He brushed the tears away gently as he continued. Reaching out with both hands, Wendell pulled her up until they stood face-to-face. He ran the back of his hand across her soft cheek, loving each spot, each wrinkle.

"Marry me, Sassy," he implored, his heart feeling as if it would burst.

"Me?" she argued. "But I'm so. . ."

He placed his finger over her lips, shushing her. "Marry me and make me the happiest man in Calista, Mississippi."

"I will," she conceded with a sigh, then leaned her head against his shoulder. "If you'll have me."

Wendell suddenly felt a joy he had never before known. "Have you?" his heart swelled. "Of course I'll have you!"

He pulled her close and wrapped his arms around her. *So this is what it feels like.* His heart pounded in his ears, sheer nerves at work, but that didn't deter him. Not this time. Wendell leaned in to kiss the woman he loved. Their lips met swiftly, and his heart swelled with a passion borne out of sixty years of waiting.

Waiting for just the right catch.

JANICE A. THOMPSON

Janice is a Christian freelance author and a true "Gulf Coast Southerner." She started writing at a young age and has published over fifty articles and short stories for Christian publications, as well as several full-length inspirational novels and non-fiction books. She's thankful for her calling as an author of Christian fiction and knows that God has brought her to this point so that she can present stories that will change people's lives. She particularly enjoyed writing *Gone Fishing* and wants readers to know that she and Sassy (the primary character) have a lot of things in common. Janice declines to comment on "which" things, in particular.

Falling for You

by Kathleen Y'Barbo

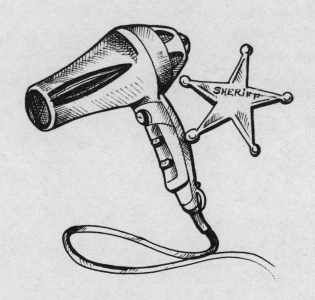

Dedication

To the ladies of Seared Hearts:
DiAnn Mills, Janice Thompson, and Martha Rogers.

And we, who with unveiled faces all reflect the Lord's glory,
are being transformed into his likeness with ever-increasing glory,
which comes from the Lord, who is the Spirit.
2 CORINTHIANS 3:18

Chapter 1

December 29

"What in the world is Sue Ellen up to now?"

Deputy Sheriff Bud Briggs swallowed the lump in his throat as he cruised past the Catfish House. Ignoring the pointed stares of the guys at the counter, he stopped his squad car at the station, directly across from the Rhonda-Vous House of Beauty, and tried not to look too obvious.

Ever since Rhonda sold out to Sue Ellen Caldwell after last fall's hurricane, strange things had been happening at the Rhonda-Vous. Today's spectacle, however, beat all.

Taking advantage of the unseasonably warm December morning, the owner herself, all decked out in form-fitting red jeans and a blue and white top with her fair hair tied up in a long ponytail, stood perched on a rickety ladder. A dozen or so yards of red ribbon draped over her shoulder and hung down her back, and a length of it spilled onto the sidewalk to puddle around the base of the ladder.

Only four days after Christmas, and she'd already removed all the blue decorations from her absurdly titled "Blue Christmas Color-and-Cut Special." Her shop tree, formerly covered in blue bows and various beauty-related items, now lay at the curb ready for the trash pickup tomorrow.

Faeoni Ledbetter, the sheriff's recently arrived sister-in-law from Bogalusa, drove by doing her customary twenty-five in a thirty-five zone, and a few stray pieces of silver tinsel glittered in her wake.

"Afternoon, Deputy," she called, waving her gloved hand in his direction.

Bud returned the gesture, then turned his attention back to Sue Ellen and the ladder, which looked none too safe. That, combined with the fact that she kept reaching just a bit farther than was safe to drape the goofy ribbon, made Bud glad he was a praying man.

A banner advertising a "New Year, New Do" special for the upcoming month of January had been hung beneath the neon pink letters of the store's original sign, and Sue Ellen seemed to be trying to deck it out in red ribbon. The place looked like the Fourth of July rather than two days before New Year's Eve.

New Year's Eve.

The reminder of the holiday, and his mission regarding it, put the lump right back into Bud's throat. Hoping to dislodge it, he took a swig from his thermos of bottled water and chased it with a vitamin E and a couple of Cs.

Why had he thought to listen to the guys down at Gus's gas station? He'd certainly never cared about having a date to anything, much less to the Camerons' New Year's Eve bash.

They teased him all the time, and generally Bud recognized it and ignored the whole lot of them. If he'd found the gumption to follow his usual procedure regarding the old coots, he'd be happily planning his final long weekend at the fish camp before it went on the market.

Instead, he had to either admit defeat to Wendell, Gus, and the boys or step out of the patrol car and ask Sue Ellen Caldwell to the big New Year's Eve party at Dottie Jean and Fletcher's new place. Pride demanded he follow through, while good sense kept him glued to the seat.

He cast a glance heavenward. *I've been meaning to deal with my pride issues, Lord, and now seems as good a time as any to start, don't You think?*

Obviously the Lord was too busy laughing at him to answer.

"What're you afraid of, Bud?" He leaned to the right a notch to adjust his sunglasses in the rearview mirror. "It's just Sue Ellen Caldwell. What's she going to do, turn you down? You two go way back."

And they did.

He and Sue Ellen Caldwell had known each other since the church nursery, where they'd spent nearly every Sunday morning together until junior high, when the pastor decided that separating the boys from the girls would better focus wandering attentions back on the Lord. Despite the inconvenience of different Sunday school rooms, Bud managed to position himself outside the church in order to arrive just as Sue Ellen and her brothers climbed out of her father's baby blue Impala.

He told himself he just wanted to be nice, but somewhere down deep he knew he wanted to get a glimpse of her smile. That always put a special shine on the Lord's Day. Of course, she put a shine on every day, even when they spent an afternoon together digging for worms to sell down at Sassy Hatchett's bait shop.

With the money they earned, they'd race to the Catfish House for chocolate shakes, then get them in carryout cups and take them to the water to drink while they caught fish. Bud still couldn't go fishing down at the fish camp without thinking about chocolate shakes, and he couldn't go fishing at all without thinking of Sue Ellen Caldwell.

Well, Sue Ellen Caldwell and Elvis. That girl sure liked to treat him and all creation to her version of every tune Elvis ever crooned, even if her singing did chase most of the fish away.

"Sue Ellen Caldwell." He tested the name, rolling it around in his head before whispering it aloud.

By high school, Bud finally admitted to himself he had it bad for her, although he would never have said a thing for fear of jeopardizing their friendship. They were pals, partners in crime in homeroom, and on the rare Saturday afternoon, still fishing buddies.

Some thought they were an item, owing in large part to the amount of time they spent with each other. The truth was, Sue Ellen's mama was one of those women of delicate nerves, and Sue Ellen's daddy was gone more than he was home. The combination of having a federal marshal for a husband and Sue Ellen for a daughter often sent the elder Caldwell female into a tizzy.

When Mama Caldwell had one of her hissy fits, Sue Ellen headed for the Briggses' house. For his part, Bud tried to pretend that it wasn't the closeness of their homes that drew her there but rather the unconfessed love she felt for him.

Either way, Bud was smart enough to know that Sue Ellen Caldwell, a cheerleader and senior class homecoming queen, was way out of his league. A girl like her didn't belong in a town like Calista anyway, so when she went off to beauty school in Biloxi and he signed up for the Marines, Bud figured he'd never see her again.

When word came to him that Sue Ellen's mama had convinced her husband to hang up his badge and buy an RV, you could've knocked Bud over with a feather. Jim Caldwell had always been somewhat of a hero to him. To think of the lawman driving around in an oversized tin box with black socks, sandals, and a camera made Bud shudder.

He should have returned home right then, for surely something was awfully wrong. Still, he'd signed on for another four years in the Corps. Sue Ellen was long gone, so what did it matter?

By the time Bud had finished his tour of duty, spent a few years on the force in Hattiesburg, then settled into the job of deputy sheriff of Calista, he should have forgotten all about Sue Ellen Caldwell. Unfortunately, he hadn't. Every blond-haired, green-eyed gal from San Diego to Savannah reminded him of her.

If he thought about it, which he tried not to, Sue Ellen Caldwell was most likely the reason he found himself single and facing thirty with no one but his hunting dogs, Bullet and

Zeke, for companionship.

You could have bowled him over when Dottie Jean down at the Catfish House showed him the letter she'd gotten last September announcing that Sue Ellen was headed home to buy what the hurricane didn't tear up of the town beauty parlor. A few new panes of glass in the front windows and a trio of brand-new shampoo bowls, and she was in business.

Over the past year, their paths had crossed more than a time or two, an unavoidable occurrence in such a small town. Each time Bud saw her, he found himself as tongue-tied as a kid on his first date, so he took to avoiding her as much as possible.

At first, Sue Ellen had acted kind of cool at his change of behavior, and that had made him rethink his policy of keeping his distance. Then she seemed to get used to his polite nod and his pretending to study something on the other side of the room whenever she came into the Catfish House. Pretty soon, she seemed to ignore him and his sorry disposition.

Bud, however, found it harder and harder to carry on his act. Lately, despite his better judgment and an application pending at the FBI Academy in Virginia, he'd begun to entertain the prospect of taking up their friendship where it had left off.

The thought sounded better than Dottie Jean's pecan pie and scared him worse than that same delicacy's cholesterol count. Running the other way seemed to be the only sane solution, at least until the boys at the gas station got involved.

So what if there had been more engagements in Calista in the past six months than he could count? So what if her best friends Dottie Jean, Berta, and even cranky old Sassy Hatchett had settled down? That didn't mean Sue Ellen was looking for a man.

The guys at the diner saw it differently, however, and they'd given Bud the idea that Sue Ellen had set her cap for him. Gus hadn't exactly confirmed it, but he hadn't exactly denied it, either. Being her grandfather, he ought to know.

The thought scared Bud to death and got his hopes up all at the same time. He felt the same way now, sitting all hunkered down in the front seat of his squad car as if he were working a stakeout.

Out of the blue, an idea struck. The time had long since passed for him to make a friendly visit to the Rhonda-Vous. Word was out that she'd done up the whole inside in some sort of wild animal print with brand-new shampoo chairs in the same color pink as the sign out front. At least that's what Tilly told him last week when he ventured into her establishment to try out her latest coffee concoction.

He ought to get out and mosey across the street. Just to be neighborly, of course.

Bud continued to watch Sue Ellen struggle with the ribbon as he worked on a plan.

Checking his watch, he noted the better part of the morning was behind him and he hadn't accomplished a single thing beyond pulling a cat out of the tree behind Patty's Posies and stopping a speeder for doing thirty-five in a school zone on Carp Court. It was Tuesday, after all, and a slow day in Calista.

But then, every day was a slow day in Calista.

"Might as well take the rest of the day off," he muttered as he unlatched his seat belt and opened the door to step out.

"Maybe I'll invite her to go fishing for old time's sake."

"Fishing! For crying out loud, Bud. Is that how you intend to charm Sue Ellen Caldwell? Do go on."

Bud whirled around to see Sassy Hatchett standing on the other side of the patrol car with a frown and a bag of groceries balanced on one hip. Obviously her engagement to the town postman hadn't softened her as much as he'd heard.

"Mornin', Miz Hatchett," he said as he failed miserably in his attempt to muster a smile. "It's a fine day, isn't it?"

"Don't you 'Mornin', Miz Hatchett' me, Bud Briggs." She shifted her groceries to the other hip and pointed a finger at him. "I know exactly what you're up to. You don't fool me for a minute."

Chapter 2

B ud Briggs didn't fool her for a minute. Sue Ellen had felt him staring ever since he pulled up in front of the police station across the street. What she didn't know was why, at least not for certain.

After all, Bud hadn't exactly been sociable to her in quite a while. In fact, she figured he'd just about decided she didn't exist.

On some days that didn't bother her a bit. Other days, it got to her worse than a burr under a saddle to think he could so easily end a friendship that had been going on, with a few minor interruptions, since they were babies in the church nursery.

Today, however, it felt nice to know he'd at least realized she still rode the same planet around the sun that he did. While Sassy Hatchett kept him busy, Sue Ellen took the opportunity to study discreetly the town's deputy sheriff.

For all his faults, chief among them being the total lack of a sense of humor and his penchant for popping vitamins like most folks popped peppermints, Bud Briggs was undeniably easy on the eye. Unlike a good number of men in their graduating class, Bud had kept all his teeth, all his sun-streaked blond hair, and most of his male charm.

Just once she'd like to get her hands on that hair of his. Although the good Lord had given him several natural streaks of pale blond, she'd like to add just a few more around the temples. And while the barber in Hattiesburg did a nice job of keeping his hair off the collar of his uniform, she knew she could do an even better job, given the ability to add a few layers and some gel to keep it in place.

Then she'd work on that sense of humor.

There wasn't a joke ever spoken or written that could make Bud Briggs laugh since he left junior high school. Somewhere between learning to drive and graduating, her friend Bud had become someone she barely knew.

It seemed like everything she did failed to make Bud smile, and the Lord knew she tried. She'd even taken to singing Elvis to chase the fish away just so they didn't have to go home so soon, but the poor man never figured it out. Nor did he think her off-tune renditions were funny.

Somewhere along the way, she started singing on key. She also found she really liked those Elvis songs.

Then there was the realization that she really liked Bud Briggs, too.

Humming her favorite, a toe-tapper about being someone's teddy bear, she gave Bud another glance, then went back to work. While the improvements to his outside would certainly add to his good looks, Bud would never allow them. Nor, did it seem, would he ever regain the ability to enjoy life that he had before adulthood changed him.

Sue Ellen shifted positions and her train of thought.

In all the time they'd spent together growing up, why hadn't he ever asked her out on a date or at least indicated a little bit of interest in her outside of catching catfish? He'd been a good friend and an even better fisherman back in the old days, but she'd been the one to come up with the most worms.

"Just like my love life," she muttered as she tossed the last of the red ribbon over the sign advertising her January special. "If there was a prize for picking the most worms, I'd win for sure. Guess the good Lord knew what He was doing when He called a halt to my social life."

For the most part, it had been easy to accept the knowledge that the Lord meant her to stay single, although she did have the occasional twinge of loneliness when she thought of her three best friends all paired up and in love. Most days, she handled the brief down moments with a prayer and a chocolate kiss or two. That and a few stanzas of "Are You Lonesome Tonight?" usually did the trick.

Looking at Bud gave her yet another twinge, one of regret.

"Don't be silly. You can't lose something you never had." She cast one last glance over her shoulder at Deputy Briggs, then turned to take a careful step down Grandpa Gus's ladder. "Or wanted," she added.

She lifted her gaze to stare into the deep blue of the winter sky. *Lord, I realize You know what's best for me and want me to stop waiting for Mr. Right to come along, but I just wish there was some way—*

"Sue Ellen, yoo-hoo." Sassy punctuated the words with a

piercing whistle, the same one she used to cheer on the Calista Cougar football team most Friday nights in the fall.

"What is it, hon?" Sue Ellen swiveled to stare at Sassy. Part of the wooden step swiveled with her, and she kicked it back into place. *Someone's going to get hurt using this old thing.* Come tax time she'd have to use her return money to buy her grandfather a new ladder.

"Come on over here and talk to this man before he makes a spectacle of himself," Sassy shouted, attracting the attention of anyone within hearing distance.

And there were plenty within hearing distance.

Sue Ellen felt the heat rising in her cheeks. Whatever Sassy had up her sleeve, it wasn't funny. She'd be sure to let her know this evening when they met for weekly Bible study.

They were supposed to discuss ideas for a new Bible study. Maybe she'd bring some suggestions for one on taming the tongue.

"I'm busy, Sassy," she answered as she took another shaky step down the ladder. "Leave me be."

"Well, I'd just love to leave you be, but if I don't help the deputy sheriff, he's gonna be sitting here all day. You know the sheriff's older than Cooter Brown and half deaf, and the good folks of Calista will be left to fend for themselves in the event of a crime wave if Bud's too busy staring at you."

Sue Ellen ducked her head and took another step toward the pavement. Oh yes, she would definitely let her so-called *friend* know just how little she appreciated the ribbing—tonight.

"Just ignore her, Bud," she said over her shoulder, tossing

her ponytail to show him how little Sassy's teasing had affected her. "She hasn't made a lick of sense since she and Wendell Meeks hooked up."

"Hooked up," Sassy said with a screeching giggle as she slapped the side of her grocery bag with her hand. "Oh, that's a good one, Sue Ellen. I get it. Bait shop, hooks, hooked up. Real funny. Now get yourself over here and have a proper conversation about spending New Year's Eve with Deputy Briggs before the whole town knows your business."

Too late for that, Sassy.

Sue Ellen offered a weak wave to Patty, who'd come out of the flower shop to see what the commotion was about.

At least Sue Ellen now knew what all the fuss was about. Dottie Jean had told her she suspected Wendell and the boys were cooking up a scheme that involved poor Bud and the New Year's Eve party they were giving. Last Tuesday at Bible study, the four of them had speculated as to just what the big joke would be, but none of them had guessed it involved Bud's asking her to the party.

Or at least none of them had admitted to knowing about it.

Sue Ellen narrowed her eyes and gave Sassy an I'll-talk-to-you-about-this-later look. No way was she getting in the middle of this. Somehow she'd have to make a graceful exit before she was forced to tell the poor, adorable, boring deputy she had plans for midnight on the thirty-first.

Plans to celebrate in her favorite pink poodle pajamas watching the ball drop in Times Square from the comfort of her cushy sofa while eating her fill of chocolate kisses. All of this after taking a steamy two-hour soak in the tub, of course.

"Like I said, ignore her, Bud," she said as she grabbed the side of the ladder and positioned her foot to take another step, thinking of the new Mango Peach Parfait bubble bath she'd purchased just that morning. "Everyone else does."

"Actually, Sue Ellen," Bud called, "I did want to talk to you about New Year's Eve."

Her heart sank. So Grandpa and the boys had been teasing Bud again. That could be the only explanation for the antisocial deputy to mention any gathering that wasn't related to church or deer hunting.

The last time Grandpa and the boys had started up on the poor man, he'd nearly been convinced that there had been a rash of late-night attempts at robbing the station. The prospect of catching the thief kept him up three nights in a row on a stakeout of the property.

Finally, Wendell Meeks took pity on the sleep-deprived deputy and confessed they'd been playing a joke on him. Bud had been so angry that he'd had them all rounded up and thrown in jail for making false reports.

The incarceration had only lasted until the sheriff returned from lunch and set them all free, but the bruises to Bud's ego had obviously endured.

"See, I told you," Sassy said. "Now, are you going with him to Dottie Jean's shindig, or what?"

Sue Ellen cast another glance over her shoulder to see Bud heading across the street toward her. For a moment she allowed herself the luxury of imagining herself decked to the nines, sequins and all, with a gussied-up Bud Briggs at her side all evening.

She might even put a rinse in her hair for the occasion, something shimmery that would wash out in a couple of shampoos. They'd laugh and have fun, visiting with the gals and their dates, talking and laughing about old times until the clock chimed midnight.

Midnight.

Sue Ellen imagined what would come next all too clearly. Then, watching the deputy sheriff dodge traffic to cross the street, she imagined it all over again. The clock would chime once, twice, three times, and then—

And then what? She bit her lip and sent a hasty apology heavenward.

And then nothing, that's what.

You told me I'm to wait for You to bring someone into my life. Spending time with a man who's not even remotely attracted to me is not what I need to do while I wait.

Maybe after Bible study, she and Berta would go get a cup of coffee at Tilly's and talk it out. Sue Ellen sighed. No, of course Berta would need to hurry home to Matt.

Another friend lost to love.

Sue Ellen paused to watch Bud wave at Patty, who now stood in the window of the flower store. Why did the deputy have to look so handsome today of all days?

Resolutely, she cast her gaze heavenward, then glanced back at Bud as she continued her trek down the ladder. *Maybe just one evening with him wouldn't hurt, Lord. It wouldn't be like we were anything more than friends.*

The answer thundered in her ears as she held tight to the rickety ladder and watched the sun glint off the silver star on his broad chest. She'd always had a particular affinity for men in uniform.

Well, that man, anyway.

Don't even think about it, Sue Ellen. You're waiting on God, and you're not going to help Grandpa and his cronies with their little joke.

Her mind made up, Sue Ellen resolved to be strong and let Bud down easy. Maybe she'd even let him in on the joke, not that he'd get it.

An evening with him was out of the question, and that's all there was to it. Still, she couldn't help taking one last long look at Bud as he stepped up on the curb and put his hand on the ladder.

That's when she fell.

Chapter 3

I appreciate your concern, but I told you I am fine." Sue Ellen gathered her pride and the remainder of the red ribbon and hurried inside the shop. Unfortunately, Sassy and the deputy followed her.

"I don't know, Sue Ellen," Bud said. "You might ought to get yourself checked out. You can't ever tell if you may have broken something."

"Humph." Sassy settled herself into the new zebra-covered shampoo chair and crossed her arms over her chest. "She landed on her rear end, Bud. What in the world do you think she might have broken?"

To his credit, Bud actually blushed before he turned his back on Sassy. "You sure you don't want me to run you over to the emergency room in Hattiesburg? It's no trouble at all."

" 'Course it's not," Sassy said. "You weren't doing anything but sitting in your car trying to get up the courage to ask her to Dottie Jean's party."

Sue Ellen dropped the ribbon into the drawer and slammed

it shut. Thankfully no one was in the waiting room. Sassy's retorts rarely bothered her. Today, however, she'd had her fill. She was about to say so when the older woman jumped to her feet and beat a path to the door.

"You two behave," she said as she slipped outside. "I got things to do that don't involve a pair of blind lovebirds."

The screen door slammed, and Sue Ellen jumped. A check of the pink neon clock, and she knew they'd only be alone a few more minutes. Fanny was due for a cut and color, and she always arrived on time, if not a few minutes early.

Poor Bud looked as if he'd been glued to the floor. His gaze wandered from the shampoo bowls to the two dryers, then finally to the baskets of curlers the older clients preferred.

"You've never been in here, have you?"

His nose wrinkled. "It smells funny."

"It smells like a beauty shop." She reached for the scissors. "As long as you're here, why don't I shape up that shaggy hair of yours?"

Bud took three steps toward the door. "You know that'll never happen. Long as there's a barbershop in Hattiesburg, you'll never get your hands on this hair."

She shook her head and set the scissors down. "You act like I want to shave you bald. Honestly," she said as she reached for the extra-large cape and draped it over the back of the chair, "I could care less that you'd look much better with a little weight off the back and all that gray covered up."

He almost fell for it. Almost, but not quite.

It might have been the fact that she could barely hide her smile that tipped him off. Whatever the reason, he began to laugh, and she couldn't do anything but join him.

"Hey, seriously," Bud finally said, "I think you ought to at least let the doc take a look at you to be sure you didn't hurt something when you fell."

"Bud, I promise the only thing I hurt was my pride."

Sue Ellen caught sight of Fanny crossing the street. "Well, like I said, I appreciate your concern, but I'm fine. You might want to head on out of here unless you want Fanny, and thus the whole town, to know you've been in here considering a haircut."

He glanced over his shoulder, then back at Sue Ellen. "Thanks for the warning. If you're sure you're all right, I'm going to head back to the office now. And for the record, I *never* considered a haircut. Not in here, anyway."

"I'm *fine*," she said to his retreating back.

"Well, of course you are, hon." Fanny yanked the screen door open just in time for Bud to press past her. "Where's he going in such a hurry?"

"Running from the truth," Sue Ellen said with a chuckle. "I told him he needed a haircut and a dye job."

Fanny wedged herself into the chair, then dipped her chin to let Sue Ellen snap the cape behind her neck. "Honey, you didn't really tell him that, did you? Not when I'm sure he just came over here to ask you to the New Year's Eve party at Dottie Jean's."

Sue Ellen ran a comb through Fanny's hair and ignored the comment. What was so important about a silly New Year's Eve party? She'd lost track of the number of years spent welcoming the new year with Dick Clark and a quart of strawberry ice cream.

Even when Mama was living, the day hadn't been an eventful one. After all, Daddy managed to miss every one. Leastwise, every one she remembered.

"So I told him I was planning to go, too, so why didn't we go together?" Fanny looked at Sue Ellen's reflection and frowned. "You didn't hear a word I said, did you?"

Sue Ellen grabbed the rat-tail comb and began sectioning off Fanny's hair. "I'm sorry. Go ahead and tell me again, and I promise I'll listen this time."

She smiled. "Honey, you don't have to apologize. If I were a younger woman, he'd fluster me, too. As it is, I think I'll stick with Gus."

"Gus? I mean, Grandpa?" Sue Ellen nearly dropped the clip. "You're going to the party with Grandpa?"

The older lady fairly beamed. "I sure am. He's just the sweetest thing. Sweeter than sugar, that grandpa of yours." Fanny made a face. "Speaking of sugar, have you heard the latest?"

Sue Ellen shook her head and proceeded to prepare Fanny's hair for the usual cut. As she grabbed the comb, she knew she'd have bruises in the places that had begun to ache.

Nothing to do but ignore it. Sue Ellen had work to do, and if she closed up shop because of a couple of aches and pains, who would see to the beauty of the women of Calista?

Perish the thought.

She began to hum "Return to Sender," her favorite mood lightener. When Fanny joined in, she switched to singing harmony through all verses—twice.

"Well, I do love the King." Sue Ellen chuckled. "Both of

them, actually, although my Savior comes first above anyone and anything."

"Oh, I get it," Fanny said. "Jesus, the King, and Elvis. You're a hoot, Sue Ellen. Say, I heard from a little birdie that we're about to get us a new restaurant in Calista." Her eyes narrowed. "Can you feature it? Someone giving the Catfish House a run for its money? I heard it was that Faeoni Ledbetter behind it. You know she's not from around here, don't you?"

"Yes, I believe I did."

In truth, Fanny had been waxing poetic about the poor Ledbetter woman ever since widowhood forced Faeoni to move in with the sheriff and his wife some six weeks ago. Sue Ellen's guess was that Fanny suspected the sheriff's sister-in-law just might steal Grandpa from her.

Not that either woman had a chance at roping the old coot.

Sue Ellen smiled at the thought of her grandfather living happily ever after with someone. Funny, but neither woman came to mind when she tried to place a bride next to him.

Sue Ellen turned Fanny away from the mirror. "I guess it's inevitable someone would come in eventually. I doubt Jenny and her mama are worried. No one's going to outcook the Catfish House."

"Yes, well, I suppose so, but I do have to admit I never expected something like this." Fanny let out a long breath. "I had high hopes we would be welcoming more good folks into the community when I heard the name of the restaurant."

"Oh?" She heard the screen door slam and looked up to see that Bud had returned. "What's it called?"

"Welcome back, Bud," Fanny said. "I was just telling Sue Ellen here about the new restaurant that's opening in the old bakery. Maybe you've heard about it? It's called Loaves and Fishes."

Bud avoided Sue Ellen's stare to study the toes of his boots. "That's a right fine name, Miss Fanny. Reckon they're Christian folks?"

"Well, of course you'd think that until you hear what kind of place it is." Her bejeweled fists grasped the arms of the chair as if she were bracing herself. "Would you believe those crazy folks are building a place that sells fresh bread on one side of the building and *sushi* on the other?"

"Sushi? So I can get my fish cooked with corn bread on one side of the street and raw with a wheat loaf on the other." Bud's smile was contagious. "Now how about that?"

"I think that's a lovely idea," Sue Ellen added. "I do love fresh bread."

"Well, who doesn't?" Fanny tapped the most prominent of her chins. "It's the sushi I'm worried about."

Bud leaned against the shampoo bowl and shook his head. "Not much to worry about with sushi, Miss Fanny. It's just prettied up raw fish on a plate. I can tell you it's good for you, but I'm sure the Catfish House won't go out of business over it."

"Well, that may be so, but I wonder if a petition might be in order. You think that would stop these people from invading the sanctity of the Catfish House? I would hate to think that the Ledbetter woman could just sashay in here and send Dottie Jean to the poorhouse."

"Now, Miss Fanny, I hardly think that's the case here." Sue Ellen fought to contain her giggle. "Maybe you ought to let

Miss Faeoni know you're worried. I'm sure she could ease your mind."

"Humph. Why in the world would I want to talk to her? Why, you know, I saw her at the Catfish House the other day, and it did not escape my attention that she was sitting just five tables over from my Gus." Fanny's eyes widened. "I mean, from your dear grandfather."

"Who's talking about the Catfish House?" Dottie Jean walked in, and Sue Ellen set the scissors aside to hug her friend.

"How was your trip? Did you and Fletcher have fun?" Bud asked, then blushed.

Chapter 4

The proprietor of the Catfish House ignored Bud's discomfort. "It's good to be back, but we did have a lovely trip." She turned to Bud. "What are you doing here, Deputy Briggs? You finally decide to let Sue Ellen do something with that hair of yours?"

"No, ma'am," was all he said.

Dottie Jean shook her head. "Don't tell me she's talked you into one of those facials. I heard tell that Wendell came in here for a haircut and came out boasting his face was as smooth as a baby's bottom after he gave in and let Sue Ellen put some goop on it."

Bud looked ready to bolt and run. "Actually, I was just passing by."

"Again," Fanny added.

"Yes, well," he stammered, "I wondered if Sue Ellen here might need her ladder fixed."

"I appreciate that, Bud," she said, "but I figured I'd let Grandpa handle it."

"No sense in that. I already hauled it behind the jailhouse." He shuffled his feet and inched toward the door. "I just figured I'd tell you where it was in case you went looking for it."

He made another move for the door, and Dottie Jean caught his sleeve. "I'm glad to see all of you here," she said. "I wanted to be sure that all my friends knew that Fletcher and I will be holding the annual New Year's Eve party at our home instead of the restaurant."

"I can't wait to see it," Fanny said. "Gus is taking me, you know."

All three sets of eyes turned toward the smiling woman in the chair. Suddenly the empty bride spot beside Grandpa was filled.

Sue Ellen blinked to remove the image of Fanny in white with a veil.

"Well, I declare—that's the best news I've heard all day," Dottie Jean said. "I'll look forward to seeing the both of you, hon. Do bring those wonderful shrimp tarts you make, will you?"

While Fanny droned on about the recipe, Dottie Jean exchanged grins with Sue Ellen. "Bud," Dottie Jean said when Fanny paused to take a breath, "you'll be there, won't you?"

"Oh, I don't know." He shook his head. "I generally volunteer to work that night. You know how the sheriff hates staying up late."

Sue Ellen watched Dottie Jean walk over to Bud and place her hand on his shoulder. "It'd mean a lot to Fletcher and me if you'd come. 'Sides, I happened to run into the sheriff on my way here. Looks like his wife's having a get-together for the ladies in her bridge group. I'd be willing to bet the poor man would do just about anything to miss that hen party."

Bud seemed to be thinking it over a minute before he nodded. "I'll go if Sue Ellen will."

"Well, of course she will. Why don't you pick her up a quarter to seven? It'll take a good ten minutes, maybe more, to get out to the house. You do know where it is, don't you, Bud? If not, I could have Fletcher get you a set of directions."

Sue Ellen stood openmouthed. What was wrong with these two? Why, they were making plans for her right under her nose without even bothering to consult her.

"No, that's all right. I know where it is," Bud said. "Would you like me to bring anything?"

"I appreciate that," Dottie Jean said, "but do you think maybe I could get back to you on that? I'm not sure, but I think Fletcher's going to handle the menfolk. He's set on grilling even though I told him he'd probably freeze."

"You never can tell." Bud shook his head. "Around here it's just as likely to be warm as it is to be cold." He turned his attention to Sue Ellen. "Be sure and bring a sweater."

"Bring a sweater?" Sue Ellen nearly took off a hunk of Fanny's bangs before she got control of the scissors and set them down. "Did either of you think I might have some say in this?"

Dottie Jean reached over to give Sue Ellen a hug. "Not particularly, hon." Dottie Jean pulled away to wink at her. "Don't forget to bring that fudge you made for the last Bible study meeting. And if you remember, bring the recipe, too."

"Oh, I'd love a copy, too." Fanny winked. "As I recall, it was quite tasty."

Sue Ellen held up both hands. "As a matter of fact, I—"

"I'm sorry to interrupt, Sue Ellen," Dottie Jean said, "but I've got need of the deputy. Bud, I wonder if you might help me with something?" She pointed to the door. "I came all the way into town to fetch some things for the party, and now I've realized I should have brought Fletcher along to help me load them into the car. If you're not too busy, would you mind?"

Sue Ellen watched speechlessly as Dottie Jean led Bud toward the door. "I never said I'd go," she said to Bud's retreating back.

"You never said you wouldn't, either," Fanny said.

"Well, I'll take care of that." She went back to styling Fanny's curls.

"While you're at it," Fanny said, "why don't you take care of telling Sassy Hatchett that we don't need her meatballs this year? Do you realize that last year the woman actually mixed in that crazy bait mix of hers by accident? I swear I thought we'd all be sick, although that goofy fiancé of hers asked for seconds. There's no accounting for love, I always say."

Once again the image of Fanny dressed in bridal gear loomed large. Or rather, extra large.

"No, Miss Fanny, you're right about that. There sure isn't any accounting for love, is there?"

When Dottie Jean called to say Bible study was canceled that night, Sue Ellen lost her chance to get a group opinion on what she should do. Of course, she already knew Dottie Jean and Sassy's thoughts on the topic.

She waited until her last customer of the day had left, then called Berta. She barely got the details of her dilemma out before Berta responded.

"Go."

"But you don't understand, Berta."

"I don't need to understand. Just go. What do you have to lose?"

Several times over the next two days, Sue Ellen thought about marching over to the sheriff's office and telling the deputy she'd made other plans, but she never did. Yesterday, she blew her chance to say no when Bud called to ask if she might be ready a half hour early.

Instead, Sue Ellen had not only said yes, but also carried on small talk about fishing and the Calista Cougar football team for a full five minutes before her next customer—Sassy, of all folks—came in.

"Dottie Jean said I won a free cut and curl." She handed Sue Ellen an envelope that read "Cut and Curl Coupon Is Invalid if Envelope Is Opened" in what looked like Dottie Jean's handwriting.

"All right, then," Sue Ellen said. "Go ahead and put that cape on. I think I'll have some peach tea. Want some?"

She scurried to the kitchenette and tore open the envelope. "Fletcher and I are paying for the services, so give Sassy the works. Love, Dottie Jean."

Sue Ellen giggled as she returned with two glasses of sweet tea. "You got it wrong, Sassy," she said. "You didn't just win a hairdo. You got the works."

Once she finished with Sassy's cut and curl, she decided to offer the woman a complimentary pedicure. What got into her,

Sue Ellen didn't know, but an hour later Sassy Hatchett left the Rhonda-Vous House of Beauty a changed woman.

Well, at least her toes were changed.

After Sassy left, Sue Ellen tried to call Bud back, but he didn't answer. Before she knew it, she'd baked two pans of fudge—one with nuts and the other without—and had picked out an outfit that said "Well groomed but not interested."

Of course, by the time Bud arrived, she'd ditched the plain Jane outfit for one that made her feel a bit more festive, and she'd even taken the curling iron to her stick-straight hair. At the last minute, she added a few highlights around her face as well.

There was no reason for a woman not to look her best even if she didn't really want to be there. Besides, she was Dottie Jean's friend, and as such, she needed to be present.

"This has nothing to do with Bud Briggs," she said to the image in the mirror. "I'm going to think of this as two friends sharing a ride. Next year, I'll drive."

That idea made her feel better, so she decided to put a little more effort into her shoe and purse selection. When the choice was made, she hummed the teddy bear song while she hobbled into the kitchen to get the fudge ready to transport.

Sue Ellen massaged her sore hip as she crimped the corners of the foil around the fudge with nuts and stacked it atop the other container. Although she'd never admit it to Bud, she had done herself a bit of bodily damage in her slide down the old ladder.

With bruises in places that no one would see, Sue Ellen felt safe in pretending she was fine. Besides, it wasn't as if she planned to do anything other than sit and count the hours until she could go home.

When the squad car pulled up behind the Rhonda-Vous House of Beauty, Sue Ellen reached for her purse. She'd just about gathered her fudge and her wits when Bud knocked on the back door.

Rather than flowers, he was carrying the mended ladder. "You want me to leave it out here, or should I bring it inside?"

"Right there's fine." Sue Ellen grabbed her purse and the fudge with nuts. "How about you get the other one?" she said as she held the door open for Bud.

He slipped past, leaving the scent of Ivory soap in his wake. "We'd better put these in the trunk," he said. "We're picking up another passenger."

Sue Ellen settled into the front seat and waited until Bud slipped behind the wheel. "Who else is riding with us?"

"The pastor," Bud said. "For some reason, Fletcher said I wasn't to tell a soul."

The reason for the secrecy became clear when they arrived at Dottie Jean and Fletcher's place.

Chapter 5

Sassy and Wendell are getting married? Does Sassy know this? She sure didn't mention it when I was—"

"Hush, Sue Ellen, or Sassy'll hear you. She thinks she's getting gussied up because she's meeting Wendell's long-lost cousin tonight. If we told her Wendell's cousin is also the judge who signed the waiver on the waiting period for the marriage license, she'd probably have a hissy fit and run for the hills."

"I've seen Sassy run, sweetheart. You could catch her." Fletcher sidled up to his bride and planted a kiss on her cheek that made Dottie Jean blush.

"Behave yourself," she said. "Can't you see we've got company?"

He smiled at Sue Ellen. "Happens every time I'm in a room with her. Would you forgive this old man's silliness?"

Sue Ellen chuckled despite the searing sense of loss she felt in the presence of this happy couple. "Well, of course. You can't blame a man in love." She looked past Fletcher to Dottie Jean.

"What I don't understand is how you got around the blood test requirement. Surely Sassy would have figured that one out."

Dottie Jean ducked her head. "Not if she thought she was giving blood for the troops."

Fletcher winked. "She felt so bad about telling that fib to Sassy that she gave Sassy that 'gift certificate' to your salon, then sent a sizable donation to the USO in Sassy's honor. I believe she gave a donation to the church, too."

"Well," Dottie Jean said, "I just couldn't figure out another way around it. I wanted her to look her best for her—"

"Anyone want to explain to me why I'm the only one who looks like a fool in this room?" Sassy's voice beat her through the door. A moment later she barged into the kitchen and stopped short, her off-white beaded dress catching the light in a thousand tiny sparkles. "And while you're at it, would you tell me how a body can walk in shoes like this?" She held up one foot to show off a strappy sandal with a kitten heel in a matching color. "It's bad enough you and Berta made me get gussied up for those weddings of yours, Dottie Jean. But this is just too much."

"Oh, those shoes are adorable," Sue Ellen said. "Did you get them here in town?"

"Who knows what torture chamber they came from? Dottie Jean loaned them to me."

"Something borrowed," Dottie Jean whispered to Sue Ellen, who nodded.

Ever the gentleman, Fletcher stepped forward to take Sassy's hand. "The only fool in this room is me. I do believe I've married the wrong woman. You look absolutely lovely."

"Oh, hush that fool talk, Fletcher Cameron. There's not a person in Calista who doesn't know you haven't spared another woman so much as a glance since you caught sight of Dottie Jean."

"Well now, you got me there, Sassy." Fletcher nodded toward the back door. "I think I'll go check on that project I've got out in the garage."

"Wendell," Dottie Jean whispered to Sue Ellen.

"Did you say something, Dottie Jean?" Sassy asked.

Their hostess straightened her spine as her husband escaped out back, where Bud was standing guard over the steaks. "I was just saying how nice it's going to be to have all of you in our new home." She fingered the diamond on her hand. "God has blessed me so. I just want the same for you."

Bud appeared at the back door, a platter of steaks in his hands. "Where do you want this, Dottie Jean?" She relieved him of the plate, and he hightailed it back outdoors.

"That's a fine man there, Sue Ellen," Dottie Jean said. "I'm glad you two decided to come to the party together."

"I didn't have much choice, now, did I?"

"Oh, I don't know about that." Dottie Jean touched her sleeve. "You sure do look pretty for someone who didn't have a choice. Is that outfit new? I'm sure Bud noticed how pretty you look."

"Dottie Jean, you're wasting your time. I'm letting the Lord find my husband for me, and so far He hasn't mentioned anything about Bud Briggs." Sue Ellen paused. "Besides, the whole town knows he's headed for the FBI."

Sassy placed her freshly manicured hand on her shoulder.

"Hon, is this about your daddy? Are you thinking about how he was gone all the time? Sue Ellen, your daddy was a hero."

"She's right, Sue Ellen," Dottie Jean said. "He spent his life doing what the Lord called him to do. Thanks to him, who knows how many bad men are behind bars?"

The lump in her throat kept Sue Ellen from responding. Thankfully, the doorbell announced Berta and Matthew's arrival, effectively changing the subject and lightening the mood.

On their heels were a group of folks, including Grandpa and Fanny. Despite her less-than-cover-girl figure, the owner of the local grocery store looked absolutely stunning. Sue Ellen shivered as the door opened wide to admit the guests.

Before she could think hard on that, her grandfather enveloped her in a bear hug. "You here alone, Susie-Q?"

"You know I'm not, Grandpa." She held him at arm's length. "I'd consider it a personal favor if you and the guys would find someone besides Bud to tease."

"Oh, come on, honey. Bud's a good sport."

She gave him a no-nonsense look. So did Fanny.

"That's right, Gus," Fanny said. "That poor deputy's got trouble enough without you fellows adding to it."

"Thank you, Miss Fanny." Sue Ellen looked up to see Bud standing nearby, then quickly returned her attention to Fanny. "I'm really glad you're here with my grandpa."

"I didn't know old Gus had such good sense, actually." Sassy's eyes narrowed. "Did you have to pay her to go on a date with you, Gus?"

"Very funny, Sassy. Speaking of dates, where's Wendell?"

Sassy glanced around the room. "Now that you mention it, I haven't seen him yet."

"Looks like my buddy may have regained his senses." Gus winked at Sue Ellen. "There's hope for him yet."

"Hush, you old fool," Sassy said, "or next Thanksgiving you can roast your own turkey."

Dottie Jean clapped her hands, commanding the attention of those gathered in the room. "Fletcher and I would like to welcome you all to our home."

Bud slid over to stand beside Sue Ellen. They exchanged looks before Dottie Jean continued.

"If you would all follow Fletcher and me, there's something waiting in the backyard. Or rather, there's some*one* waiting in the backyard."

Sue Ellen fell in line behind her grandpa with Bud at her side. Sassy brought up the rear, complaining with every step of her borrowed shoes.

"Why in the world are we traipsing back to the pasture when Dottie Jean and Fletcher have a perfectly lovely. . . Oh my word. Wendell, is that you?"

Chapter 6

Wendell stood in the center of a gazebo that had been draped in white tulle tied with white ribbons. How Dottie Jean had kept this a secret, Sue Ellen had no idea.

"It is, my love. Come join me."

"Don't be silly. It's too cold. Now come on inside."

"It's warm over here." He held out his hands to Sassy. "I promise. Fletcher was kind enough to install heaters. I'm not sure if it's that or the fact I'm looking at you, but I am positively overheated."

Sue Ellen started to giggle, and Bud grasped her wrist. "Shh," he said, much to her surprise. "Let them have their moment."

Sassy stood her ground, hands on her hips. "Wendell Meeks, come down from there this instant. You're going to catch your death out here." She paused. "Say, is that Reverend Jordan up there?"

Wendell stepped to the edge of the platform and stared his

bride-to-be down. It was all Sue Ellen could do not to giggle at the formerly meek Wendell's new me-Tarzan attitude.

"Sassy Hatchett, get up here and marry me this instant before I change my mind."

The pastor stepped to the edge of the platform, Bible in hand. "It is, and I'm prepared to conduct a wedding unless Wendell changes his mind."

Sassy met Sue Ellen's gaze and shrugged. Her blue-gray eyes twinkled. "Guess it's a good thing you painted my toes this afternoon. Looks like I'm getting hitched."

"It sure looks like it." The image of Sassy swam with the tears that threatened—tears of both joy and disappointment. Never had she been so certain she'd never know such happiness as she saw on Wendell's and Sassy's faces.

"Oh, honey, what's wrong?"

Sue Ellen gave Sassy a hug. "I'm just so happy for you."

Sassy returned the hug. "It'll be your time someday soon." She reached for Bud's shoulder and gave him a shake. "If you'd worry less about your vitamins and that blasted FBI job and more about the woman God put right under your nose, maybe—"

"Sassy!"

"Coming, Wendell, honey." She paused. "Wait, I can't get married without my son and daughter here."

"I'm right here, Mom." Tilly pressed past Sue Ellen to give her mother a one-armed embrace. With her other hand, she presented Sassy with a bouquet of daisies. "I brought the flowers."

"Daisies." Sassy looked up at Tilly. "Did you do that on purpose?"

"Sure did." Tilly winked at Sue Ellen. "I figure Daddy's smiling at the two of you. You know all he ever wanted was for you to be happy." She paused. "You are happy, aren't you?"

"I am, honey," she said. Then her expression turned wistful. "I just wish your brother was here. 'Course, if you all told him New Year's Eve, he'll most likely turn up round Easter Sunday."

"That was the old Tucker. This one's here right on time to walk you down the aisle."

Sue Ellen watched a handsome man with his mother's eyes lift Sassy a full foot off the ground before setting her down. In between a couple of "put me downs" and one well-placed swat on the back of Tucker's head, Sue Ellen thought she noticed a tear as it fell from Sassy's eyes.

When she quit complaining, Sassy held her son at arm's length. "You don't look any different, Tucker Hatchett."

"Probably not," the young man replied, "since it's mostly on the inside. Although I did land a job with Bobby Jim Penty's pit crew."

"Bobby Jim Penty? The NASCAR driver from Biloxi?"

"That's right, Mama." Tucker smiled, and Sue Ellen realized he now looked even more like his mother.

"Well, hallelujah. Finally, some use for all those tires in the backyard."

"Mama, that's not funny," he said, although his face clearly showed he thought the opposite. "One of these days when you're not busy getting married, I'll tell you all about it. Right now, let's get you hitched."

The wedding was beautiful, and afterward, Sue Ellen

couldn't be sure who cried harder, the bride or the groom. She shed a few tears, too, and strangely into Bud's handkerchief. He'd handed it to her midway through the part where Sassy stumbled over the phrase "love, honor, and obey."

The I do's were quickly followed by Dottie Jean's statement that a proper feast awaited the group inside. It took two announcements to break the lip-lock between Sassy and Wendell.

The wedding dinner consisted of a variety of meats, courtesy of Fletcher and Bud's grilling expertise, along with more vegetables, breads, and side dishes than the law should have allowed. Dessert was Sue Ellen's fudge topped with Tilly's homemade mocha ice cream. For those who were more calorie conscious, Dottie Jean provided fresh fruit and fat-free vanilla yogurt.

As far as Sue Ellen could tell, Bud was the only one who partook of the low-fat fare.

So as not to have her date—and oh, how she hated to call Bud that—cast aspersions on her choice of dessert, Sue Ellen took her fudge and mocha concoction back outside. The gazebo beckoned, so she found a hiding spot behind the yards of tulle and ribbon that swayed in the fresh evening breeze.

So, she thought as she stabbed at the mound of molten sugar, *another year come and gone almost.* Sue Ellen checked her watch.

A quarter to ten.

One hour and fifteen minutes until the ball landed in Times Square. Another hour after that until the city fathers set off the fireworks on the riverbank, signaling the coming of the new year to Calista.

Sue Ellen looked down at the dessert plate. "Guess I'd better chew slow."

Heavy footsteps echoed on the steps. "Is there room in there for me?"

" 'Course there's room, Bud," Sue Ellen said in an exasperated tone. "Dessert hasn't gone to my hips yet. Most of it's still on my plate."

"I didn't reckon it had." Bud peered around the wall of tulle and ribbons. Sure enough, his plate held a decent smattering of pineapple chunks, orange slices, and pieces of apple and banana.

Figures.

Then she saw it. A single chocolate-covered almond wobbling dangerously close to the remains of a dab of fat-free yogurt.

"Why, Bud Briggs." She pointed to his plate. "Is that what I think it is?"

He had the decency to look surprised. "Wonder who put that on my plate?"

"Here, let me help you with that." She reached for the offending chocolate delicacy only to be stopped when Bud beat her to it.

Bud popped the almond in his mouth. "That's what you call removing the evidence."

Chapter 7

The sugar in that one bite would set him back for a week. Bud was about to calculate the calorie content when a strange thing happened.

He just didn't care.

Try as he might to berate himself for allowing a sugary treat into his regimen, he couldn't. This was certainly a new state of affairs.

New and distinctly uncomfortable. But then, Sue Ellen made him feel uncomfortable on a regular basis. Why should today be any different?

"What's wrong, Bud? Adding up how many extra hours you'll have to spend in the gym tomorrow?"

"Tomorrow I run. It's not a gym day." Bud knew by the look on Sue Ellen's face that this was the wrong answer. He tried again. "Besides, I already know it will add precisely thirteen minutes and seventeen seconds."

This answer seemed to do the trick, as Sue Ellen went back to gazing off in the direction of the river. It was dark, too dark to see anything but the slightest glint of moonlight on the slow-moving water, but she seemed to be studying it intently. Every once in a while, she would pause from her contemplation to take a bite of the ice cream–covered chocolate goo.

On one of those occasions, Bud decided to break the silence. "Nice wedding."

She made one of those *humph* sounds that let a body know disagreement was in the air. Bud waited a minute to see if she'd elaborate.

When she bit into another piece of fudge, he decided to press on with polite conversation. "Sure do like New Year's Eve. It always feels good to go out with the old and in with the new."

Another *humph*, this time a bit louder.

Bud gave her a sideways look and took her expression as a challenge. If Sue Ellen Caldwell thought she could get away with wallowing in a foul mood on New Year's Eve, she had another thing coming.

Slowly he developed his plan. With a skill and precision gleaned from his years in the Marine Corps, Bud gripped his fork and aimed for a particularly appealing slice of pineapple on the easternmost edge of his plate. At the last second, his hand changed directions, and he snagged a bite of Sue Ellen's dessert.

Before she could complain, he'd swallowed it whole.

Sue Ellen's mouth gaped open, and she made a funny squeaking noise. "Bud Briggs," she finally managed, "I've known you since we were both knee-high to a grasshopper. I'd be willing to bet you haven't had that much chocolate since junior high."

Bud leaned back against the fancy fabric-covered post and savored the flavor of the forbidden treat. Sue Ellen was wrong, of course. Diet and exercise hadn't been the priority during his military days. Staying alive had.

He'd never tell her that, though. No sense in ruining a perfectly good night talking about the past. Time to lighten the mood and change the subject.

Setting his plate aside, Bud turned to face Sue Ellen. "So, are you making any resolutions this year, Sue Ellen?"

"I hate resolutions."

"Oh, come on," Bud said. "Resolutions are a good way to make positive changes."

"Give me a break, Bud." Sue Ellen finished the last of her dessert, then set her plate on the floor beside her. "I figure it this way. If I don't start the year telling myself what I can't do, I won't finish the year wishing I'd kept my resolutions." She looked up at him. "Make sense?"

"None whatsoever," he said.

She made that *humph* sound again.

On the outside, Sue Ellen Caldwell was as pretty as a woman could be. Inside, she had to be suffering the consequences of years of junk food. "What if I told you that you *could* keep your resolutions? Better yet, you give me one month and I'll promise you will *want* to keep them."

Sue Ellen chuckled. "I'd say you weren't nearly as smart as you look."

He pretended to be offended, then broke down and laughed. "Come on, Sue Ellen. What do you have to lose?"

"A month of good food?" Her eyes narrowed. "Stop looking at me like that."

Bud held his stare until she relented.

"All right." She held her hands up in a gesture of surrender, then stood and gathered her plate and fork. "I'll listen to what you have to say, but I'm not making any promises."

"That's all I ask." Bud trotted behind Sue Ellen until they reached the house, then he raced ahead to open the door for her.

"But not tonight." She glanced at him over her shoulder. "Tonight I'm going to enjoy myself, and if that means I shock you with chocolate-covered almonds and sweet tea, then so be it. The shop's closed on Monday. How about we meet over at the Catfish House for lunch on Tuesday and you can educate me?" She shook her head. "No, wait, let's make it a week from Tuesday. The first week of the year's always a busy one because I run my New Year, New Do special."

"All right," he said as the sound of the guests' chatter made conversation nearly impossible. "A week from Tuesday it is. You won't be sorry. I promise."

"I think I already am," she shouted, but her face belied her statement.

While Sue Ellen rejoined the party, Bud hung back to watch. There was something special tonight about the cranky beautician. More than just pretty, Sue Ellen Caldwell was, well, the word escaped him.

He pondered a few choices as Sue Ellen carried on an animated conversation with Berta and Matt. Elegant. Yes, that's the word his mama probably would have used. And fancy. Far too fancy for Calista, Mississippi.

The fact she'd returned to small-town life after so many years away perplexed him. The only family she had left here was Gus. If she felt as though she needed to take care of the old coot, she was most likely about to be relieved of her duties. At least, that's the way things appeared tonight.

As far as Bud could tell, Fanny hadn't left Gus's side all night.

When Fanny caught him staring and waved, he returned the gesture, then went back to thinking about Sue Ellen. It was possible surviving the hurricane last year in Biloxi caused her to want to come back and set down roots in Calista.

"I reckon staring's the next best thing to speakin', but I wouldn't recommend it long term." Wendell clamped his hand on Bud's shoulder. "Take it from me, Deputy. If you want a woman, you just have to pull yourself up by your bootstraps, head yourself in the right direction, and take no prisoners. *Semper fi*, Marine."

Bud looked down at the little man and tried to decipher his statement. Wendell, however, had already turned his attention to his bride. When the new groom wandered away toward Sassy, Bud could only watch in amazement.

If anyone doubted God was in control, they only had to look at the new Mr. and Mrs. Wendell Meeks. No one but the Lord Himself could have made that match.

Then there was the improbable match between Gus Caldwell and Calista's favorite grocer. Last Bud heard, Gus had declared himself a bachelor for life.

Showing up at the party of the year with Fanny meant one of two things: Either Gus had changed his mind, or Gus was up to something.

Bud would bet his badge the truth lay somewhere in the second option.

Chapter 8

"Hey, Bud, it's almost time." Gus slapped Bud on the shoulder and grinned. "You'd better not be thinkin' you're gonna pair off with my granddaughter for a kiss come midnight. You hear?"

"Until tonight, I would've said that's about as likely as you pairing off with Fanny." He grinned. "Say, what was it you said about never marrying again?" Bud gestured to Gus's date, who was currently in the kitchen with Dottie Jean, Berta, and Sue Ellen talking women talk. "Looks like you might have forgotten to tell someone. From what I hear, Fanny sure doesn't know."

"Did I hear my name?" Fanny waved from the kitchen. "Are you boys watching the clock?"

Gus gave Bud a look, then turned to face his date. "We're letting you women watch the clock."

"Don't count on me, Grandpa," Sue Ellen called. "Far as I'm concerned, midnight's just the time the clock chimes. It certainly doesn't mean anything special."

There was no missing the look Sue Ellen gave him. He

almost grinned when Dottie Jean swatted at Sue Ellen with a dish towel. Words were exchanged, but in a whisper. From their expressions, it looked as though Dottie Jean was explaining to Sue Ellen just how wonderful Bud Briggs was.

Or at least he hoped that was the case.

"How 'bout you and me take this conversation a little farther away from the females?" Gus headed for the front porch and motioned for Bud to follow.

Bud stepped into the brisk air and sucked in a deep breath. Somewhere between dessert and now, the temperature had plummeted. Tomorrow morning's run would be a good one, but he'd probably need a second layer under his sweatshirt.

Gus took up pacing and only stopped when the door closed behind them.

"Here's the thing, Bud," Gus said. "I figure I'm about done for in the wife department. I had me the best, and we spent a lot of good years together."

Unsure of the correct response, Bud kept it neutral. "I reckon you did."

"I'm not sayin' that a body don't get lonely. And my wife, rest her soul, she made me promise I'd marry up again if I felt the Lord a-leadin' me to it." He started pacing again. "I figured I could ease my way through what's left of my life here on earth without having to worry about any of this. Then the competition started."

"Competition?" Bud chuckled. "Over you?"

"Yeah, I know." Gus halted his pacing. "It don't make no sense, does it? The trouble all started when the new widow woman came to town."

"You mean Miz Ledbetter?"

"That's the one. Ever since she came to town, Fanny's been working twice as hard to get my attention. Guess she thinks she's got to best the sheriff's sister-in law." He shook his head. "Faeoni Ledbetter's a fine woman, but I don't cotton to her or Fanny as the next Mrs. Caldwell."

"If you're not looking, Gus, why're you here with Fanny?"

He shrugged. "I figure to nip this silliness in the bud. If I pay attention to Fanny, maybe Faeoni won't think she's got a chance and will drop out of the race. Once Fanny spends time with me, I figure she'll lose interest, too. I don't figure you'd know this, Bud, but I'm not the easiest man to live with."

It was Bud's turn to laugh. "Why're you telling me this?"

"Laugh all you want, young man, " Gus said. "Let's just see if you're laughing when it happens to you."

A shiver snaked down Bud's spine, and he wished for his jacket. "If that's all you're worried about, then we can go back inside."

"Maybe so, maybe not." He paused. "I figure if my granddaughter takes a shine to you and you don't cotton to settlin' down with her, you'll know how to handle the situation."

"Let me get this straight. You think I'm in danger of having your granddaughter fall for me?"

"I'd say it's more than a danger." Gus leaned closer. "She's here with you, ain't she?"

The old man looked so solemn, Bud almost bought it. Almost, but not quite.

Had it not been so cold out, he might have stuck around and argued the point for the craziness it was. Instead, he decided to cut to the chase.

Bud took a step back and shook his head. "All right. You got me, Gus. Where are the rest of the guys?"

"What're you talkin' about, Bud? It's just you and me out here."

"Sure it is." He gave Gus a sideways look. "You're ribbing me again, and this time I won't be fooled. You got me here by challenging me to ask your granddaughter to the party, then prodding my ego until I took the bait." He stomped his feet to get the circulation going. "I did that, but I shouldn't have. Sue Ellen and I are like matches and dry kindling."

Gus had the audacity to laugh. "I know that, boy. Been knowin' that since the two of you were knee-high to a grasshopper."

He did a quick check of the shrubs lest the others in Gus's crowd were hiding there. The sound of laughter from somewhere inside drifted past.

"I'm going back in, Gus, and I don't want to hear any more of this nonsense. You do whatever you want about Fanny and Miz Ledbetter, but leave me out of it. And as for Sue Ellen—"

"What about Sue Ellen?" a familiar female voice asked.

Bud cringed. Of course the woman would come outside just now.

"Nothing, darlin'," Gus said. "Bud and me were just jawin'. Say, what's this I hear about you takin' a tumble off my ladder?"

Sue Ellen approached and wrapped her arm around her grandfather's waist, then gave Bud a look. "Did you tell on me?"

"Of course not, girl. That boy's got more sense than to tell on you. He knows I'd have had your hide for being on the ladder at all." He looked down at Sue Ellen. "Where did you find that thing anyway?"

"It was leaning behind the garage." Sue Ellen frowned. "It's cold out here."

"I told you to wear your sweater," Bud said.

Another look and then Fanny came to the door.

"Gus, honey, are you planning to stay out there all night?"

Berta knocked on the window and gestured for Sue Ellen to come inside. Bud watched her go, helpless to find the words to keep her with him.

"One minute," Gus said. "Bud and me aren't quite finished with our business."

Gus's date looked disappointed, but she merely nodded and disappeared inside. When the door closed, Gus clamped his hand on Bud's shoulder.

"You've got to get hold of your senses, Bud Briggs, else you're going to ruin it for the rest of us bachelors."

"What're you talking about?" He watched Sue Ellen through the window as she appeared to be deep in conversation with Berta. My, but she looked pretty with her hair done up like that.

"Now that's exactly what I'm talkin' about. The last fella who went around with that hangdog look ended up married— *tonight*."

Bud swallowed hard. He tried to protest, but there wasn't any use. Gus had him caught, and good.

"I can't help it," he said. "That girl's been a thorn in my side long as I can remember."

Gus shook his head. "Well, all I got to say is fish or cut bait. Me, I'm going back inside."

The older man made good on his statement, and Bud followed. It was warm inside but crowded. He hated crowds.

The idea of leaving now appealed to him, but in reality it defeated the purpose. In order to make his exit, he'd have to take Sue Ellen and Reverend Jordan with him.

"Pondering the great mysteries of the universe?" Sue Ellen tapped him on the shoulder, then yawned. "I hate to be a party pooper, but I think I'm going to head home." She gestured to the hulk of a man standing near the door. "Bubba Lee said he'd be glad to run me home, since it's on his way."

Bud exchanged nods with the new owner of Bert's Dirts, a man who, back on the high school football team, threw blocks so Bud could run for touchdowns. Without a word to Sue Ellen, Bud made his way to the door and Bubba.

He shook hands with the burly fellow, making sure his handshake was every bit as strong as Bubba's. When Bud saw the big man wince, he released his grip.

"I 'preciate the offer to take Sue Ellen home," Bud said, "but I'll be seein' her home tonight." *You got a problem with that?*

Bubba caught on quick. "All right, then."

"All right, then," Bud added.

Reverend Jordan chose that moment to come between the men. Thankfully, he needed a ride home, and Bubba made his services available. "Yes," the reverend explained. "I promised my wife I'd get home in time to watch the ball drop in Times Square."

"I'm particular fond of watching that myself," Bubba added. "Might ought to get on out of here, then. I'd hate to miss it."

Bubba opened the door for the reverend, and just before following the preacher outside, he gave Bud a smile and a big thumbs-up.

Bud palmed his keys and checked his watch. Twenty minutes to twelve. If he hurried, he could have Sue Ellen home before the clock struck.

"You ready to go?"

"Oh no, you can't leave yet, Bud Briggs," Sassy said. "You've got to stay here until midnight."

"Who's leaving before midnight?" Dottie Jean grasped Sue Ellen's wrist. "Are you feeling ill? Have you caught cold?" She stepped back to give Sue Ellen the once-over. Apparently satisfied, Dottie Jean let her go. "Bud told you to bring a sweater."

Although he could have said more, Bud only nodded.

"I'm fine, Dottie Jean," Sue Ellen said. "Just a little tired. I thought I might—"

"Go home and watch the year change on television?" Dottie Jean shook her head. "I declare that's what's wrong with the two of you. Instead of watching life on television or from the inside of a squad car, why don't you start actually living it?"

Speechless, Bud turned to Sue Ellen. She seemed to be trying to form a protest but having no luck.

"Well, neither of you is going anywhere until the clock strikes midnight." Fletcher wrapped his arm around his bride's waist. "The squad car's blocked in by a half dozen vehicles." He shrugged. "Hazard of coming early, I guess."

It didn't take a specialist in criminal behavior to note the twinkle in his host's eyes. "You did that on purpose, didn't you, Fletcher?"

"I refuse to answer that question." The older man shrugged. "I suppose in your line of work, Deputy, that would be called taking the fifth."

Chapter 9

Sue Ellen looked around the room for a diversion and found none.

Bud jammed his keys back into the pocket of his jeans and rubbed his palms together. "Least we can do is make the best of it."

"S'pose so," she responded.

"Another fifteen minutes and I can take you home."

She shrugged. "Better figure on more than that, Deputy. You're assuming all these folks are leaving at midnight. What you don't know is that Dottie Jean's got a whole other course of desserts and appetizers to serve after the clock strikes. Oh, and don't forget the fireworks. I heard tell that Fletcher went all the way to Biloxi for them."

Bud groaned.

"Hey, a girl could be insulted by a man who's that anxious to leave her company."

His expression softened. "I could say the same for me. That is, for you." He shook his head. "What I mean is, you sure were in a hurry to get home. A guy might be insulted by that, too."

Sue Ellen chewed on that statement for a minute. "Fair enough. How about we make the best of the rest of the evening?"

Bud looked around at the milling crowd and saw few prospects for enjoying himself. "What do you have in mind?"

Her smile was contagious as her gaze swept the room. "Since Bubba and the reverend left, looks like we're the only ones who aren't a couple. What say we find a television somewhere in this place and watch the ball drop?"

"Oh, I don't know, Sue Ellen. I doubt Dottie Jean wants us wandering around her home."

She grabbed his wrist and dragged him toward the nearest exit, a hallway that led away from the noise of the crowd. "Which door shall we try?" she whispered as she looked at doors on the right, then on the left. "How about that one?"

Bud stopped short and refused to budge as Sue Ellen tried the first door on the left. "Have you lost your mind?"

Turning the knob, she pushed the door open to find a linen closet. "Hush. If you're not going to help, at least keep quiet."

She tried another door and found what looked like a guest bedroom. On the third attempt, she hit the jackpot. A cozy den, done up in dark wood paneling, beckoned. A leather sofa dominated the center of the room, while a large flat-panel television sat above the fireplace.

"Bud, get in here."

Sue Ellen stepped inside the room and inhaled deeply of the vanilla scent, a fat white candle sitting on the oversized coffee table being the obvious culprit. Beside the candle was what looked like a remote control for the television.

"Any idea how to. . . Bud?" She retraced her steps to find the deputy still standing in the hallway. "What are you *doing*?"

"You're trespassing, Sue Ellen, and I won't be a part of—"

Before he could complete the sentence, Sue Ellen had him inside the room with the door shut tight. "Now all we need to do is figure out how to get this thing working." She thrust the remote in his direction, but he refused to take it. "Come on, Bud. Loosen up. Do you honestly think Dottie Jean and Fletcher will care that we're watching their television instead of standing around out there making small talk?"

"I don't know," he said slowly. "But I just don't think. . . Say, is that a flat screen? Is that surround sound?"

Sue Ellen chuckled as she handed him the remote, then led him to the sofa. "Sit here, techno dude, and fire that puppy up. Dick Clark's not getting any younger."

Three clicks of the remote and they were watching a sports wrap-up of the evening's bowl games. Sue Ellen grabbed for the remote, but Bud was too fast for her. He switched from the sports talk to a John Wayne movie.

"Oh man, this looks amazing in HD," he said as he made himself comfortable on the sofa. "I wish we'd thought to bring popcorn."

"Hey," Sue Ellen said as she made another reach for the remote, "you're going to make us miss the big moment. Cut that out."

"Oh, all right," he said, "but I don't think you fully understand what I'm giving up so that you can watch that show. Don't you realize this movie is the Duke's personal favorite?"

She gave him an I-don't-care look, then made a grab for the

remote. He easily dodged her and turned the channel to the golf channel.

"Bud!"

He gave her a wicked grin as he clutched the remote to his chest. "Quiet, Sue Ellen, or we'll be found out."

"Why, Bud Briggs, that was spoken like a true criminal."

His brows shot up in mock offense. "Excuse me, ma'am," he said in an exaggerated drawl, "but last time I checked, I was the law around here."

Before she could protest, Bud switched the channel to the correct program. Sue Ellen settled into the cushy leather sofa and watched a popular actor and his on-screen costar freezing on a balcony overlooking Central Park while chatting about their latest romantic comedy. While half listening to the staged banter, Sue Ellen cast a furtive glance at her companion.

The flickering light of the television cast a myriad of colors across his face, and the light of the single lamp cast soft gold highlights into his already golden hair. While her fingers itched to improve the straight lines of the barber's cut, she also wondered how the blond strands would feel to the touch.

He obviously bought his hair products at the grocery store, and whatever he used did not have a good conditioner in it. Probably one of those shampoo-and-conditioner-in-one items. Given the right cut and a deep conditioning, the deputy would be drop-dead gorgeous.

Who was she kidding? He already was.

If only he had a sense of humor. Sue Ellen sighed again. There was nothing more tragic than a man who'd forgotten how to have fun.

A commercial featuring a talking lizard came on, and Bud chuckled. He always did have a nice smile.

Lord, You've thrown Bud and me together since we were just kids. Why is it that I feel like I'm just now seeing him for the first time?

What would it take to keep Bud Briggs in Calista? She sighed. Certainly more than the promise of a romance with her.

Much as she hoped she could change the situation, unless the Lord intervened, Bud Briggs would be headed out of Calista as soon as he heard back from the FBI Academy. And thanks to a recommendation from her daddy, he was all but certain to get in.

"Thanks, Dad," she muttered.

"What's that?" Bud hit the MUTE button. "Did you say something?"

"No, nothing." *At least nothing I meant for you to hear.*

The New Year's Eve program came back on, and Bud clicked off the MUTE button. "You're not old enough to start talking to yourself, and I'm not deaf," she thought he said.

"What's that?" She caught his grin as it disappeared.

"Nothing at all. Just making an observation." He pointed to the television. "Look, isn't that the guy from. . ."

Bud kept talking, and Sue Ellen did her best to give the on-screen antics her full attention. Something about the man sitting less than an arm's length away kept her thoughts skittering in two directions.

"Five more minutes," Bud said without removing his gaze from the screen.

She didn't reply.

"Any last-minute resolutions you want to make?" He swiveled to view her profile. "Other than a full month of following my every command."

Butterflies crashed about in Sue Ellen's stomach, and she clasped her trembling hands. Then good sense took over. Much as she wanted to be a blob of simpering emotions, she did have her pride.

"As I recall, I didn't commit to anything. I said I'd listen to what you had to say over lunch."

He shrugged. "Fair enough. But don't think you're ordering the fried catfish."

Sue Ellen worked up a look of pretend anger. "I predict by the end of the month I'll have you eating fried catfish and begging for more."

Another chuckle. "How about we make this an official challenge?" He leaned forward. "One month is all I ask. After that you'll thank me."

"Well, I don't know." She gave him a sideways glance. "What's in it for me? Seems like you're the one who benefits, given the fact you'll be spending quality time with me."

"You do have a point." This time his grin lasted much longer. "What did you have in mind?"

"My first inclination is to require you to submit to my scissors and do something with that hair. I mean, honestly, Bud. Nobody ever died from a deep-conditioning treatment." She held up her palms to silence his protest. "However, I've come up with something slightly—and only slightly, mind you—more valuable to your personal growth in the new year."

He quirked a brow. "Oh? What's that?"

"I'm going to teach you how to have fun, Bud Briggs, and if you don't agree to one month under my complete command, I'm backing out of my end of the deal."

"Hey, I'm fun." The deputy actually looked a bit wounded.

Sue Ellen tried to soften her words with a sensitive look. "Name the last time you did something just for the pure fun of it." Before he could speak, she shook her head. "And exercising and deer hunting don't count."

He opened his mouth twice but said nothing. For a second she thought he might have a response.

"And working on cars doesn't count, either."

"Not fair. Who's making these rules, anyway?"

"I am." She squared her shoulders. "You got a problem with that?"

"If it gives me a chance to improve your diet and health, no, I guess I don't. Still, I think I'm a fun guy."

She gave him a look that told him exactly how fun she thought he was. "Stop stalling, Deputy. Fish or cut bait."

It didn't take him but a second to grasp her hand. "Deal," he said. "On the condition that anything you ask of me isn't illegal, immoral, or fattening."

"Bud Briggs, you know me better than that."

"All right, strike the first two." His eyes narrowed. "But I'm sticking to the third one."

"No deal," she said. "I refuse to put caloric restrictions on fun. Shake on it or forget it."

On TV, the ball began its slow descent to the cheers of the crowd in Times Square.

"No restrictions," he said slowly. "All right, but that goes

326

both ways, you know." Bud slowly held out his hand to shake.

"All right," she said as she met him halfway. Palm to palm they sat, with only the glow of the magnificent crystal globe to light the room.

On the other side of the closed door, the countdown began. "Ten, nine, eight. . ."

Bud tightened his grip on her fingers.

"Seven, six, five. . ."

"Happy New Year, Bud," Sue Ellen whispered.

"Four, three, two. . ."

"Happy New Year, Sue Ellen."

And then he shook her hand.

Chapter 10

H e shook your hand?" Dottie Jean swiped at the air with her dish towel. "I just don't believe it."

Sue Ellen perched on the stool nearest the cash register while Dottie Jean, filling in for Jenny, counted change. A half hour from now, the Catfish House would be full of customers. For now, however, the dining room was blissfully empty.

"I know. I thought. . . Well, that is, I hoped. . ."

"You hoped he'd come out of whatever fog he's been in since high school? Good luck, Sue Ellen. That man's near to impossible to figure out."

The door jangled and shut behind Berta. "What're you doing in town, honey?" Dottie Jean called. "I thought you'd be gone the rest of the week."

"We were miserable worrying about what was going on back home." She shrugged. "I had no idea how attached I'd become to those sweet folks. It's good to be back to our family, unique as it is."

After exchanging hugs with her friend, Sue Ellen climbed back onto her stool to sip her coffee. "Ever wonder how the Lord managed to decide that you'd be the one to end up married to a man who came with a whole houseful of elderly folks?"

Berta chuckled. "God's all over that for sure, because I never would have dreamed it. To think I can teach music all day and come home to a husband I love is amazing enough, but to know we're providing a home for sweet older folks who had nowhere to go after the hurricane is just beyond belief."

Dottie Jean set a steaming cup of coffee in front of Berta, then leaned her hip against the counter. "We were just talking about how Sue Ellen and Bud rang in the New Year."

Berta's brows shot up. "Do tell, honey. Did he kiss you?"

Sue Ellen sighed. "No, he shook my hand."

Her friend nearly choked on her coffee. "Stop teasing me," she said when the coughing fit subsided.

"Oh, she's serious," Dottie Jean said. "That boy's a blame fool, and I, for one, would like to give him a piece of my mind. Why, for once I wish Sassy were here instead of in Hawaii with Wendell. She'd have just the right thing to say about a man who settles for a handshake with a pretty girl instead of a New Year's kiss."

Berta chuckled.

"What's so funny?" Sue Ellen asked.

"I just had an image of Sassy in her overalls with a grass skirt and coconut top on over them." She dissolved into a fit of giggles. "Oh, and Wendell in a pair of flowered swim trunks."

"His trunks were a solid color, thank you very much, and I, for one, wore a string bikini under my grass skirt."

"Sassy!" Dottie Jean laughed out loud. "Don't even ask me to look at those vacation pictures."

"As if I'd ask you. Some things are just private, you know?" Sassy gave Berta a squeeze, then enveloped Sue Ellen in a hug. "Now what's this I hear about you getting a handshake instead of a New Year's kiss?"

"Bud shook her hand, Sassy. Can you feature it?"

Sassy lowered herself gingerly onto the bar stool beside Sue Ellen, then winced. "Girls, I never did know a sunburn to hurt like this one."

"But you don't look sunburned," Berta said.

"That's cause I put lotion on every place I could reach. Guess I missed a spot or two." She paused to take a sip from her mug, her face a mask of innocence. "That's good coffee, Dottie Jean. Not like that sissy stuff my Tilly serves." She slapped herself on the forehead, as if to remind herself. "You know, I've got to stop talking like that. Tilly's a sweet girl—and I must confess even her coffee's improved since she gave her heart to the Lord."

"Amen to that," Sue Ellen agreed. "I tried her Cinnamon Streusel Delight. It's my personal favorite."

"She is a good girl." Sassy's lips turned up in a smile. "And the proof's in the pudding. Did I tell you that she's offered the use of her place for the youth on Sunday morning? She told me on the way in from the airport that Reverend Jordan was thrilled with the idea."

"That's wonderful," Sue Ellen said. "Especially with the way our youth group is growing."

"I agree." Sassy's lower lip began to quiver. "And that Fred. . ." She shook her head and wiped away a tear. "He's been the next best thing to sliced bread for that daughter of mine. I do hope he proposes soon."

"Why, Sassy Hatchett!" Sue Ellen put a hand over her mouth, realizing her mistake. "I mean *Meeks*. Sassy Meeks." She let out a little giggle. "I thought you were opposed to the idea of Tilly marrying Fred because they scarcely knew each other."

"I'm over that." Sassy grinned from ear to ear. "I'm a firm believer in marriage. And besides"—she took another sip of the coffee—"I've already talked to Pastor Jordan. He thinks Fred would make a great youth pastor. Can you imagine my Tilly Mae, a youth pastor's wife?" She slapped her knee and let out a deep-throated laugh. "My goodness, would Tilly's father get a chuckle out of that?"

"I do believe he would," Sue Ellen agreed. "I do believe he would."

Sassy patted Sue Ellen's arm. "I didn't mean to get off on all that. Why, I'm not paying a bit of attention to what happened to you." She looked over at Dottie Jean. "You say this pretty girl only got a handshake at midnight?" When Dottie Jean nodded, Sassy frowned. "I'd say we ought to string him up, but likely as not, doing harm to a deputy sheriff is probably a bad idea."

"Oh, I don't know," Berta said. "I kind of like the idea."

"I've got a plan," Sue Ellen said, "so don't you worry."

"Do tell, child," Sassy encouraged.

"Excuse me, ladies," Dottie Jean said. "Much as we'd all like to teach our deputy sheriff a lesson, I suggest we keep it to ourselves."

"Why's that, Dottie Jean?" Sue Ellen asked.

She gestured toward the plate glass window advertising the best catfish east of the Mississippi. " 'Cause here he comes, crossing the street."

"Be nice, all of you." Sue Ellen took a deep breath and let it out slowly. "I've got this under control."

"Of course you do," Dottie Jean said as she shared a grin with Sassy.

"Just act natural," Sue Ellen said. "All of you. I mean it." That last comment she directed at Sassy, who looked to be trying to scoot off the stool.

"You don't want me to act natural, Sue Ellen." Sassy wiggled back onto the stool, then winced as she straightened her overall strap. "I just might say something to offend somebody." When the others giggled, she shrugged. "Hey, you never know."

"Please," Sue Ellen said. "Berta, talk to me about something. I don't want him to think I'm waiting for him."

"But you are," Sassy said.

"Stop it, Sassy." Dottie Jean reached under the counter to deposit a stack of cloth and silverware in front of Sassy. "Get a handful of those napkins and set to work. Me, I'm going back to my hush puppies."

By the time the bell on the diner door jingled, Sue Ellen and Berta were engrossed in a discussion of the latest Christian concert coming to Hattiesburg, while Dottie Jean was up to her elbows in hush puppy dough.

Sassy gave up the pretense of rolling napkins before the door shut. "Well, look who's here. It's Handshake Bud—I mean, Deputy Bud."

"How do, Miss Sassy?" He shook his head. "I guess I ought

to start calling you Mrs. Sassy."

"And I reckon I ought to start calling you—"

"Sassy!" Dottie Jean gave her a warning glare. "Can I speak to you back in the office? It's about that thing for church."

"That thing?" Sassy looked to Berta. "Do you know what she's talking about?"

"Excuse us, you two." Berta rose to help Sassy off her stool.

"Help yourself to some coffee, Bud," Dottie Jean called. "I'll be right back to take your lunch order."

Sue Ellen watched her friends disappear into the office. "No hurry, Dottie Jean. Bud and I have some work to do first."

"What's wrong with Sassy?" Bud asked. "She looks like she's limping."

"Sunburn." She waved away his questions with a sweep of her hand. "Don't ask."

Gathering up her purse and notepad, Sue Ellen led the way to a table in the corner farthest from the office. The three amigos were likely leaning against the door trying to listen. No sense in making it any easier for them.

Bud poured himself a cup of coffee and strolled across the dining room to join her. Sue Ellen's fickle heart jumped as the uniformed officer settled into the seat across from her.

"Shall we go over the rules?" Bud pulled a piece of folded paper from his shirt pocket. Her expression must have conveyed her feelings. "Honestly, Sue Ellen, this is for your own good." He paused to take a sip of coffee before sliding the paper across the table toward her. "It's only a few items, I promise."

Sue Ellen scanned the list, then looked back up at Bud.

"Diet, exercise, and plenty of sleep." She folded the paper. "Piece of cake." Giggling, she amended her comment. "Sorry. Piece of lettuce."

"I'm glad you think so." He pulled a second piece of paper from his pocket. "Here's the rest of the program."

This time she didn't accept the paper with quite so much anticipation. The page was divided into sections, each marked with detailed information on the topic. Notable were the sentences highlighted in bold.

"No more chocolate?" She tried not to look distraught, certain that would only amuse him. "Daily exercise?"

"Not every day. You get Sundays off, of course."

"Of course." Sue Ellen caught sight of Sassy peering around the office door and glared at her.

"That's the basics. I sent the rest to you on a spreadsheet in an e-mail attachment."

He looked so proud of himself that it was impossible to say a word about how she actually felt. Rather, she mumbled a brief thanks.

"So I suggest you take a few days to look over all the information, then we can get started."

Sue Ellen almost took him up on his offer of a grace period. Then she thought better of it. The sooner she got started, the sooner the whole crazy experiment would end.

"What about tomorrow?"

Bud shook his head. "I've already made the schedule out. We start Saturday."

"Ah, the schedule." *We'll see how long you stick to schedules, Bud Briggs.*

334

"I'll be there bright and early Saturday morning. Check the e-mail for running times."

"Running?"

"Yes, you know. Faster than walking, slower than racing? I suggest you drive into Hattiesburg and get fitted for a proper pair of running shoes. Believe it or not, it's not how cute they are that matters." He reached for the menu as Dottie Jean approached. "Two grilled catfish platters with vegetables and salad, oil and vinegar on the side, please." He paused. "And two waters."

Sue Ellen's eyes narrowed as she expelled a long breath. "*Fried* catfish platter, with french fries and a salad." She paused. "Ranch dressing. Oh, and sweet tea. Peach if you have it. And I think I'll wrap it up with a piece of your pecan pie, Dottie Jean."

"Sue Ellen." The warning in Bud's voice could not be mistaken. "You sure about that?"

She pretended to consider his question for a moment. "Bud's right, Dottie Jean. Let me change that."

Dottie Jean hid her grin behind her menu pad. "Go ahead," she finally said.

"All right, add ice cream, and don't forget to heat the pie. I love it when the homemade vanilla drips down the sides." Sue Ellen offered Bud a broad smile. "It's not Saturday yet."

Chapter 11

I t *cannot* be morning." Sue Ellen slapped at the ringing
sound, certain it was just some fool who got up with the
chickens but dialed as if still asleep.

"Wrong number," she muttered into her cell.

And yet the ringing continued.

"I've got to get Tilly to show me how to download a better
ring tone. This one sounds just like the alarm clock."

Sue Ellen buried the phone under one pillow and her head
under the other. That worked for a few seconds.

Then she realized that, however faint the sound, the phone
was still ringing. "Why isn't my voice mail picking up?"

She tossed the pillows off and sat bolt upright, then groaned
and fell back on the mattress. "The alarm clock."

Rolling onto her side, Sue Ellen hit the snooze button.
Then the phone rang for real.

"Hello?" she whispered.

"Good morning."

"Bud," she managed in a hoarse whisper. "Go away."

Throwing the sheet over her head, Sue Ellen waited for the click that signaled the deputy had given up. The silence on the other end lasted only long enough for Sue Ellen to close her eyes.

"We had a deal. Now get up, put on your running shoes, and meet me in front of the salon."

"Fine," she said as she threw off the sheet, "but I'll need some coffee first."

"After," he said firmly. "I'll treat you to a cup at Tilly's. I've penciled in a half hour to go over your plans for me, then another hour to implement them. Will that work?"

"Pencil this in, Bud. We run to Tilly's, grab a latte, then I run home and take a nice hot bubble bath."

"Look, I know you're a little cranky this morning. I'm sure you're used to sleeping in on Saturdays."

"Not likely, Deputy. You have no idea how early the seniors over at Berta's place get up. I'm usually out there by nine every other Saturday. This, however, was going to be my sleeping-in Saturday." She leaned over to lift the blinds a notch. "It's still dark outside. Are you kidding me?"

"Stop procrastinating, or you'll miss out on whatever torture you planned for me."

"All right." Sue Ellen rose and promptly tripped over the pillows. Thankfully she made a soft landing on the goose down.

"You all right?" Bud asked.

"No, Bud, I am not all right." She tossed the pillows back onto the bed. "It's dark. It's early. It's Saturday."

"Don't make me come up there after you, Sue Ellen Caldwell."

She hung up the phone, then ignored it when Bud called back. Five minutes later, she'd brushed her teeth, yanked her hair into a ponytail, and slipped into her new running shoes and matching jogging suit—all in the same shade of pink as her shop sign.

As an accent, she'd bought a top in a black and white leopard print and a matching thingie to put her house key in. The best surprise of all was the leopard print shoelaces she'd found to complete the ensemble.

Bud was partly right, she decided as she checked her image in the closet's full-length mirror. The shoes did fit nicely, but it didn't hurt that they were cute, too.

The look on Bud's face when she let herself out the front door of the shop was worth every penny she spent on the outfit.

"Before you can run," Bud said when he'd recovered his senses, "you have to stretch." He took her through a few stretches, then pointed her in the direction of Carp Court. "I figured we'd just run until we get tired and see how far we get."

"Fine by me, Deputy Briggs. I just hope you can keep up."

"It's chilly. Don't you think you ought to get some gloves?"

"Couldn't find any that matched." She shot out like an Olympic runner, then realized when Bud caught up that she probably ought to slow down.

"Couldn't find any that *matched*?" Bud shook his head. "Lord, I don't think I've ever dared to pray this, but could You give me patience? And fast?"

Pride kept Sue Ellen moving at the brisk pace until they reached a red light. Despite the fact there wasn't a single soul coming in either direction, Bud pushed the button and waited until the WALK sign turned green.

Tinges of orange faded to pink as the morning stole away the night. Sue Ellen watched the sun peer over the Catfish House and smiled. In all her years, she'd never taken notice of a sunrise until today.

"Sue Ellen, check your pace," Bud said. "Can you talk while running at this speed?"

"I don't know. Ask me something and see if I can answer."

She knew she'd have a hard time saying anything right now, but the combination of a rocket pace and a shortened night of sleep would surely have that effect on anyone.

"Tell me about Biloxi and why you're back."

His sideways glance told her the statement held more meaning than just a request for geographical information. Information she wasn't quite ready to give.

"Tell me why you're so all-fired excited about leaving Calista." She hurdled over a manhole, then veered toward the sidewalk that ran beside Tilly's. "Then maybe I'll tell you why I came back. That's what you really want to know, isn't it?"

Bud stopped short, and it took Sue Ellen a minute to notice. She doubled back to join him on the sidewalk. "What's wrong?"

He shook his head. "You took me by surprise with that question," he said. "How about I buy you that cup of coffee you wanted, and we can talk about the answer?"

A man wanting to talk? Now that had to be a first. Sue Ellen gladly let him steer her into the wacky interior of the Café Latte, Calista's best—and only—coffee shop.

"Well, good morning, you two. You're the first customers of the day." Tilly turned her attention to Sue Ellen. "You're up early. What happened? Lose a bet?"

While Sassy's daughter giggled, Sue Ellen scanned the menu. "Better than that, Tilly." She leaned toward the coffee shop owner. "I've been given a rare opportunity to actually change a man."

"Oh, really?" Tilly's many earrings glittered beneath the overhead beam. "How so?"

"Actually, it's me who has the rare opportunity." He gestured toward Sue Ellen. "She would like a cup of coffee, black. Give me the same."

Tilly looked at Sue Ellen. "No White Chocolate Cinnamocha with sprinkles?"

"I'm afraid not."

She looked doubtful. "All right, Sue Ellen, but please don't let it get out that you're giving up the sugar. It'd be bad for business." Tilly snapped her fingers. "Say, speaking of business, did you hear about the new bakery and sushi bar that's going in?"

"Yes, I believe Fanny mentioned something about it in the shop awhile back."

Setting two steaming fish-themed mugs on the counter, Tilly smiled. "Well, I bet she doesn't know this. You know my Fred, right?" When Sue Ellen nodded, Tilly continued, "It seems as though Faeoni Ledbetter, the new owner, decided she'd pack up and move back to Bogalusa. Something about there being a shortage of eligible men. Anyway, guess who's going to be the new manager?"

Sue Ellen took a wild guess. "Fred?"

Tilly clapped her hands. "Yes," she said with a glee that could only be achieved by a morning person. "Isn't that wonderful?"

She left Tilly with a hug and a brief prayer that not only would Fred succeed in his job at Loaves and Fishes, but the Lord would lead him into a youth ministry position at the church. A silent but obvious prayer was that the fellow would also have the good sense to realize the prize he had in Tilly and marry her before she changed her mind.

Sue Ellen took her sweaty self over to the table where Bud waited. "Biloxi?" he reminded her when she'd settled in.

"Biloxi." She sighed as she wrapped her fingers around the mug. "The truth is, I realized one day that while I was out looking for wings, what I really needed was roots."

Bud's confused look told Sue Ellen he didn't understand. "Translation: I missed home and realized everything I was looking for is right here." She let the statement hang between them for a moment. "Your turn, Deputy. Why is it you're set on leaving? What's the FBI got that's so much better than what's right here in Calista?"

Chapter 12

Bud gave her an answer outlining the fine history of the Federal Bureau of Investigation, then went on to add how his military training made him a perfect candidate for the job. It was a lame response, and she knew it, but he seemed to believe every word he said.

Later, when he walked her home, he avoided the topic, and she let him. Rather, they discussed the warming trend that had turned frigid into only moderately chilly almost overnight, the cost of pole beans at the farmers' market, and which John Wayne movie was really the best.

By the time they stopped in front of the Rhonda-Vous, he'd just about run out of words, or so it seemed. She fumbled with the silly key holder until Bud took pity on her. "Stick your foot up here."

She obliged, balancing on his shoulder as she raised her ankle within his reach. In no time, he had the contraption open and had placed the key in her hand.

Was it her imagination, or had he let his fingers linger a

bit longer than necessary when he placed the key in her palm? Maybe it was just wishful thinking.

"See you at three," he said, and of course he was back promptly at the appointed time.

Sue Ellen slipped into the passenger seat of the squad car and handed him a map before tossing an oversized garbage bag and a smaller grocery-sized bag into the back.

"Any questions?"

"Nope," he said as he studied the map. "Hey, that's the high school football field."

"Sure is," she said. "Nice breeze today?"

"Um, I suppose."

Before long, they were standing in the end zone of the Calista Cougar football team with a pair of red, white, and blue striped kites. "Do you remember how to fly a kite, Bud?"

He looked doubtful but soon followed her lead. While hers soared, however, his sank.

"Here, let me get yours flying. Take mine." She thrust the string in his hand, then took his kite and began to run. Soon she had Bud's kite floating at the same altitude as hers.

A swift breeze tangled their strings, causing both kites to plummet. In the process, Sue Ellen got caught in the string. She reached for Bud to stay upright, and they both fell.

Then the strangest thing happened.

Bud Briggs laughed. Not a polite chuckle or a guarded smile. He laughed out loud—a belly laugh that was contagious.

She heard that laugh again two days later when they played miniature golf. The next Saturday, when the alarm went off, Sue Ellen skipped the snooze button. A full week of jogging had done something to her. She actually had begun to *like* the dreaded activity. Not that she'd admit it to Bud, of course.

The following Saturday, Bud let her sleep until nearly seven before his wake-up call came.

By the end of the month, they'd settled into a routine. Running every morning but Sunday followed by coffee at the Café Latte. Three evenings a week, they piled into Bud's squad car and headed out to do such varied things as lying on their backs watching a meteor shower and bowling at the lanes in Hattiesburg. The fourth evening was always reserved for playing board games.

Today, however, their month together would come to an end. Bud's call came a full hour before their customary time. It was still dark when Sue Ellen met him at the curb in her favorite pink jogging suit and began to warm up.

"How about we skip our run today?"

Sue Ellen did a double take, then walked over to feel his forehead. "Are you sick or something?"

Bud captured her wrist and lifted her fingers, almost but not quite brushing them to his lips. "Our chariot awaits." He gestured to the vintage muscle car across the street.

"Is that your car from high school?" She wandered over to touch the black paint, noting how the color shone under the streetlamp. "It is, isn't it?"

"I've been working on restoring it." He nodded as he helped her into the passenger seat. "One of those things I'd been putting off until I met you. Well, until you and I struck this deal, that is."

A moment later, they were roaring past the Catfish House,

then away from town with Elvis's greatest hits playing on the oversized speakers. The sun was just rising and Elvis was finishing the Hawaiian love song with the funny words in the chorus when they reached a familiar spot.

"Bud, this is where we used to dig for worms."

"Sure is." He trotted around to help Sue Ellen out of the car, then reached into the backseat to retrieve a hamper and an oversized lantern. "Follow me."

"What, no jogging today?" she asked as she trotted behind him.

"Did you want to?" He glanced over his shoulder. "Because we can skip breakfast and run if you'd like."

"Are you kidding me?"

He stopped at the water's edge. "We had a lot of fun here, didn't we, Sue Ellen?"

"Yes," she said softly as she came to stand beside him, "we sure did."

A fish popped up in the moonlight, then hit the water with a splash, breaking the spell. Bud headed for the end of the pier, where he set the basket down and pulled out what looked like a tablecloth from the Catfish House.

Bud patted the place beside him, and Sue Ellen obliged. "I have a confession to make."

"You didn't cook breakfast?" Sue Ellen nudged Bud with her elbow. "I'm not surprised."

"No," he said slowly, "although you're right. Dottie Jean packed the breakfast for me. Biscuits and gravy, I believe."

"Why, Bud Briggs. You mean you're going to indulge in an artery-clogging breakfast? How positively amazing."

"No," he said slowly, "actually, you're amazing."

Well now, she never saw that coming. "Pass the gravy, Bud, and stop being silly."

"Not yet." He paused to reach for her hand. "You asked me a question a month ago, and I never did answer you."

The full moon dispelled any need for the lantern, a fact for which Sue Ellen was grateful. Moonlight definitely became Bud Briggs.

"You asked what the FBI had that was better than anything I had in Calista." Bud shifted positions to face Sue Ellen. "I gave you a whole line of nonsense about facts and figures. What I didn't count on was that you would show me there's something a whole lot more important than all that."

She glanced down at her hand, enveloped in the warmth of Bud's fingers. Just beyond the edge of the Biloxi, a slice of orange sun peeked through.

"What's that, Bud?" she whispered on a contented sigh.

"You," he said softly.

His response startled her. "Me?"

"You. I turned down the FBI, Sue Ellen, and I have to tell you it feels right." Bud moved closer. "Remember New Year's Eve?"

"Yes." Despite her good sense, she moved an inch in his direction. "I believe I do."

"Well, there was a moment there when I missed an opportunity."

Like a moth to the flame, Sue Ellen allowed Bud to draw her into his embrace. "Was there?" she managed.

"Oh yes. I believe it started something like this." He paused.

"Ten, nine, eight, seven. . ."

Time slowed, and the world seemed to stand still. A cool breeze blew across the pier, bringing with it the scent of morning. "Oh my," Sue Ellen whispered.

"Six, five, four. . ."

"Sue Ellen?"

His lips were close. Too close. And yet not close enough. "Yes?"

"If you're not falling for me, now's the time to say so."

She met his gaze. "Three, two. . ."

"One," was his response.

And then he kissed her.

KATHLEEN Y'BARBO

Kathleen is a multi-published, award-winning author of Christian fiction who also writes under the name Kathleen Miller. A tenth-generation Texan, she holds a marketing degree from Texas A&M University and a certificate in Paralegal Studies. She is the former treasurer of American Christian Fiction Writers Guild, as well as a member of Words for the Journey Christian Writers Guild, Inspirational Writers Alive, Fellowship of Christian Writers, Writers Information Network, the Houston Paralegal Association, and the Writers Guild. The proud mother of a daughter and three sons, she makes her home in Texas (where else?).

A Letter to Our Readers

Dear Readers:

In order that we might better contribute to your reading enjoyment, we would appreciate your taking a few minutes to respond to the following questions. When completed, please return to the following: Fiction Editor, Barbour Publishing, Inc., P.O. Box 719, Uhrichsville, OH 44683.

1. Did you enjoy reading *Sugar and Grits*?
   ❑ Very much—I would like to see more books like this.
   ❑ Moderately—I would have enjoyed it more if _____

   _____

   _____

2. What influenced your decision to purchase this book?
   (Check those that apply.)
   ❑ Cover   ❑ Back cover copy   ❑ Title   ❑ Price
   ❑ Friends   ❑ Publicity   ❑ Other

3. Which story was your favorite?
   ❑ *Mississippi Mud*   ❑ *Gone Fishing*
   ❑ *Not on the Menu*   ❑ *Falling for You*

4. Please check your age range:
   ❑ Under 18   ❑ 18–24   ❑ 25–34
   ❑ 35–45   ❑ 46–55   ❑ Over 55

5. How many hours per week do you read? _____

Name _____

Occupation _____

Address _____

City_____ State_____ Zip_____

E-mail_____

If you enjoyed
Sugar and Grits
then read

SWEET HOME
Alabama

Paige Winship Dooly, Pamela Griffin,
Lisa Harris & Pamela Kaye Tracy

ONE ANONYMOUS LOVE POEM MISTAKENLY
FINDS ITS WAY INTO FOUR COUPLES' LIVES

Head Over Heels
The Princess and the Mechanic
Matchmaker, Matchmaker
Ready Or Not

If you enjoyed

Sugar and Grits

then read

Bayou
BRIDES

Janet Spaeth ❧ Lynette Sowell
Janet Lee Barton ❧ Kathleen Miller

*Four Generations of Couples
Are Bound by Love, Faith, and Land*

Capucine: Home to My Heart
Joie de Vivre
Language of Love
Dreams of Home